THE FREEDOM TRAP

This story concerns the activities of a highly organized gang whose business is arranging for the escape from jail of certain selected long-term prisoners who can afford the price. It was the rapid growth and startling success of this latest criminal 'industry' that prompted Lord Mountbatten's investigation and report on prison security. But when rumours circulate that Slade, the notorious traitor-spy who was jailed for forty years (*vide* the author's *Running Blind*) is planning to escape from a top-security prison, M.I.5 cannot wait for the usual ponderous Home Office action. This dangerous gang must be smashed at all costs, so the bait is laid along a trail that starts in London and leads by way of Ireland and Gibraltar to a night of spectacular fireworks in Malta. The twists and turns of this gripping novel make it easily the most accomplished of Desmond Bagley's thrillers to date.

THE
FREEDOM TRAP

★

DESMOND BAGLEY

THE
COMPANION BOOK CLUB
LONDON

This edition, published in 1972 by
The Hamlyn Publishing Group Ltd,
is issued by arrangement with
William Collins, Sons & Co. Ltd.

*Made and printed in Great Britain
for the Companion Book Club
by Odhams (Watford) Ltd.*
SBN600871533
10.72/253

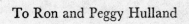
To Ron and Peggy Hulland

CHAPTER ONE

I

MACKINTOSH'S OFFICE was, unexpectedly, in the City. I
had difficulty in finding it because it was in that warren of
streets between Holborn and Fleet Street which is a maze to
one accustomed to the grid-iron pattern of Johannesburg. I
found it at last in a dingy building; a well-worn brass plate
announcing innocuously that this Dickensian structure held the
registered office of Anglo-Scottish Holdings, Ltd.

I smiled as I touched the polished plate, leaving a smudged
fingerprint. It seemed that Mackintosh knew his business; this
plate, apparently polished by generations of office boys, was a
sign of careful planning that augured well for the future—the
professional touch. I'm a professional and I don't like working
with amateurs—they're unpredictable, careless and too
dangerous for my taste. I had wondered about Mackintosh
because England is the spiritual home of amateurism, but
Mackintosh was a Scot and I suppose that makes a difference.

There was no lift, of course, so I trudged up four flights of
stairs—poor lighting and marmalade-coloured walls badly in
need of a repaint—and found the Anglo-Scottish office at the
end of a dark corridor. It was all so normal that I wondered if
I had the right address but I stepped forward to the desk and
said, 'Rearden—to see Mr Mackintosh.'

The red-headed girl behind the desk favoured me with a
warm smile and put down the tea-cup she was holding. 'He's
expecting you,' she said. 'I'll see if he's free.' She went into the
inner office, closing the door carefully behind her. She had
good legs.

I looked at the scratched and battered filing cabinets and
wondered what was in them and found I could not possibly
guess. Perhaps they were stuffed full of Angles and Scots. There

were two eighteenth-century prints on the wall—Windsor Castle and the Thames at Richmond. There was a Victorian steel engraving of Princes Street, Edinburgh. All very Anglic and Scottish. I admired Mackintosh more and more—this was going to be a good careful job; but I did wonder how he'd done it—did he call in an interior decorator or did he have a pal who was a set dresser in a film studio?

The girl came back. 'Mr Mackintosh will see you now—you can go right through.'

I liked her smile so I returned it and walked past her into Mackintosh's sanctum. He hadn't changed. I hadn't expected him to change—not in two months—but sometimes a man looks different on his home ground where he has a sense of security, a sense of knowing what's what. I was pleased Mackintosh hadn't changed in that way because it meant he would be sure of himself anywhere and at any time. I like people I can depend on.

He was a sand-coloured man with light gingery hair and invisible eyebrows and eyelashes which gave his face a naked look. If he didn't shave for a week probably no one would notice. He was slight in build and I wondered how he would use himself in a rough-house; flyweights usually invent nasty tricks to make up for lack of brawn. But then Mackintosh would never get into a brawl in the first place; there are all sorts of different ways of using your brains.

He put his hands flat on the desk. 'So you are,' he paused, holding his breath, and then spoke my name in a gasp, 'Rearden. And how was the flight, Mr Rearden?'

'Not bad.'

'That's fine. Sit down, Mr Rearden. Would you like some tea?' He smiled slightly. 'People who work in offices like this drink tea all the time.'

'All right,' I said, and sat down. He went to the door.

'Could you rustle up another pot of tea Mrs Smith?'

The door clicked gently as he closed it and I cocked my head in that direction. 'Does she know?'

8

'Of course,' he said calmly. 'I couldn't do without Mrs Smith. She's a very capable secretary, too.'

'Smith?' I asked ironically.

'Oh, it's her real name. Not too incredible—there are plenty of Smiths. She'll be joining us in a moment so I suggest we delay any serious discussion.' He peered at me. 'That's a rather lightweight suit for our English weather. You mustn't catch pneumonia.'

I grinned at him. 'Perhaps you'll recommend a tailor.'

'Indeed I will; you must go to my man. He's a bit expensive but I think we can manage that.' He opened a drawer and took out a wad of currency. 'You'll need something for expenses.'

I watched unbelievingly as he began to count out the fivers. He parted with thirty of them, then paused. 'We'd better make it two hundred,' he decided, added another ten notes, then pushed the wad across to me. 'You don't mind cash, I trust? In my business cheques are rather looked down upon.'

I stuffed the money into my wallet before he changed his mind. 'Isn't this a little unusual? I didn't expect you to be so free and easy.'

'I dare say the expense account will stand it,' he said tolerantly. 'You are going to earn it, you know.' He offered a cigarette. 'And how was Johannesburg when you left?'

'Still the same in a changing sort of way,' I said. 'Since you were there they've built another hundred-and-sixty-foot office block in the city.'

'In two months? Not bad!'

'They put it up in twelve days,' I said dryly.

'Go-ahead chaps, you South Africans. Ah, here's the tea.'

Mrs Smith put the tea tray on to the desk and drew up a chair. I looked at her with interest because anyone Mackintosh trusted was sure to be out of the ordinary. Not that she looked it, but perhaps that was because she was disguised as a secretary in a regulation twin-set—just another office girl with a nice smile. Yet in other circumstances I thought I could get on very well with Mrs Smith—in the absence of Mr Smith, of course.

9

Mackintosh waved his hand. 'Will you be mother, Mrs Smith?' She busied herself with the cups, and Mackintosh said, 'There's no real need for further introductions, is there? You won't be around long enough for anything but the job, Rearden. I think we can get down to cases now.'

I winked at Mrs Smith. 'A pity.'

She looked at me unsmilingly. 'Sugar?' was all she asked.

He tented his fingers. 'Did you know that London is the world centre of the diamond business?'

'No, I didn't. I thought it was Amsterdam.'

'That's where the cutting is done. London is where diamonds are bought and sold in all stages of manufacture from uncut stones to finished pieces of jewellery.' He smiled. 'Last week I was in a place where packets of diamonds are sold like packets of butter in a grocer's shop.'

I accepted a cup of tea from Mrs Smith. 'I bet they have bags of security.'

'Indeed they have,' said Mackintosh. He held his arms wide like a fisherman describing the one that got away. 'The safe doors are that thick and the place is wired up with so many electronic gimmicks that if you blink an eyelash in the wrong place at the wrong time half the metropolitan police begin to move in.'

I sipped the tea, then put down the cup. 'I'm not a safe cracker,' I said. 'And I wouldn't know where to begin—you need a peterman for that. Besides, it would have to be a team job.'

'Rest easy,' said Mackintosh. 'It was the South African angle that set me thinking about diamonds. Diamonds have all the virtues; they're relatively anonymous, portable and easily sold. Just the thing a South African would go for, don't you think? Do you know anything about the IDB racket?'

I shook my head. 'Not my line of country—so far.'

'It doesn't matter; perhaps it's for the better. You're a clever thief, Rearden; that's why you've stayed out of trouble. How many times have you been inside?'

I grinned at him. 'Once—for eighteen months. That was a long time ago.'

'Indeed it was. You change your methods and your aims, don't you? You don't leave any recurring statistics for a computer to sort out—no definite *modus operandi* to trip over. As I say—you're a clever thief. I think that what I have in mind will be just up your street. Mrs Smith thinks so, too.'

'Let's hear about it,' I said cautiously.

'The British GPO is a marvellous institution,' said Mackintosh inconsequentially. 'Some say ours is the best postal system in the world; some think otherwise if you judge by the readers' letters in the *Daily Telegraph*, but grousing is an Englishman's privilege. Insurance companies, however, regard the GPO very highly. Tell me, what is the most outstanding property of the diamond?'

'It sparkles.'

'An uncut diamond doesn't,' he pointed out. 'An uncut stone looks like a bit of sea-washed bottle glass. Think again.'

'It's hard,' I said. 'Just about the hardest thing there is.'

Mackintosh clicked his tongue in annoyance. 'He's not thinking, is he, Mrs Smith? Tell him.'

'The size—or the lack of it,' she said quietly.

Mackintosh pushed his hand under my nose and curled his fingers into a fist. 'You can hold a fortune in your hand and no one would know it was there. You could put diamonds worth a hundred thousand pounds into this matchbox—then what would you have?'

'You tell me.'

'You'd have a parcel, Rearden; a package. Something that can be wrapped up in brown paper with enough room to write an address and accept a postage stamp. Something that can be popped into a letter-box.'

I stared at him. 'They send diamonds through the *post*?'

'Why not? The postal system is highly efficient and very rarely is anything lost. Insurance companies are willing to bet large sums of money on the efficiency of the GPO and those boys know what they're doing. It's a matter of statistics, you know.'

He toyed with the matchbox. 'At one time there was a courier system and that had a lot of disadvantages. A courier would personally carry a parcel of diamonds and deliver it to its destination by hand. That fell through for a number of reasons; the couriers got to be known by the wide boys, which was very sad because a number of them were severely assaulted. Another thing was that human beings are but human, after all, and a courier could be corrupted. The supply of trustworthy men isn't bottomless and the whole courier system was not secure. Far from it.

'But consider the present system,' he said enthusiastically. 'Once a parcel is swallowed into the maw of the Post Office not even God can extract it until it reaches its destination. And why? Because nobody knows precisely where the hell it is. It's just one of millions of parcels circulating through the system and to find it would *not* be like finding a needle in a haystack—it would be like searching a haystack for a particular wisp of hay. Do you follow me?'

I nodded. 'It sounds logical.'

'Oh, it is,' said Mackintosh. 'Mrs Smith did all the necessary research. She's a very clever girl.' He flapped his hand languidly. 'Carry on, Mrs Smith.'

She said coolly, 'Once the insurance company actuaries analysed the GPO statistics regarding losses, they saw they were on to a good thing provided certain precautions were taken. To begin with, the stones are sent in all sizes and shapes of parcel from matchbox size to crates as big as a tea chest. The parcels are labelled in a multitude of different ways, very often with the trade label of a well-known firm—anything to confuse the issue, you see. The most important thing is the anonymity of the destination. There are a number of accommodation addresses having nothing to do with the diamond industry to which the stones are sent, and the same address is never used twice running.'

'Very interesting,' I said. 'Now how do we crack it?'

Mackintosh leaned back in his chair and put his fingertips together. 'Take a postman walking up a street—a familiar sight. He carries a hundred thousand pounds' worth of diamonds but—and this is the interesting point—he doesn't know it and neither does anyone else. Even the recipient who is eagerly awaiting those diamonds doesn't know when they'll arrive because the postal authorities don't guarantee delivery at any specific time, regardless of what they might say about first-class post in their specious advertising. The parcels are sent by ordinary post; no special delivery nonsense which would be too easy to crack open.'

I said slowly, 'It seems to me that you're painting yourself into a corner, but I suppose you have something up your sleeve. All right—I'll buy it.'

'Have you ever done any photography?'

I resisted the impulse to explode. This man had more ways of talking around a subject than anyone I had ever known. He had been the same in Johannesburg—never talking in a straight line for more than two minutes. 'I've clicked a shutter one or twice,' I said tightly.

'Black-and-white or colour?'

'Both.'

Mackintosh looked pleased. 'When you take colour photographs—transparencies—and send them away for processing, what do you get back?'

I looked appealingly at Mrs Smith and sighed. 'Small pieces of film with pictures on them.' I paused and added, 'They're framed in cardboard mounts.'

'What else do you get?'

'Nothing.'

He wagged his finger. 'Oh yes, you do. You get the distinctive yellow box the things are packed in. If a man is carrying one of those boxes in his hand you can spot it across a street and you say to yourself, "That man is carrying a box of Kodachrome transparencies." '

13

I felt a thrill of tension. Mackintosh was coming to the meat of it. 'All right,' he said abruptly, 'I'll lay it out for you. I know when a parcel of diamonds is being sent. I know to where it is being sent—I have the accommodation address. Most important of all, I know the packaging and it's unmistakable. All you have to do is to wait near the address and the postman will come up to you with the damn thing in his hand. And that little yellow box will contain one hundred and twenty thousand quid in unset stones which you will take from him.'

'How did you find out all this?' I asked curiously.

'I didn't,' he said. 'Mrs Smith did. The whole thing is her idea. She came up with the concept and did all the research. Exactly *how* she did the research is no concern of yours.'

I looked at her with renewed interest and discovered that her eyes were green. There was a twinkle in them and her lips were curved in a humorous quirk which smoothed out as she said soberly, 'There must be as little violence as possible, Mr Rearden.'

'Yes,' agreed Mackintosh. 'As little violence as possible commensurate with making a getaway. I don't believe in violence; it's bad for business. You'd better bear that in mind.'

I said, 'The postman won't hand it to me. I'll have to take it by force.'

Mackintosh showed his teeth in a savage grin. 'So it will be robbery with violence if you get nabbed. Her Majesty's judges are hard about that kind of thing, especially considering the amount involved. You'll be lucky to get away with ten years.'

'Yes,' I said thoughtfully, and returned his grin with interest.

'Still, we won't make it too easy for the police. The drill is this; I'll be near by and you'll pass the package to me smartly, and then you'll keep on going. The stones will be out of the country within three hours of the snatch. Mrs Smith, will you attend to the matter of the bank?'

She opened a folder and produced a form which she pushed across the desk. 'Fill that in.'

It was a request to open an account at the *Züricher Ausführen*

Handelsbank. Mrs Smith said, 'British politicians may not like the gnomes of Zürich but they come in handy when needed. Your number is very complicated—write it out fully in words in this box.'

Her finger rested on the form so I scribbled the number in the place she indicated. She said, 'That number written on the right cheque form in place of a signature will release to you any amount of money up to forty thousand pounds sterling, or its equivalent in any currency you wish.'

Mackintosh sniggered. 'Of course, you'll have to get the diamonds first.'

I stared at them, 'You're taking two-thirds.'

'I did plan it,' Mrs Smith said coolly.

Mackintosh grinned like a hungry shark. 'She has expensive tastes.'

'Of that I have no doubt,' I said. 'Would your tastes run to a good lunch? You'll have to suggest a restaurant, though; I'm a new boy in London.'

She was about to answer when Mackintosh said sharply, 'You're not here to play footsie with my staff, Rearden. It wouldn't be wise for you to be seen with either of us. Perhaps when it's all over we can have dinner together—the three of us.'

'Thanks,' I said bleakly.

He scribbled on a piece of paper, 'I suggest that after lunch you . . . er . . . "case the joint"—I believe that is the correct expression. Here is the address of the drop.' He pushed the paper across the desk, and scribbled again. 'And this is the address of my tailor. Don't get them mixed up, there's a good chap. That would be disastrous.'

2

I lunched at the Cock in Fleet Street and then set out to look up the address Mackintosh had given me. Of course I walked in the wrong direction—London is the devil of a place to get around in if you don't know it. I didn't want to take a taxi because I always play things very cautiously, perhaps even too cautiously. But that's why I'm a success.

Anyway, I found myself walking up a street called Ludgate Hill before I found I'd gone wrong and, in making my way into Holborn, I passed the Central Criminal Court. I knew it was the Central Criminal Court, because it says so and that surprised me because I always thought it was called the Old Bailey. I recognized it because of the golden figure of Justice on the roof. Even a South African would recognize that—we see Edgar Lustgarten movies, too.

It was all very interesting but I wasn't there as a tourist so I passed up the opportunity of going inside to see if there was a case going on. Instead I pressed on to Leather Lane behind Gamage's and found a street market with people selling all kinds of junk from barrows. I didn't much like the look of that —it's difficult to get away fast in a thick crowd. I'd have to make damned sure there was no hue and cry, which meant slugging the postman pretty hard. I began to feel sorry for him.

Before checking on the address I cruised around the vicinity, identifying all the possible exits from the area. To my surprise I found that Hatton Garden runs parallel with Leather Lane and I knew that the diamond merchants hung out there. On second thoughts it wasn't too surprising; the diamond boys wouldn't want their accommodation address to be too far from the ultimate destination. I looked at the stolid, blank buildings and wondered in which of them were the strong-rooms Mackintosh had described.

I spent half an hour pacing out those streets and noting the various types of shop. Shops are very useful to duck into when you want to get off the streets quickly. I decided that Gamage's might be a good place to get lost in and spent another quarter-hour familiarizing myself with the place. That wouldn't be enough but at this stage it wasn't a good thing to decide definitely on firm plans. That's the trouble with a lot of people who slip up on jobs like this; they make detailed plans too early in the game, imagining they're Master Minds, and the whole operation gets hardening of the arteries and becomes stiff and inflexible.

I went back to Leather Lane and found the address Mackintosh had given me. It was on the second floor, so I went up to the third in the creaking lift and walked down one flight of stairs. The Betsy-Lou Dress Manufacturing Co., Ltd, was open for business but I didn't trouble to introduce myself. Instead I checked the approaches and found them reasonably good, although I would have to observe the postman in action before I could make up my mind about the best way of doing the job.

I didn't hang about too long, just enough to take rough bearings, and within ten minutes I was back in Gamage's and in a telephone booth. Mrs Smith must have been literally hanging on to the telephone awaiting my call because the bell rang only once before she answered, 'Anglo-Scottish Holdings.'

'Rearden,' I said.

'I'll put you through to Mr Mackintosh.'

'Wait a minute,' I said. 'What kind of a Smith are you?'

'What do you mean?'

'Don't you have a first name?'

There was a pause before she said, 'Perhaps you'd better call me Lucy.'

'Ouch! I don't believe it.'

'You'd better believe it.'

'Is there a Mr Smith?'

Frost formed on the earpiece of my telephone as she said icily, 'That's no business of yours. I'll put you through to Mr Mackintosh.'

There was a click and the line went dead temporarily and I thought I wasn't much of a success as a great lover. It wasn't surprising really; I couldn't see Lucy Smith—if that was her name—wanting to enter into any kind of close relationship with me until the job was over. I felt depressed.

Mackintosh's voice crackled in my ear. 'Hello, dear boy.'

'I'm ready to talk about it some more.'

'Are you? Well, come and see me tomorrow at the same time.'

'All right,' I said.

'Oh, by the way, have you been to the tailor yet?'

'No.'

'You'd better hurry,' he said. 'There'll be the measurements and at least three fittings. You'll just about have time to get it all in before you get slapped in the nick.'

'Very funny,' I said, and slammed down the phone. It was all right for Mackintosh to make snide comments; he wasn't going to do the hard work. I wondered what else he did in that shabby office apart from arranging diamond robberies.

I took a taxi into the West End and found Austin Reed's, where I bought a very nice reversible weather coat and one of those caps as worn by the English country gent, the kind in which the cloth crown is sewn on to the peak. They wanted to wrap the cap but I rolled it up and put it into the pocket of the coat which I carried out over my arm.

I didn't go near Mackintosh's tailor.

3

'So you think it's practicable,' said Mackintosh.

I nodded. 'I'll want to know a bit more, but it looks all right so far.'

'What do you want to know?'

'Number one—when is the job to be?'

Mackintosh grinned. 'The day after tomorrow,' he said airily.

'Christ!' I said. 'That's not allowing much time.'

He chuckled. 'It'll be all over in less than a week after you've set foot in England.' He winked at Mrs Smith. 'It's not every-one who can make forty thousand quid for a week's not very hard work.'

'I can see at least one other from here,'' I said sarcastically. 'I don't see that you're working your fingers to the bone.'

He was undisturbed. 'Organization—that's my forte.'

'It means I've got to spend the rest of today and all tomorrow studying the habits of the British postman,' I said. 'How many deliveries a day?'

Mackintosh cocked his eye at Mrs Smith, who said, 'Two.'

'Have you any snoopers you can recruit? I don't want to spend too much time around Leather Lane myself. I might get picked up for loitering and that would certainly queer the pitch.'

'It's all been done,' said Mrs Smith. 'I have the timetable.'

While I was studying it, she unrolled a plan on to the desk. 'This is a plan of the entire second floor. We're lucky on this one. In some buildings there's a row of letter-boxes in the entrance hall, but not here. The postman delivers to every office.'

Mackintosh put down his finger with a stabbing motion. 'You'll tackle the postman just about here. He'll have the letters for that damnably named clothing company in his hand ready for delivery and you ought to see whether he's carrying the package or not. If he isn't you pass it up and wait for the next delivery.'

'That's what's worrying me,' I said. 'The waiting bit. If I'm not careful I'll stick out like a sore thumb.'

'Oh, didn't I tell you—I've rented an office on the same floor,' said Mackintosh blandly. 'Mrs Smith went shopping and all home comforts are installed; an electric kettle, tea, coffee, sugar and milk, and a basket of goodies from Fortnum's. You'll live like a king. I hope you like caviare.'

I blew out my breath sharply. 'Don't bother to consult me about anything,' I said sarcastically, but Mackintosh merely smiled and tossed a key-ring on the desk. I picked it up. 'What name am I trading under?'

'Kiddykar Toys Limited,' said Mrs Smith. 'It's a genuine company.'

Mackintosh laughed. 'I set it up myself—cost all of twenty-five quid.'

We spent the rest of the morning scheming and I didn't find any snags worth losing any sleep over. I found myself liking Lucy Smith more and more; she had a brain as sharp as a razor and nothing escaped her attention, and yet she contrived to retain her femininity and avoid bossiness, something that seems difficult for brainy women. When we had just about got everything wrapped up, I said, 'Come now; Lucy isn't your real name. What is?'

She looked at me with clear eyes. 'I don't think it really matters,' she said evenly.

I sighed. 'No,' I admitted. 'Perhaps not.'

Mackintosh regarded us with interest, then said abruptly, 'I said there was to be no lally-gagging around with the staff, Rearden; you just stick to doing your job.' He looked at his watch. 'You'd better leave now.'

So I left the gloom of his nineteenth-century office and lunched again at the Cock, and the afternoon was spent in the registered office of Kiddykar Toys, Ltd, two doors away from the Betsy-Lou Dress Manufacturing Co., Ltd. Everything was there that Mackintosh had promised, so I made myself a pot of coffee and was pleased to see that Mrs Smith had supplied the real stuff and not the instant powdered muck.

There was a good view of the street and, when I checked on the timetable of the postman, I was able to identify his route. Even without the telephone call Mackintosh was to make I ought to get at least fifteen minutes' notice of his arrival. That point settled, I made a couple of expeditions from the office, pacing the corridor and timing myself. There really was no point in doing it without knowledge of the postman's speed but it was good practice. I timed myself from the office to Gamage's, walking at a fair clip but not so fast as to attract attention. An hour in Gamage's was enough to work out a good confusing route and then work was over for the day and I went back to my hotel.

The next day was pretty much the same except I had the postman to practise on. The first delivery I watched from the office with the door opened a crack and a stopwatch in my hand. That might seem a bit silly; after all, all I had to do was to cosh a man. But there was a hell of a lot at stake so I went through the whole routine.

On the second delivery of the day I did a dummy run on the postman. Sure enough, it was as Mackintosh had predicted; as he approached Betsy-Lou's door the letters for delivery were firmly clutched in hand and any box of Kodachromes should be clearly visible. I hoped Mackintosh was right about the diamonds; we'd look mighty foolish if we ended up with a photographic record of Betsy-Lou's weekend in Brighton.

Before I left I telephoned Mackintosh and he answered the telephone himself. I said, 'I'm as ready as I'll ever be.'

'Good!' He paused. 'You won't see me again—apart from the hand-over of the merchandise tomorrow. Make a neat job of that, for God's sake!'

'What's the matter?' I asked. 'Got the wind up?'

He didn't answer that one. Instead, he said, 'You'll find a present awaiting you at your hotel. Handle with care.' Another pause. 'Good luck.'

I said, 'Give my sincere regards to Mrs Smith.'

He coughed. 'It wouldn't do, you know.'

'Perhaps not; but I like to make my own decisions.'

'Maybe so—but she'll be in Switzerland tomorrow. I'll pass on your message when I next see her.' He rang off.

I went back to the hotel, picked up a small package at the desk, and unwrapped it in my room. Nestling in a small box was a cosh, lead-centred and rubber-padded with a non-skid grip and a neat strap to go round the wrist. A very effective anaesthetic instrument, if a bit more dangerous than most. Also in the box was a scrap of paper with a single line of typescript: HARD ENOUGH AND NO HARDER.

I went to bed early that night. There was work to do next day.

Next morning I went into the City like any other business gent, although I didn't go so far as to wear a bowler and carry the staff of office—the rolled umbrella. I was earlier than most because the first postal delivery of the day was before office hours. I arrived at Kiddykar Toys with half an hour in hand and immediately put on the kettle for coffee before inspecting the view from the window. The stallholders of Leather Lane were getting ready for the day's sales and there was no sign of Mackintosh. I wasn't worried; he'd be around somewhere in the neighbourhood keeping an eye open for the postman.

I had just finished the first cup of coffee when the phone rang. Mackintosh said briefly, 'He's coming.' There was a click as he hung up.

In the interests of his leg muscles the postman had put in a bit of time and motion study on this building. It was his habit to take the lift to the top floor and deliver the letters from the top down on the theory that walking downstairs is easier than climbing them. I put on my coat and hat and opened the door a couple of inches, listening for the whine of the lift. It was ten minutes before I heard it go up, and then I stepped out into the corridor, carefully drawing the office door closed but not quite shut so that the least push would swing it open.

It was very quiet in the building at that hour and, as I heard the postman clattering down the stairs to the second floor, I retreated down the flight of stairs to the first floor. He hit the second floor and turned away from Betsy-Lou's door to deliver the post to other offices. That was his usual routine and so I wasn't worried.

Then I heard him coming back a few steps at a time, the intervals punctuated by the metallic bangs of swinging letter-box flaps. Just at the right time I came up the stairs and headed for the Kiddykar office which brought me facing him. I stared at his hands but there was no little yellow box to be seen.

'Morning,' he said. 'Lovely day, isn't it?' He went past at a quick pace and I fumbled my way into the office, faking the opening of the door with a key. As I closed it behind me I found that I was sweating slightly; not much but enough to show that I was under tension. It was ridiculous, I suppose—I had only to take a little box away from an unsuspecting man, which should have been the easiest thing in the world and no occasion for nerves.

It was the contents of that box which set up the tension. A hundred and twenty thousand quid is a hell of a lot of money to be at stake. It's rather like the man who can walk along a kerbstone unconcernedly and never put a foot wrong, yet let him try the same thing with a two-hundred-foot drop on one side and he'll break into a muck sweat.

I walked over to the window and opened the casement, not so much to get fresh air as to signal to Mackintosh that the first delivery was a bust. I looked down into Leather Lane and saw him in his appointed place. He was standing before a fruit and vegetable stall prodding tomatoes with a nervous forefinger. He flicked his eyes up at the window then swung around and walked away.

I lit a cigarette and settled down with the morning papers. There was quite a while to wait before the second post.

Two hours later the telephone rang again. 'Better luck this time,' said Mackintosh, and hung up.

I went through the same routine as before—there was no harm in it as this would be a different postman. I waited on the landing just below the second floor and listened intently. It would be more difficult now that the building was inhabited and a lot depended on whether I could catch the postman alone in the corridor. If I could then it was easy, but if there was anyone else present I would have to grab the box and run for it.

Steady footsteps warned me that he was coming and I trotted up the stairs at the critical moment. I swung my head back and forwards like someone about to cross a street and found that all was clear—no one in the corridor except for me and the postman. Then I looked at his hands.

He was carrying a bundle of letters and right on top of the bundle was a little yellow box.

I stepped right in front of him as he drew abreast of the Kiddykar office. 'Have you anything for me?' I asked. 'I'm in there.' I pointed to the door behind him.

He turned his head to look at the name on the door and I hit him behind the ear with the cosh, hoping to God he hadn't an unusually thin skull. He grunted and his knees buckled. I caught him before he fell and pushed him at the door of the office which swung open under his weight, and he fell over the threshold spilling letters before him. The Kodachrome box fell to the floor with a little thump.

I stepped over him and hauled him inside, pushing the door closed with my foot. Then I grabbed the yellow box and dropped it into the innocuous brown box that Mackintosh had had specially tailored to fit it. I had to pass it on to him in the street and we didn't want that conspicuous yellow to be seen.

In less than sixty seconds from the time I greeted the postman I was outside the office and locking the door on him. As I did so someone passed behind me in the corridor and opened the door of the Betsy-Lou office. I turned and went downstairs, not moving too fast but not dawdling. I reckoned the postman wouldn't come round for two or three minutes, and then he still had to get out of the office.

I came out on to the street and saw Mackintosh staring at me. He averted his eyes and half-turned away and I strode across the street among the stalls in his direction. It was easy enough, in the throng, to bump him with my shoulder, and with a muffled 'Sorry!' I passed the packet to him and continued in the direction of Holborn.

I hadn't gone far when I heard the smash of glass behind me and a confused shouting. That postman had been smart; he had wasted no time on the door but had broken the window as a means of drawing attention to himself. Also he hadn't been unconscious for as long as I had hoped—I hadn't hit him nearly hard enough.

But I was safe—far enough away not to be spotted by him and moving farther all the time. It would take at least five minutes to sort out the confusion and by that time I intended to get thoroughly lost—and I hoped Mackintosh was doing the same. He was the hot one now—he had the diamonds.

I ducked into the rear entrance of Gamage's and made my way through the store at an easier pace, looking, I hoped, like a man who knows where he's going. I found the men's room and locked myself into a cubicle. My coat came off and was reversed—that so carefully chosen coat with the nicely contrasting colours. The natty cap came from my pocket and the hat I was wearing was regretfully screwed into a shapeless bundle. It wouldn't do it much good to be jammed into my pocket but I didn't want to leave it lying around.

Clothes make the man and a new man left that men's room. I wandered casually about the store, drifting towards the front entrance, and on the way I bought myself a new tie just to have a legitimate reason for being in Gamage's, but that precaution was unnecessary. I emerged on to the pavement of Holborn and set off to walk west. No taxis for me because taxi-drivers would be questioned about pick-ups in the area at that time.

Half an hour later I was in a pub just off Oxford Street near the Marble Arch and sinking a thankful pint of beer. It had been a good smooth job but it wasn't over yet, not by a hell of a long way. I wondered if I could trust Mackintosh to do his half of the job properly.

5

That evening, as I was preparing to go out on the town, there came a firm knock at the door of my room. I opened it and was confronted by two very large men dressed very conservatively and in the best of taste. The one on the right said, 'Are you Joseph Aloysius Rearden?'

I didn't have to bend my brain too far to realize that these two were coppers.

I gave a twisted grin. I'd rather forget the Aloysius.'

'We are police officers.' He flipped a wallet in front of me negligently. 'We hope you can assist us in our enquiries.'

'Hey!' I said. 'Is that a warrant card? I've never seen one of those before.'

Reluctantly he flipped open the wallet again and let me read the card. He was Detective-Inspector John M. Brunskill and indubitably the genuine article. I babbled a bit. 'You see these things happening at the bioscope; I never thought it would happen to me.'

'Bioscope?' he said dubiously.

'The films—we call a cinema a bioscope in South Africa. That's where I'm from, you know. I don't know how I can help you in any enquiries, Inspector. I'm a stranger to London —in fact, I'm a stranger to England. I've been here only a week—less than that, really.'

'We know all that, Mr Rearden,' said Brunskill gently.

So they'd checked on me already. These boys moved fast— the British police are wonderful.

'May we come in, Mr Rearden? I think you *will* be able to help us.'

I stood on one side and waved them into the room. 'Come in and take a seat. There's only one chair so one of you will have to sit on the bed. And take your coats off.'

'That won't be necessary,' said Brunskill. 'We won't be staying long. This is Detective-Sergeant Jervis.'

Jervis looked an even harder nut than Brunskill. Brunskill was polished and had the suavity that maturity brings, while Jervis still had his sharp corners and was all young, rock-hard cop. But Brunskill would be the more dangerous—he'd be tricky.

I said, 'Well, what can I do for you?'

'We are making enquiries about the theft of a package from a postman in Leather Lane this morning,' said Brunskill. 'What can you tell us about it, Mr Rearden?'

'Where's Leather Lane?' I asked. 'I'm a stranger here.'

Brunskill looked at Jervis and Jervis looked at Brunskill and then they both looked at me. 'Come, Mr Rearden,' said Brunskill. 'You can do better than that.'

'You've got a record,' said Jervis suddenly.

This was the shot across the bows. I said bitterly, 'And you johns will never let me forget it. Yes, I've got a record; I did eighteen months in Pretoria Central—eighteen months of stone cold jug—and that was a long time ago. I've been straight ever since.'

'Until perhaps this morning,' suggested Brunskill.

I looked him straight in the eye. 'Don't pull the old flannel on me. You tell me what I'm supposed to have done, and I'll tell you if I did it—straight out.'

'Very good of you,' murmured Brunskill. 'Don't you think so, Sergeant?'

Jervis made a nasty noise at the back of his throat. Then he said, 'Mind if we search your room, Rearden?'

'It's Mr Rearden to sergeants,' I said. 'Your boss has better manners than you. And I most certainly do object to you searching my room—unless you have a warrant.'

'Oh, we have that,' said Brunskill calmly. 'Go ahead, Sergeant.' He took a document from his pocket and slapped it into my hand. 'I think you'll find that in order, Mr Rearden.'

I didn't even bother to look at it, but just tossed it on to the dressing-table and watched Jervis do an efficient overhaul of the room. He found nothing—there wasn't anything for him to find. At last he gave up, looked at Brunskill and shook his head.

Brunskill turned to me. 'I must ask you to come to the police station with me.'

I was silent and let the pause lengthen for a long time before I said, 'Well, go ahead and ask.'

'We've got ourselves a joker here, sir,' said Jervis. He looked at me with dislike.

'If you do ask I won't come,' I said. 'You'll have to arrest me to get me anywhere near the nick.'

27

Brunskill sighed. 'Very well, Mr Rearden; I arrest you on suspicion of being involved in an assault on a postman on premises in Leather Lane at about nine-thirty this morning. Does that satisfy you?'

'It'll do to be going on with,' I said. 'Let's go.'

'Oh, I almost forgot,' he said. 'Anything you say will be noted and may be used in evidence.'

'I know the form,' I said. 'I know it only too well.'

'I'm sure you do,' he said softly.

I expected them to take me to Scotland Yard but I found myself in quite a small police station. Where it was I don't know—I don't know London at all well. They put me into a small room unfurnished except for a deal table and two bentwood chairs. It had the same institutional smell of all police stations anywhere in the world. I sat in a chair and smoked one cigarette after another, watched by a uniformed copper who stood with his back to the door, looking undressed without his helmet.

It was nearly an hour and a half before they got around to doing anything and it was tough boy Jervis who started the attack. He came into the room and waved abruptly at the uniformed john who did a disappearing act, then he sat down at the other side of the table and looked at me for a long time without speaking. I ignored him—I didn't even look at him and it was he who broke first. 'You've been here before, haven't you, Rearden?'

'I've never been here before in my life.'

'You know what I mean. You've sat on hard wooden chairs with a policeman the other side of the table many, many times. You know the drill too well—you're a professional. With another man I might pussyfoot around—use a bit of psychology, maybe—but that wouldn't work with you, would it? So I'm not going to do it. There'll be no tact, no psychology with you. I'm going to crack you like a nut, Rearden.'

'You'd better remember Judges' Rules.'

He gave a sharp bark of laughter. 'See what I mean? An honest man wouldn't know Judges' Rules from Parkinson's Law. But you know, don't you? You're a wrong 'un; you're bent.'

'When you're finished with the insults I'll go,' I said.

'You'll go when I say you can,' he said sharply.

I grinned. 'You'd better check with Brunskill first, sonny.'

'Where are the diamonds?'

'What diamonds?'

'That postman is in a bad way. You hit him a bit too hard, Rearden. The chances are he'll cash in his chips—and where will that put you?' He leaned forward. 'You'll be inside for so long that you'll trip over your beard.'

I must say he was trying hard but he was a bad liar. No dying postman could have busted that window in the Kiddykar office. I just looked him in the eye and kept my mouth shut.

'If those diamonds aren't found it'll go hard for you,' said Jervis. 'Maybe if the diamonds turn up the judge will be a bit easier on you.'

'What diamonds?' I asked.

And so it went on for a good half hour until he got tired and went away and the uniformed man came back and took up his old stance in front of the door. I turned and looked at him. 'Don't you get corns? Isn't this job bad for your feet?' He looked at me with a bland face and expressionless eyes and said exactly nothing.

Presently a bigger gun was brought to bear. Brunskill came in carrying a thick folder bulging with papers which he put on the table. 'I'm sorry to have kept you waiting, Mr Rearden,' he said.

'I wouldn't like to bet on it,' I said.

He gave me a pitying, though understanding smile. 'We all have our jobs to do, and some are nastier than others. You mustn't blame me for doing mine.' He opened the folder. 'You have quite a record, Mr Rearden. Interpol have a fat dossier on you.'

'I've been convicted once,' I said. 'Anything else is not official and you can't use it. What anyone might have to say about me isn't proof of a damned thing.' I grinned and, pointing at the folder, quoted: ' "What the policeman said isn't evidence." '

'Just so,' said Brunskill. 'But it's interesting all the same.' He mused over the papers for a long time, then said, without looking up, 'Why are you flying to Switzerland tomorrow?'

'I'm a tourist,' I said. 'I've never been there before.'

'It's your first time in England, too, isn't it?'

'You know it is. Look here, I want an attorney.'

He looked up. 'I would suggest a solicitor. Have you anyone in mind?'

From my wallet I took the scrap of paper with the telephone number on it which Mackintosh had given me with this eventuality in mind. 'That'll find him,' I said.

Brunskill's eyebrows lifted when he read it. 'I know this number very well—he's just the man to tackle your type of case. For a man who's been in England less than a week you know your way around the fringes.' He put the paper on one side. 'I'll let him know you're here.'

My throat was dry from smoking too many cigarettes. 'Another thing,' I said. 'I could do with a cup of tea.'

'I'm afraid we can't run to tea,' said Brunskill regretfully. 'Would a glass of water be all right?'

'It'll do.'

He went to the door, gave instructions, and then came back. 'You people seem to think that we spend all our time in police stations drinking tea—running a continuous cafeteria for old lags. I can't think where you get it from unless it's from television.'

'Not me,' I said. 'We have no TV in South Africa.'

'Indeed!' said Brunskill. 'How curious. Now, about those diamonds. I think that . . .'

'What diamonds?' I broke in.

And so it went on. He shook me more than Jervis because he was trickier. He wasn't stupid enough to lie about something

30

I knew to be true, as Jervis had done, and was better at the wearing down process, being as persistent as a buzzing fly. The water came—a carafe and a tumbler. I filled the tumbler and drank thirstily, then refilled it and drank again. Brunskill watched me and said at last, 'Had enough?'

I nodded, so he reached out and took the tumbler delicately in his fingertips and carried it out. When he came back he looked at me sorrowfully. 'I didn't think you'd fall for that chestnut. You know we can't fingerprint you until you're booked. Why did you let us have them?'

'I was tired,' I said.

'Too bad,' he said sympathetically. 'Now, to get back to those diamonds . . .'

Presently Jervis came into the room and beckoned to Brunskill and they stood by the door and talked in low voices. Brunskill turned around. 'Now, look here, Rearden; we've nailed you. We have enough evidence now to send you up for ten years. If you help us to get back those stones it might help you when the judge sentences you.'

'What diamonds?' I asked tiredly.

His mouth shut with a snap. 'All right,' he said curtly. 'Come this way.'

I followed, the meat in a sandwich between Brunskill and Jervis. They escorted me to a large room occupied by a dozen men lined along one wall. Jervis said, 'No need to explain what this is, Rearden; but I will because the law says I must. It's a line-up—an identification parade. There are three people coming in to see you. You can insert yourself anywhere in that line, and you can change your position in the intervals if you like. Got it?'

I nodded and walked over to the wall, putting myself third in line. There was a pause in the action and then the first witness came in—a little old lady, someone's darling mother. She went along the line and then came straight back to me and pointed at my chest. 'That's the one.' I'd never seen her before.

They took her out, but I didn't bother to change position. There wasn't any point, really; they had me nailed just as Brunskill had said. The next one was a young man of about eighteen. He didn't have to go all the way along the line. He stopped in front of me. 'That's 'im,' he said. ''E did it.'

The third witness didn't have any trouble either. He took one look at me and yelled, 'This is the boyo. I hope you get life, mate.' He went away rubbing his head. It was the postman— not nearly as dead as Jervis would have me believe.

Then it was over and Jervis and Brunskill took me back. I said to Jervis, 'You'd make a good miracle-worker; you brought that postman back to life pretty smartly.'

He gave me a sharpish look and a slow smile spread over his face. 'And how did you know that was the postman?'

I shrugged. My goose was cooked whichever way I looked at it. I said to Brunskill, 'Who is the bastard of a nark that shopped me?'

His face closed up. 'Let's call it "information received", Rearden. You'll be charged tomorrow morning and you'll go before a magistrate immediately. I'll see that your solicitor is in attendance.'

'Thanks,' I said. 'What's his name?'

'By God!' he said. 'But you're a cool one. Your solicitor is a Mr Maskell.'

'Thanks again,' I said.

Brunskill whistled up a station sergeant who put me in a cell for the night. I had a bite to eat and then stretched out and went to sleep almost immediately.

It had been a tiring day.

CHAPTER TWO

I

MASKELL was a short, stout man with shrewd brown eyes and an immense air of dignity. He was introduced to me just before the charge was laid and did not seem at all perturbed at the prospect of acting for a criminal. The law is a strange profession in which ordinary morality goes by the board; a well liked and generally respected barrister will fight like a tiger for his client, who may well be a murderer or a rapist, and will receive well-merited congratulations on an acquittal. Then he will go home and write a letter to the editor of *The Times* fulminating about the rise in crime. A schizophrenic profession.

I said as much to Maskell once when I knew him better. He said gently, 'Mr Rearden, to me you are neither guilty nor innocent—the people who decide that are the twelve men in the box. I am here to find out the facts and present them to a barrister who will argue the case—and I do it for money.'

We were in court at the time and he waved his hand largely. 'Who says crime doesn't pay?' he asked cynically. 'Taking all in all, from the court ushers to his Lordship up there, there are at least fifty people directly involved in this case, and they're all making a living out of it. Some, such as myself and his Lordship, make a better living than others. We do very well out of people like you, Mr Rearden.'

But at this time I didn't know Maskell at all. It was a hurried introduction, and he said hastily, 'We will talk in more detail later. First we must find what this is all about.'

So I was taken and charged. I won't go into all the legal language but what it all boiled down to was robbery with violence—an assault on the person of John Edward Harte, an employee of the GPO, and the theft of diamonds, the property of Lewis and van Veldenkamp, Ltd, valued at £173,000.

33

I nearly burst out laughing at that. It had been a bigger haul than Mackintosh had expected, unless Mr Lewis and Meneer van Veldenkamp were trying to sting their insurance company. But I kept a straight face and when it was over I turned to Maskell and asked, 'What now?'

'I'll see you in the Magistrates' Court in about an hour. That will be a mere formality.' He rubbed his chin. 'There's a lot of money involved here. Have the police recovered the diamonds?'

'You'd better ask them. I know nothing about any diamonds.'

'Indeed! I must tell you that if the diamonds are still—shall we say *at large*?—then it will be very difficult for me to get you out on bail. But I will try.'

The proceedings in the Magistrates' Court were brief, lasting for about three minutes. They would have been even briefer but Brunskill got on his hind legs and argued against the granting of bail. 'The diamonds have not yet been recovered, your Honour, and if the prisoner is released on bail I fear they never will be. Further, if the prisoner had not been apprehended last night he would have been in Switzerland this morning.'

The magistrate flapped his hand. 'You think the prisoner will jump bail?'

'I do,' said Brunskill firmly. 'And there is one thing more, your Honour; the prisoner is in the dock on a charge of violence and he has a police record in which violence figures largely. I fear the intimidation of witnesses.'

He nearly overreached himself. 'You think he will leave the country *and* intimidate witnesses?' asked the magistrate with polite incredulity. 'I doubt if his violent arm would reach so far. However, on the balance of evidence and especially in respect of the missing property I am inclined to agree with you. Bail is denied.'

Brunskill smiled and was about to sit down when the magistrate said, 'Detective-Inspector Brunskill; an officer of your seniority surely must know that it is entirely improper to refer to a past criminal record at this point in the proceedings

34

and I am surprised that you have done so. I draw the attention of your superiors to this lapse and I direct that the reference should be struck from the record.'

Brunskill sat down with a red face and Maskell shrugged and stuffed some papers back into his briefcase. And so I was remanded for trial at the Central Criminal Court. I was going to see the inside of the Old Bailey, after all.

Maskell had a few words with me before I was taken away. 'Now I can find out the strength of the police case against you. I'll have a word with the prosecution and then you and I can sit down together and discuss this whole thing. If you want anything ask that I be informed, but I shall probably see you tomorrow, anyway.'

A prisoner on remand is theoretically an innocent man. Practically, he is regarded neutrally as neither guilty nor innocent. The food was good, the bed soft and there were no irksome restrictions—except one. I couldn't get out of the nick. Still, you can't have everything.

Maskell came to see me the following afternoon and we sat in one of the interviewing rooms. He regarded me thoughtfully, then said, 'The case against you is very strong, Mr Rearden; very strong, indeed. Unless you can prove conclusively and without equivocation that you could not have committed this crime, then I fear you will be convicted.'

I was about to speak, but he raised his hand. 'But we can go into that later. First things first. Now, have you any money?'

'About a hundred and fifty pounds. But I haven't paid my hotel bill—I wasn't given the chance. I don't want hotel bilking to be added to the charge sheet, so it'll be nearer a hundred pounds I have to play around with.'

Maskell nodded. 'As you may know, my own fee has been taken care of. But I am not the man who will fight your case in court; that will be done by a barrister, and barristers come even more expensive than I do, especially barristers of the calibre needed to win this case. A hundred pounds would come nowhere near the amount necessary.'

I shrugged. 'I'm sorry; it's all I've got.' That wasn't exactly true but I could see that even the best barrister in the business couldn't get me out of this one and there wasn't any point in throwing my money away.

'I see. Well, there is provision for a case like yours. A barrister will be appointed by the Court to act for you. The trouble is that he will be not of your choice; yet I am not without influence and I will see if I have any strings to pull that will get us the best man.'

He took a folder from his briefcase and opened it. 'I want you to tell me exactly what you did on the morning in question.' He paused. 'I already know you did not have breakfast at your hotel.'

'I didn't sleep well that night,' I said. 'So I got up early and took a walk.'

Maskell sighed. 'And where did you walk to, Mr Rearden?'

I thought it out. 'I went into Hyde Park and walked up as far as the Round Pond. There's a famous building up there— Kensington Palace—but it was closed. It was very early in the morning.'

'I shouldn't imagine there would be many people in Hyde Park or Kensington Gardens so early. Did you speak to anyone —make enquiries—at Kensington Palace? Did you ask the time of opening, for instance?'

'There wasn't anyone around to ask.'

'Very well; what did you do then?'

'I walked back through the park to Hyde Park Corner and over into Green Park. Then up Bond Street into Oxford Street. I was doing a bit of window shopping, you see.'

'And what time would this be?'

'Oh, I don't know. Say, about nine-fifteen. I was dawdling a bit. I had a look at a place called Burlington Arcade, then I went on up Bond Street looking at the shops, as I said. It's marvellous—nothing like it in South Africa.'

'And you didn't speak to anyone at all?'

'If I'd known I needed an alibi I would have,' I said bitterly.

'Just so,' said Maskell. 'So you arrived at Oxford Street—what did you do then?'

'Well, I hadn't had breakfast and I felt a bit peckish so I found a pub and had some sandwiches and a pint. I was chatting to the barman, an Irishman. He ought to remember me.'

'And what time was this?'

'It must have been after ten o'clock because the pub was open. Say, half past ten.'

'That alibi comes a little late,' said Maskell. 'It's not relevant.' He consulted a sheet of paper from the folder. 'I must tell you that the police version differs from yours substantially—and they have a great deal of evidence to show.' He looked me in the eye. 'Do I have to point out the dangers of lying to your lawyer?'

'I'm not lying,' I said indignantly.

He spoke gravely. 'Mr Rearden, let me say that you are in deep trouble. I gather you want to enter a plea of not guilty at your trial, but I must warn you that, on the evidence now extant, you are likely to lose the case. Public concern about crimes of violence of this nature has been increasing and this concern is reflected by the heavy sentences imposed by the courts.'

He paused to collect his thoughts and then went on in measured tones. 'Now, as your solicitor I cannot prejudge this case, but I would like to say this: If the diamonds were to be returned, and if you entered a plea of guilty, then the court would be inclined to leniency and, in my opinion, your sentence would be not more than five years and possibly as little as three years. With a remission of sentence for good behaviour you could be out of prison in as little as two years.

'On the other hand, if the diamonds are *not* returned and if you enter a plea of not guilty then your sentence is going to be very heavy—assuming you are convicted, an assumption which on the evidence I have is very likely. If I may use slang I would say that his Lordship is going to throw the book at you; he'll lock you up and throw away the key. I doubt if you would get

37

away with much under fourteen years, and I assure you that I have great experience in these forecasts and I do not speak lightly.'

He cleared his throat. 'Now, what do you say, Mr Rearden? What shall we do about this?'

'The only diamonds I saw that morning were in the shop windows of Bond Street,' I said distinctly.

He looked at me in silence for a long time then shook his head. 'Very well,' he said quietly. 'I will go about my business —and yours—but with no great hope of success. I ought to warn you that the police have such evidence that will be very difficult for defence counsel to refute.'

'I'm innocent,' I said obstinately.

He said no more but collected his papers and left the room without a backward glance.

2

So there I was in the dock of the Central Criminal Court—the Old Bailey. There was much pomp and circumstance, robes and wigs, deferences and courtesies—and me popping up from the bowels of the earth into the dock like the demon king in a pantomime, the centre of attraction. Of course, I had competition from the Judge. It seems that when a man gets to sit on the Bench he feels that he's entitled to be a licensed jester and he loves nothing more than to have the audience rolling in the aisles at his witticisms. I've seen worse music-hall turns than a Criminal Court judge. Still, it does lighten the atmosphere— a court would be a pretty grim place without the comic bits— and the Chief Comic isn't prejudiced; he aims his barbs at prosecution and defence alike. I found that I quite enjoyed it and laughed as much as anyone else.

Maskell was there, of course, but in a minor role; defence counsel was a man called Rollins. Maskell had tried again, just before the trial, to get me to alter my plea of not guilty. He said, 'Mr Rearden, I want you to consider once more the consequences of losing this case. You will not only receive a long sentence but there are certain other implications. Long term prisoners are invariably regarded as high risk prisoners, especially those who are regarded as having financial backing. In the absence of diamonds to the value of £173,000 you would undoubtedly come into that category. A high risk prisoner is treated very differently from the ordinary prisoner and I understand that the circumstances can be rather unpleasant. I would think of that if I were you.'

I didn't have to think of it. I hadn't a hope in hell of getting the diamonds back and that was the crux of the matter. Even if I pleaded guilty I'd get a stiff sentence in the absence of the diamonds. The only thing to do was to put on a brave face and make the best of it. It struck me that Mackintosh was a very smart man and that maybe Mrs Smith was even smarter.

I said, 'I'm sorry, Mr Maskell, but I'm innocent.'

He looked puzzled. He didn't believe a word I said but he couldn't figure out why I was keeping my mouth shut. But then a wintry smile came to his face. 'I hope you don't think the investment of so many years of your life is worth the money. Too much time in prison is apt to change a man for the worse.'

I smiled at him. 'I thought you said you wouldn't prejudge the case.'

'I think you are a very foolish young man,' he said. 'But you have my best wishes in your unfortunate future.'

The trial got under way laboriously. First, the jury details were settled and then the action began, the prosecution getting first crack. The prosecuting counsel was a tall, thin man with a face like the blade of a hatchet, and he fairly revelled in his job. He led off with a rather skimpy introduction and then began to lay on the prosecution witnesses, while Rollins, my counsel, looked on with a bored expression on his face. I had met Rollins only twice and he had been offhanded on both occasions. He knew this was one he wasn't going to win.

The prosecution witnesses were good—very good, indeed—and I began to see why the prosecuting counsel was looking so cheerful despite the misfortune of his face. Expert police witnesses introduced photographs and drawings of the scene of the crime and, that groundwork laid, the pressure was applied.

There was the motherly old soul who had identified me at the police station line-up. 'I saw him strike the postman,' she testified, the light of honesty shining from her eyes. 'I was standing in the corridor and saw the accused hit the postman with his fist, grab a yellow box from him, and push him into an office. Then the accused ran down the stairs.'

The prosecutor offered her a plan of the second floor. 'Where were you standing?'

She indicated a place in the corridor and looked across the court straight at me as guileless as you please. The sweet old lady was lying like a flatfish, and she knew that I knew she was lying. She couldn't have been standing in the corridor because I'd checked, and the details of her evidence were all wrong, anyway. There wasn't a thing I could do about it, though.

Another highlight was a man from Fortnum and Mason who testified to having sent a packed picnic basket to a certain hotel. The order was telephoned in by a Mr Rearden. Questioned by the defence he said he couldn't be certain that the Mr Rearden who ordered the basket was the accused.

A hotel employee testified that the accused stayed at his hotel and that a basket had been delivered addressed to Mr Rearden. Asked what had happened to it he said he didn't know but presumably the accused had collected it. There was a bit of argument about that and part of his answer was struck out.

A detective produced a picnic basket in court and testified that he had found it in the office of Kiddykar Ltd. It had been identified as coming from Fortnum's. Another police witness testified that the basket was liberally covered with the accused's fingerprints, as were other items in the room; to wit

—an electric kettle, a coffee pot and several pieces of crockery and cutlery.

Then there was the police witness who said he had been interested in tracking down the ownership of Kiddykars Ltd. Apparently it was a genuine company but not doing any business. The lines of ownership were very tangled but he had finally cracked it with the helpful assistance of the South African police. The owner proved to be a Mr Joseph Aloysius Rearden of Johannesburg. No, he had no means of knowing if the Joseph Aloysius Rearden of Kiddykars was the Joseph Aloysius Rearden who stood in the dock. That would be taking him further than he was prepared to go.

The jury drew its own conclusions.

The postman gave his evidence fairly. I had hit him and he had recovered consciousness in the Kiddykar office. There was nothing in that which contradicted the perjured evidence of Old Mother Hubbard. The third eye-witness was the office boy from Betsy-Lou; he said he saw me lock the office door and run downstairs. I remembered him vaguely as the person who had walked behind me at that time. But I hadn't *run* downstairs—that was his imagination working overtime.

Brunskill was a star witness.

'Acting on information received I went, with Detective-Sergeant Jervis, to see the accused at his hotel. His answers to my questioning were such that I arrested him on suspicion of having been concerned in this crime. Subsequently I obtained his fingerprints which matched prints found in the office of Kiddykars Ltd. Further enquiries were made which resulted in three witnesses coming forward, all of whom identified the accused. More extensive enquiries led to the further evidence that has been presented to the Court relating to the picnic basket and the ownership of Kiddykars Ltd.'

The prosecutor sat down with a grin on his face and Rollins bounced to his feet for cross-examination.

Rollins: You spoke of 'information received', Inspector. How did this information come to you?

Brunskill: (hesitantly) Must I answer that, my Lord? The sources of police information may be prejudicial to . . .

Rollins: (quickly) This goes to the malice of a person or persons unknown which may prejudice the case for the accused, my Lord.

Judge: (in Churchillian tones) Mr Rollins; I don't see how your case *can* deteriorate much further. However, I am inclined to let the question go. I am as interested as anybody. Answer the question, Inspector.

Brunskill: (unwillingly) There was one telephone call and one letter.

Rollins: Both anonymous?

Brunskill: Yes.

Rollins: Did these communications indicate that the accused had committed this crime?

Brunskill: Yes.

Rollins: Did they indicate where he was to be found?

Brunskill: Yes.

Rollins: Did they indicate that the basket found in the Kiddykar office had been purchased by the accused at Fortnum and Mason?

Brunskill: . . . er . . . Yes.

Rollins: Is it a crime to purchase foodstuffs from that eminent firm of retailers?

Brunskill: (sharply) Of course not.

Rollins: Did these anonymous communications indicate that the firm of Kiddykars Ltd was owned by the accused?

Brunskill: (uncomfortably) Yes.

Rollins: Is it a crime to own such a firm as Kiddykars Ltd?

Brunskill: (with ebbing patience) No.

Judge: I am not so sure. Anyone who so maltreats the English language as to arrive at so abominable a name ought to be treated as a criminal.

(Laughter in court)

Rollins: Inspector, would you not say it was true that all your work had been done for you in this case? Would you not say it was true that without these malicious communications the accused would not be standing in the dock at this moment?

Brunskill: I cannot answer that question. He would have been caught.

Rollins: Would he? I admire your certitude.

Brunskill: He would have been caught.

Rollins: But not so speedily.

Brunskill: Perhaps not.

Rollins: Would you not characterize your mysterious communicant as someone who 'had it in' for the accused at worst—or a common informer or stool pigeon at best?

Brunskill: (smiling) I would prefer to think of him as a public-spirited citizen.

Very funny! Mackintosh—a public-spirited citizen! But, by God, the pair of them had been infernally clever. The first time I had laid eyes on that picnic basket had been in the Kiddykars office, and I certainly hadn't telephoned Fortnum's. Mrs Smith had done her shopping to good effect! Nor did I own Kiddykars Ltd—not to my own knowledge; but I'd have a hell of a time proving it. They had delivered me to the law trussed up like a chicken.

There wasn't much after that. I said my piece, futile though it was; the prosecutor tore me into shreds and Rollins half-heartedly tried to sew up the pieces again without much success. The judge summed up and, with one careful eye on the Appeal Court, directed the jury to find me guilty. They were out only for half an hour—just time enough for a much-needed smoke—and the answer was predictable.

Then the judge asked if I had anything to say, so I spoke up with just two words: 'I'm innocent.'

Nobody took much notice of that—they were too busy watching the judge arrange his papers and gleefully anticipating how heavy he'd be. He fussed around for a while, making sure that all attention would be on him, and then he began to speak in portentous and doomladen tones.

'Joseph Aloysius Rearden, you have been found guilty of

stealing by force diamonds to the value of £173,000. It falls to me to sentence you for this crime. Before I do so I would like to say a few words concerning your part in this affair.'

I could see what was coming. The old boy couldn't resist the chance of pontificating—it's easy from a safe seat.

'An Englishman is walking the streets in the course of his usual employ when he is suddenly and unexpectedly assaulted —brutally assaulted. He is not aware that he is carrying valuables which, to him, would undoubtedly represent untold wealth, and it is because of these valuables that he is attacked.

'The valuables—the diamonds—are now missing and you, Rearden, have not seen fit to co-operate with the police in their recovery in spite of the fact that you must have known that the court would be inclined to leniency had you done so. Therefore, you cannot expect leniency of this court.

'I have been rather puzzled by your recalcitrant attitude but my puzzlement abated when I made an elementary mathematical calculation. In the normal course of events such a crime as yours, a crime of violence such as is abhorrent in this country, coupled with the loss to the community of property worth £173,000, would be punished by the heavy sentence of fourteen years' imprisonment. My calculation, however, informs me that for those fourteen years you would be receiving an annual income of not less than £12,350—tax free—being the amount you have stolen divided by fourteen. This, I might add, is considerably more than the stipend of one of Her Majesty's Judges, such as myself—a fact which can be ascertained by anyone who cares to consult Whitaker's Almanack.

'Whether it can be considered that the loss of fourteen years of freedom, and confinement to the hardly pleasant environs of our prisons, is worth such an annual sum is a debatable matter. You evidently think it is worth while. Now, it is not the function of this court to make the fees of crime worth while, so you can hardly blame me for endeavouring to reduce your annual prison income.

'Joseph Aloysius Rearden, I sentence you to twenty years'

preventive detention in such prison or prisons as the appropriate authority deems fit.'

I'd bet Mackintosh was laughing fit to bust a gut.

3

The judge was right when he referred to 'the hardly pleasant environs of our prisons.' The one in which I found myself was pretty deadly. The reception block was crowded—the judges must have been working overtime that day—and there was a lot of waiting about apparently pointlessly. I was feeling a bit miserable; no one can stand in front of a judge and receive a twenty-year sentence with complete equanimity.

Twenty years!

I was thirty-four years old. I'd be fifty-four when I came out; perhaps a bit less if I could persuade them I was a good boy, but that would be bloody difficult in view of what the judge had said. Any Review Board I appeared before would read a transcript of the trial and the judge's remarks would hit them like a hammer.

Twenty long years!

I stood by apathetically while the police escort read out the details of my case to the receiving officer. 'All right,' said the receiving officer. He signed his name in a book and tore out a sheet. 'Here's the body receipt.'

So help me—that's what he said. 'Body receipt.' When you're in prison you cease to be a man; you're a body, a zombie, a walking statistic. You're something to be pushed around like the GPO pushed around that little yellow box containing the diamonds; you're a parcel of blood and guts that needs feeding at regular intervals, and you're assumed not to have any brains at all.

'Come on, you,' said the receiving officer. 'In here.' He unlocked a door and stood aside while I walked in. The door slammed behind me and I heard the click of the lock. It was a crowded room filled with men of all types, judging by their clothing. There was everything from blue jeans to a bowler and striped trousers. Nobody was talking—they just stood around and examined the floor minutely as though it was of immense importance. I suppose they all felt like me; they'd had the wind knocked out of them.

We waited in that room for a long time, wondering what was going to happen. Perhaps some of us knew, having been there before. But this was my first time in an English gaol and I felt apprehensive. Maskell's words about the unpleasant circumstances that attend the high risk prisoner began to worry me.

At last they began to take us out, one at a time and in strict alphabetical order. Rearden comes a long way down the alphabet so I had to wait longer than most, but my turn came and a warder took me down a passage and into an office.

A prisoner is never asked to sit down. I stood before that desk and answered questions while a prison officer took down the answers like the recording angel. He took down my name, birthplace, father's name, mother's maiden name, my age, next-of-kin, occupation. All that time he never looked at me once; to him I wasn't a man, I was a statistics container—he pressed a button and the statistics poured out.

They told me to empty my pockets and the contents were dumped on to the desk and meticulously recorded before being put into a plastic bag. Then my fingerprints were taken. I looked around for something with which to wipe off the ink but there was nothing. I soon found out why. A warder marched me away and into a hot, steamy room where I was told to strip. It was there I lost my clothes. I wouldn't see them again for twenty years and I'd be damned lucky if they'd be in fashion.

After the bath, which wasn't bad, I dressed in the prison clothing—the man in the grey flannel suit. But the cut was terrible and I'd rather have gone to Mackintosh's tailor.

A march up another corridor led to a medical examination, a bit of bureaucratic stupidity. Why they can't have a medical examination while a man is stripped after his bath is beyond me. However, I undressed obligingly and dressed again, and was graded for labour. I was top class—fit for anything.

Then a warder took me away again into an immense hall with tiers of cells lining the walls and with iron stairs like fire escapes. 'I'll tell you once,' said the warder. 'This is "C" Hall.'

We clanked up some stairs and along a landing and he stopped before a cell and unlocked it. 'This is yours.'

I went inside and the door slammed with a cold sound of finality. I stood for some time, not looking at anything in particular. My brains had seized up—gone on strike. After, maybe, fifteen minutes I lay on the bed and damn near cried my eyes out.

After that I felt better and was able to bring some intelligence to bear on the situation. The cell was about twelve feet by seven, and perhaps eight feet high. The walls were distempered—institutional cream and Borstal green—and in one of them was a small barred window set high. The door looked as though it could withstand artillery fire and there was a Judas hole set in it.

The furnishing was sparse: an iron-framed bed, a wooden table and a chair, a washstand with jug, basin and chamber-pot, and a bare shelf. Exploring a prison cell is one of the quickest tasks a man can set himself. Within three minutes I had checked everything there was to find—three blankets, two sheets, a lumpy mattress, another shirt, a pair of felt slippers, a thin non-absorbent towel, a spoon and a mug. Hanging on a nail in the wall by a loop of string was a copy of the Rules and Regulations governing HM Prisons together with an informational pamphlet.

Three minutes and I knew practically everything there was to know about that cell. I wondered what I was going to do for the next twenty years. Right there and then I decided I'd have to ration my curiosity—shut down the dampers on thought. There would be too much time and not enough happening, and every new experience would have to be jealously hoarded.

The walls of that prison suddenly had physical meaning. I

47

felt them looming all about me, thick and strong. It was a claustrophobic quarter-hour before the feeling receded.

I immediately broke my promise about rationing curiosity by beginning to read the informational pamphlet, but that was absolutely necessary. I was a new boy in this school and the sooner I learned the ropes the better. There were too many tricks that could be played on the newcomer by the old hands and I didn't want to fall for any of them.

It was an interesting compilation of data. I discovered that the spare shirt in the cell was to be used as a night shirt, that lights-out was ten-thirty, that the waking call was six-thirty in the morning, that I was to be issued with a razor blade to be returned after shaving. There were other helpful hints even to the point of finding a way out of prison.

For instance, I could refer my case to the Court of Criminal Appeal and, if that failed, I could apply to the Attorney-General to put the case before the House of Lords. At any time I could petition the Home Secretary and I was permitted to write to my Member of Parliament.

I couldn't see myself doing any of those things. I wasn't pally enough with the Home Secretary to enter into any kind of extended correspondence and my Member of Parliament was a shade too far away to do any good—6,000 miles away.

I read the booklet through and then started on it again from the beginning. I had nothing else to do so I decided to memorize the whole goddamn thing. I was still reading it when the light went out.

4

The bell clanged and I opened my eyes and was confused until I remembered where I was. I dressed hurriedly and made the bed, then hoisted it up so that it stood on end in a corner of the cell. I sat on the chair and waited. Presently there was a slight metallic sound from the door and I knew someone was watching through the Judas hole.

There was a sharp snap from the lock and the door opened. I stood up and the warder came in. He looked appraisingly around the cell and then fixed me with a hard eye. 'You're new here. You've been reading that thing, haven't you?' He nodded to the booklet on the table.

'Yes, I have.'

'Your bed's in the wrong corner, and the book should be hanging on the wall where you found it. You'll learn. Take a tip from me; do just what you're told and you'll be all right. Now, pick up your chamber-pot and get ready for slopping out.'

'I haven't used it,' I said.

'It gets slopped out whether you've used it or not,' he said curtly. 'Remember what I told you—do as you're told with no arguments. That's lesson number one.'

I picked up the chamber-pot and followed him on to the landing which was full of men, all lined up and each holding his pot. 'All right,' someone shouted. 'Move along.'

There was mephitic stink in the air. I trudged along and found that I was expected to empty the pot into one sink and wash it in another. I went through the motions and returned to my cell, taking my cues from what the others were doing.

The warder came back. 'You can eat in your cell if you like. You'll be served with the others down in the hall, but you can bring your tray up here if you don't feel like joining the party just yet.'

I didn't feel like talking to anyone at all right then. I was too busy trying to keep a firm hold on myself. 'Thanks,' I said, and heard my voice crack.

He was ironic. 'Don't thank me; it's regulations for new prisoners. And another thing, you'll be seeing the Governor this morning. A trusty will take you to his office.'

The trusty came just before ten o'clock and I went with him out of 'C' Hall. 'You're Rearden,' he said. 'I've heard about you.'

'Have you?'

'I'm Simpson.' He nudged me in the ribs with a sharp elbow. 'You're going before the Reception Board. Don't volunteer anything—that's my tip.'

'What happens?'

'Oh, it's just the big boys giving you the once-over. The Governor, the Bible-Slapper, the Senior Screw, the Welfare Officer—people like that. The Governor's not too bad if you keep on the right side of him, but Gawd help you if you don't. Some of the others'll try to feed you a load of old cod's wallop —a crowd of flaming do-gooders. But watch out for Hudson— he's a right bastard.'

'Who's he?'

'The Chief Screw. Gawd help us all if he is made Governor.'

Simpson took me into a waiting room in which half a dozen other prisoners were sitting. They all looked dispirited. Simpson chuckled. '*You* won't have to wait your turn, mate. You're on first; you're someone special.'

I stared at him. 'What's so special about me?'

'You'll see. The Governor'll explain it all very nicely.'

I was about to pursue that a bit further but a warder came into the room. 'Rearden, come this way. Simpson, get back to "C" Hall.'

There were five men seated around a large table, two of them prison officers in uniform. It's a funny thing about prison officers—they never take off their caps, not even when sitting in the Governor's office. Perhaps it's a tradition of the service. One of the civilians wore a dog-collar, so he'd be Simpson's Bible-Slapper—the Prison Chaplain.

The military-looking man in the middle spoke up first. 'Rearden, I'm the Governor of this prison. You are here because you have committed a crime and society has decided that you cannot be allowed to remain at large. How you get on in this prison is your own affair. There are two ways of looking at a prison—as a place of punishment and as a place of rehabilitation. The choice is up to you; we have ample facilities for both modes of operation. Do I make myself clear?'

'Yes, sir.'

He picked up a paper from the table. 'It is normally my practice to treat all prisoners alike. However, I have received notification from the Home Office that you are to be treated as a high risk prisoner and that entails certain restrictive modifications of your treatment here. For instance, you were brought to this office by a Star Class trusted prisoner; that will never happen again. In future, if you have to move about inside the prison you will be escorted by a prison officer. You will also wear coloured patches upon your clothing. I have prepared a list here of all the other restrictions appertaining to a high risk prisoner which you will study and to which you will conform.'

He handed me the paper and I folded it and put it into my pocket.

He cleared his throat. 'You must understand, Rearden, that whether you remain in the high risk category depends entirely upon yourself. The position is reviewed at regular intervals and my recommendations are forwarded to the Home Office. You must also understand that the Home Office is at liberty to disregard my recommendations. The fact that you are a high risk prisoner is entirely of your own doing, and if there is any way you can convince the police authorities that you are not a risk then I strongly recommend that you do so.'

He meant the diamonds, of course. They still wanted those bloody diamonds. 'Yes, sir,' I said woodenly. 'I'll try to think of something, sir.'

The Governor turned his head. 'Anything from you, Padre?'

The chaplain smiled. 'My name is Clark. I note you claim to have no religion.'

'That's right, sir.'

'I'm not one for pushing religion down a man's throat,' said Clark. 'But do you mind if I come to see you from time to time?'

'No, sir.'

The Governor said, 'This is Mr Anderson, our Welfare

Officer. He can do a lot for you if you will let him. Any time you want to see him ask your landing officer. Have you anything you would like to ask him now?'

'Yes, sir. How do I get writing material and books?'

Anderson said easily, 'The writing materials—pens and paper—you will buy in the canteen shop with money you will earn by doing work in the prison. You will be paid a minimum of one shilling and eightpence a day, but you can improve on that if you choose to. Books you can obtain from the prison library.'

'Thank you, sir,' I said. 'Is it possible to get books from outside?' I hesitated. 'I'll be here for a long time—I want to study. I want to improve myself.'

Anderson started to speak but checked himself and looked at the Governor, who said, 'Very commendable, but we'll have to see about that. That will depend upon your general conduct and, as you say, you'll be here a long time.' He nodded to the uniformed officer at the end of the table. 'This is Mr Hudson, the Senior Prison Officer responsible for prison discipline. Have you anything to say, Mr Hudson?'

'Just one thing, sir.' said Hudson. He had a hard face and eyes like chips of glass. 'I don't like high risk prisoners, Rearden. They upset prison routine and cause trouble among the other prisoners. Don't give me any trouble, that's all. If you do it will be the worse for you.'

I kept my face studiously blank. 'I understand, sir.'

'I sincerely hope you do,' said the Governor. 'You have a visitor—a police officer from Scotland Yard.' He signalled to a warder standing by the door. 'You know where to take him.'

I expected to see Brunskill but it was another detective. 'Detective-Inspector Forbes,' he said. 'Sit down, Rearden.'

I sat down, facing him over the table, and he said pleasantly, 'I expect the Governor has broken the news that you have been classified as a high risk. Do you know what that means?'

I shook my head. 'Not really.'

'You'd better find out,' Forbes advised. 'The Governor must have given you a copy of the high risk rules. I'll give you five minutes to read it.'

I took the sheet of paper from my pocket and smoothed it out on the table. It was immediately apparent after a cursory reading that life was going to be made quite a bit tougher. The light in my cell was going to be on all night, for one thing. All my clothes, except for shirt and slippers, were to be deposited outside the cell door each night. Any letters I wrote I would have to hand to a prison officer—copies would be made and only photostats would be sent to the ultimate destination, the originals to be filed in the prison. Any conversations with visitors were to be monitored by a prison officer.

I looked up at Forbes. He said, 'Those are only the rules which concern you directly, of course. There are other things. You'll be moved from cell to cell without warning; your cell will be searched—and so will you—at a moment's notice. It will all be very harassing.'

'And what is it to you?' I asked.

He shrugged. 'Nothing really—except that I feel sorry for you. If you weren't so stupid you could get yourself out of this jam.'

'Out of this nick?'

'I'm afraid not,' he said regretfully. 'But the Review Board would look upon you very kindly if you co-operated with us.'

'What sort of co-operation?'

'Come off it, Rearden,' he said tiredly. 'You know what we want. The diamonds, man; the diamonds.'

I looked him in the eye. 'I've never seen any diamonds.' Which was the exact truth—from the start to the finish of the caper I never saw the diamonds at all.

'Look, Rearden; we know you did it, and we've proved it conclusively. Why try to act the innocent? My God, man; you've been sentenced to a quarter of a lifetime in prison. Do you think you'll be good for anything when you come out? The judge was right—the game isn't worth the candle.'

53

I said, 'Do I have to sit here and listen to you? Is that part of my punishment?'

'Not if you don't want to,' Forbes said. 'I don't understand you, Rearden. I don't understand why you're taking all this so calmly. All right, let's try another tack. How did you know the drop? How did you know where the diamonds were being sent? That's of some interest, too.'

'I don't know anything about it.'

'You don't know anything about it,' he repeated. 'Do you know—maybe that's true. You could be telling the truth.' He stared at me. After a few moments he began to laugh. 'Oh, no!' he said. 'It couldn't be as simple as that! You couldn't have been double-crossed, could you, Rearden?'

'I don't know what you're talking about.'

Forbes tapped the table. 'You arrive in England out of the blue, and four days later you do the snatch. It must have been set up for you—you couldn't have laid it all on in three days. Then we pick you up and there are no diamonds. So where are they? Obviously, someone else must have them.'

He chuckled. 'Could it be the same someone who made a telephone call and wrote an anonymous letter? You passed on the diamonds and then got shopped, Rearden. Your brainy pal who planned all this made a patsy of you—isn't that the truth?'

I sat mute.

'What!' he said. 'Honour among thieves? Don't be as big a fool as you make out to be. Your friend sold you to the law for a few thousand lousy quid and you're standing for it.' He sounded disgusted. 'Don't think you're going to get out of here to go looking for him; it's not going to be as simple as that. I'm to make recommendations to the Home Office, too, you know; and I'm going to report a total lack of co-operation. And that will mean that you'll be a high risk prisoner for a hell of a long time—no matter what the Governor may recommend. You can be a good boy in here—you can be the perfect prisoner—but it will cut no ice with the Review Board after they read my report.'

I said hesitantly, 'I'll think about it.'

'You do that,' he said forcibly. 'Any time you want to see me just pass word to the Governor. But don't try to play the fool with me, Rearden. Don't waste my time. You give us what we want and we'll nail your friend for you. We'll crucify him. And *you'll* be off the hook as far as high risk is concerned. What's more, I'll see to it personally that the Review Board gives your case every favourable consideration. I can't do more than that, can I?'

Privately, I doubted if he could do as much. A detective-inspector is pretty small fry at Scotland Yard and if he thought I couldn't see what he was up to he must have thought I was a dumb bunny. All that Forbes wanted was to clear the case and get a good conduct tick on his card—the man who recovered the unrecoverable. And once he'd done it then I could go to hell as far as he was concerned. I wouldn't count; I was just another bent villain, and you don't have to keep promises to crooks. Talk about honour among thieves!

I said slowly, 'Twenty years is a long time. I'll think about it very seriously, Mr Forbes.'

'You won't be sorry,' he said expansively. 'Here, have a cigarette.'

CHAPTER THREE

I

I SUPPOSE a man can get used to anything. They tell me the Jews even got used to living—and dying—in Belsen and Dachau. Well, this was no Dachau, crummy though it was. I was fed well, if a bit monotonously, and there were one or two things about being a long-term prisoner which alleviated the strain in spite of the high risk harassments. For instance, I was allowed a radio in my cell which did a lot to preserve my sanity. At first I used it to keep up with the news of the outside world, but news of outside soon palled because it had ceased to have any direct relationship with me, and what I was left with was the blessed solace of music. I used to listen to symphony concerts by the hour.

But I didn't get the radio until I'd been in for quite a while.

At the end of the first week I no longer had my meals in the cell but joined with the others in eating in the Hall. It was then I discovered that I was a personality. There's a very strong caste system in a prison largely based on criminal achievement and, oddly enough, on the lack of achievement which results in a long sentence. Roughly speaking, the long-term prisoners, such as myself, were at the top of the heap with the high risk boys as the *élite*. They're looked up to and respected; they hold their little courts and can command the favour of many parasites and hangers-on.

That is one classification. Another is by type of crime. The brainy boys—the con men and professional frauds—are on top with safe-breakers running them close. At the bottom of this heap are the sex criminals whom nobody likes. The honest burglar is a much respected man, more for his workmanlike and unassuming ways than anything else.

I was in a position to command a lot of respect, had I so

56

wished it. My status stemmed from the fact that not only was I a long-term man but that I'd diddled the johns and hadn't grassed on my mysterious pal. You can't keep a secret in prison and everyone knew the facts of my case. Because I kept my mouth shut about the diamonds and because everyone knew what pressure Forbes was exerting I was reckoned to be one of the all right boys; an oddity, but one to be respected.

But I steered clear of all entanglements and alliances. I was being a good boy because I didn't want my high risk status to continue for any longer than it had to. The time would come when I was going to escape and I had to get rid of the constant surveillance—the singling out of attention on Rearden. Not that I was the only high risk prisoner—there were others—about half a dozen in all. I steered clear of the lot of them.

Because I was high risk they gave me the job of looking after the tidiness of 'C' Hall where I was under the eye of the Hall screw permanently on duty. Otherwise they would have had to provide a warder to escort me to the workshops instead of going with the others in a gang supervised by a trusty. They were short-staffed and this was a convenient arrangement. I didn't object; I mopped the floors and scrubbed the tables and worked with a will. Anything to be a good boy.

Homosexuals are the bane of prison life. One of them rather fancied me and pursued me to the extent that the only possible way of dissuading him was to give him a thump on the nose which I didn't want to do because that would have been a black mark on my record sheet. It was Smeaton, my landing screw, who got me out of that predicament. He saw what was happening and warned off the queer with a few choice and blasphemous threats, for which I was thankful.

Smeaton was typical of the majority of prison officers. He hadn't interfered because he particularly wanted to prevent my corruption. He'd done it for the sake of a quiet life. The screws looked upon us neutrally for the most part and to them we were just a part of the job. Over the years they had learned a technique—stop it before it starts; keep the temperature

57

down; don't let trouble spread. It was a very effective technique.

So I kept to myself and out of trouble. Not that I didn't mix with the others at all; if I drew attention as a loner then the prison psychiatrist would fix his beady eye on me. So, during the free association periods, I played a few games of cards and improved my chess considerably.

There were others to talk to besides one's fellow criminals. There were the unofficial visitors. Why these were called unofficial I never found out because they had to be authorized by the Governor. They were the prison visitors, the do-gooders and penal reform crowd, and a mixed bag they were. Some of them thought the way to reform a criminal was to moralize at him solemnly by the hour as though a steady drip of pre-digested religious pap would wash away the canker of the soul. Others were better than that.

Fortunately they weren't obligatory and one could pick and choose to some extent. I discarded a couple before finding a good one. He used to come and chat with me about all sorts of things without ever once trying to fill me up with a lot of guff or trying to convert me. He, also, had lived in South Africa and so we had something in common. Of course, since I was a high risk prisoner, all these conversations were under the watchful eye and listening ear of a screw. Once I popped in a sentence in Afrikaans to which my visitor replied in the same language. The screw soon put a stop to that and we were both reprimanded by the Governor. But no black mark for Rearden, thank God.

Clark, the Prison Chaplain, also came to see me occasionally. He, also, was no toffee-nose and we got on together quite well. Basically, he was a very religious man and so found himself in a dilemma. He found it hard to reconcile the Christian precept of 'Love thy enemies' with the task of ministering to his flock who were locked up in a big cage. I think it was wearing him down a bit.

The best of the lot was Anderson, the Welfare Officer. He

did quite a lot for me and I think his reports to the Governor were encouraging. It was through him that I got the radio, something for which I had worked assiduously. I had been going to the library once a week, as per regulations, and each visit needed the supervision of a screw. I asked Anderson why I couldn't take out a double ration of books and halve the number of library visits, thus taking a bit of strain off the overworked staff.

He saw the point and quickly agreed. I think I managed successfuly to give him the notion that I was playing along and trying to help. When I applied for permission to have a radio there was no opposition and, soon after that, I was given permission to start correspondence courses through the prison educational system. After all, if you are doing twenty years' bird you have to fill in the time somehow.

I chose English Literature and Russian. There was a bit of doubt about the Russian but it went through all right in the end. I had no intention of finishing either course if I could help it; it was all a bit of wool-pulling to make them think Rearden was reconciled to his fate. Still, I buckled down and worked hard. It had to look good and, besides, it was something to do.

The only other prisoner I got close to at this time was Johnny Swift who was doing a 'cut' for burglary. In prison jargon a 'sleep' is a sentence of from six months to two years; a 'cut' is from two to four years, and a 'stretch' is anything over four years. Johnny had been sent up for three years for having been found on business premises after closing time, so he was doing a cut and I was doing a stretch.

More shrewd than intelligent, he gave me lots of tips about the minor rackets that go on in prison and the best ways of keeping out of trouble. Once, when I had changed cells for the umpteenth time, I was a bit grouchy about it. He laughed. 'The penalty of being famous,' he said. 'I know one cell you'll never be put in.'

'Which is that?'

'That one over there in the corner. Snooky's cell.'

Snooky was an odd little man with a permanent smile; he also was in for burglary. 'And why shouldn't I go in there?'

Johnny grinned. 'Because the main sewer runs under there —right across the corner of the Hall. It's big enough to crawl through if you could dig down to it.'

'I see,' I said thoughtfully. 'But they'll trust your burglar mate, Snooky.'

'Burglar!' said Johnny in disgust. 'He's no more a burglar than my Aunt Fanny. He's nick-struck—that's what he is. Every time he's discharged tears roll down his cheeks as they push him through the gate. Then he goes and does a job and bungles it so he can get back in here.'

'He *likes* it here?'

'If you'd been brought up like Snooky you'd find this place a home from home,' said Johnny soberly. 'But I agree he's not all there.'

Another time Johnny said, 'Be careful who you talk to in here. I wouldn't trust a bloody soul myself.'

'Even you?'

He chuckled. 'Especially me, mate. But seriously, watch out for Simpson—he's a proper arse-creeper. If you find him hanging around, clip his bloody earhole.'

He pointed out others I should beware of, and some of them surprised me. 'That gang would peach on anyone if they thought it would get them in good with the Governor so he'll put in a good word to the Review Board. But they're wasting their time; he's too fly for them. He knows what goes on in here without those narks helping him.'

Johnny was philosophical about doing time. To him, his work was his profession and prison an occupational hazard. 'I've done two sleeps and a cut,' he said. 'Next time it'll be a stretch.'

'Aren't you worried about that?'

'A bit,' he admitted. Like an economist discussing the effect of government legislation on industrial activity he began to analyse the situation. 'It's these bloody do-gooders,' he said.

'They've knocked out capital punishment and they've got to put something in its place. So you get long terms for murderers. But a bloke serving a long term doesn't like it and wants to get out, so they class him as a high risk.'

He grinned. 'And they've got to find a special place to put him. Nicks like this are no good—you could get out of here with a bent pin—so they're building high risk nicks special like. But when you've got a place like that there aren't enough killers to fill it—there's a bit of space going waste—so they begin to get a bit harder on the sentences. That's where you felt the draught, chum.'

I said, 'But why put me in here to do my bird if it isn't safe?'

'Because the special nicks aren't ready yet. You wait until they've built those places on the Isle of Wight that Mountbatten's been going for. You'll be whizzed out of here in no time. In the meantime they spread you high risk blokes around thin, a few in each nick, so you can be watched easy.'

I looked around 'C' Hall. 'If this place is so easy to get out of why haven't you tried?'

He looked at me incredulously. 'Think I'm a mug, mate? I'm only doing a cut, and that means I'm out of here in just over two years from start to finish—if I don't lose me temper and clobber that bastard, Hudson. You got no idea what it's like when you go over the wall and you know that every bluebottle in England is looking for you. It ain't worth it, chum; not with all those bloody dogs. They use helicopters, too, and radio. It's like a bloody army exercise.'

He tapped my arm. 'Could be different for you, though. You ain't got as much to lose. But it wouldn't be as easy for you to go over the wall as it would be for me, 'cause they're watching you all the time. They're on to you, mate. And if you *did* get over the wall you'd get nowhere without an organization.'

That sounded interesting. 'Organization! What organization?'

'You got to have planning on the outside,' said Johnny. 'You don't want to be like those mugs who find themselves on the

61

Moor running in circles and eating raw turnip and listening for the dogs.' He shuddered slightly. 'Those bloody dogs! No, you got to have an organization that'll get you clean away. How do you suppose Wilson, Biggs, Blake and the others did it?'

'All right,' I said. 'I'll buy it. How did they get away?'

He rubbed the side of his nose. 'Like I said—organization and outside planning. But it takes the shekels; you got to have a lot of money.' He looked around to see if there was anyone within earshot, and lowered his voice. 'You ever hear of the scarperers?'

'*Scarperers?*' I shook my head. 'Never heard of them.'

'Well, it's only a rumour and I could be wrong, but the griff is that there's a mob specially set up for it—helping you long-term blokes.' He chuckled. 'Could call it a new kind of crime. But you got to have the bees.'

That didn't need much working out; the bees and honey—the money. 'How do I contact them?'

'You don't,' said Johnny bluntly. 'They contact you. This is a very exclusive mob; very picky and choosy. But I hear on the grapevine that they do a guaranteed job—you get clear away or no pay—barring expenses. Course, they don't bother about blokes like me because they know it ain't worth me while, but you could be different.'

I hesitated. 'Johnny, this isn't my country and I don't know the ropes. I was in England for less than a week before I was picked up. But if you put it out on the grapevine that there's a bloke in this nick who could do with a bit of help it might do me some good. No names, mind!'

'Think I'm a mug?' he asked. 'No names it is.' He looked at me speculatively. 'Can't say that I blame you, chum. Twenty years' bird would send me round the twist. Trouble with you is that you didn't cough up nicely when asked; you slapped 'em in the face with it and they didn't like it.'

He sighed heavily. 'As I said, next time I'm up before the beak it'll be a stretch. Time was when I could reckon on five or seven years, but that was before the beaks got bloody-minded. Now I don't know what they'll do—could be ten, twelve or even fifteen years' bird. I don't know if I could do fifteen years. It unsettles a man, it really does, not having a dependable stretch to rely on.'

I said, 'Maybe you'd better call it a day when you get out.'

'What else can I do?' he said despondently. 'I'm not brass-faced enough to go on the con; besides, I ain't got the voice—you need to be la-di-da for that. And I'm too old to learn how to dip. And I hates the protection bit—too soft-hearted to beat anybody up. No, I'm an inside man—up the old drainpipe, that's me.'

'You could turn honest,' I suggested.

He looked at me incredulously. 'That's for peasants. Can you see me as a nine-to-fiver? Can you see me working in the corner garage getting me hands black?' He was silent for a while. 'Not that I'm *relying* on getting boobed, you understand. I'm not like Snooky, you know. But I know it's in the cards and I got to face it.'

He stared blindly into the middle distance as though seeing a very bleak future. 'And the scarperers won't do nothing for me,' he said softly. 'I ain't got the bees—I never have had.'

As far as I could see there wasn't much difference between Snooky and Johnny Swift—they both faced the same end.

2

The months went by.

I mopped and scrubbed and polished 'C' Hall in a continual round of endeavour; it was like cleaning out the Augean stables because of some of the pigs who lived in it. I had one or two arguments on that score but nothing serious enough to get me a black mark.

Forbes tried to con me a couple of times into narking about the diamonds but when he saw he wasn't getting anywhere he gave it up. I suppose I was written off as incorrigible.

63

Maskell came to see me a couple of times. The first time he asked if I wanted to appeal against my sentence. I said, 'Is there any point?'

'A technicality,' he said. 'You may remember that the judge told Rollins that he didn't see how your case could deteriorate much further. That was an unfortunate remark and could be construed on appeal as having undue influence on the jury. On the other hand, your attitude about the missing property has not been an encouraging feature.'

I smiled at him. 'Mr Maskell, if I knew nothing about the diamonds then I couldn't help in the way I'm expected to, could I?'

We did nothing about the appeal.

The second time he came I saw him in the Governor's office. The Governor said, 'Your solicitor is asking that you should sign a power of attorney.'

Maskell broke in smoothly. 'Mr Rearden had certain assets in South Africa which have now been liquidated and transferred to England. It is natural that he have an advisor to handle the investment of these funds since he is incapable of doing it himself.'

'How much is involved?' asked the Governor.

'A little over £400,' said Maskell. 'A safe investment in trustee funds should turn it into over £1,000 in twenty years—something for Mr Rearden to look forward to, I hope.' He produced a document. 'I have Home Office approval.'

'Very well,' said the Governor, so I signed the power of attorney. Someone had to pay for the radio I had been granted permission to have—they aren't supplied free of charge. And it was nice to know I hadn't been forgotten. I thanked Maskell warmly.

The time came when I was able to strike day number 365 from my calendar—only another 19 years to go. I had heard nothing from Johnny about the so-called scarperers and was becoming despondent about my chances.

I was still classified as high risk with all the attendant

irritants. By now I had got used to sleeping with the light on and it had become an automatic and unthinking reaction to put my clothes outside the cell door before Smeaton locked up for the night. I changed cells irregularly and kept a record, wondering if I could detect a pattern but there were no regularities as far as I could see, either in the timing or in the particular cell I was transferred to next. I think they randomized it by pulling numbers out of a hat or some such method. That kind of thing is unbeatable.

It was about this time that I first met Slade. He was a new boy inside for a first offence and he'd got forty-two years, but I don't believe the First Offenders Act covers espionage. I had heard about him before, of course; the news broadcasts had been full of the Slade Trial. Since most of the juicy bits had been told *in camera* no one really knew what Slade had been up to, but from all accounts he was the biggest catch since Blake.

He was a pallid man and looked as though he had been bigger at one time but had shrunk, so that his skin was baggy and ill-fitting, something like the skin of a bloodhound. He walked with two sticks and I later learned that he'd been shot through the hips and had spent eight months in hospital before being put on trial. A spy leads an interesting life—sometimes too interesting.

At the trial it had come out that he was really Russian but to speak with him you wouldn't think so because his English was perfect, if a little too public school. His forty-two year stretch should have made him the doyen of the prison but it didn't work out that way. Surprisingly, the most hardened criminal can be patriotic and, to a large extent, he was given the cold shoulder.

Not being English that didn't worry me too much. He proved to be a most interesting conversationalist, cultured and knowledgeable, and was instantly prepared to help me with my Russian lessons when I asked him. He looked at me blandly when I put the question. 'Certainly I speak Russian,' he said.

'It would be very odd if I didn't under the circumstances.'
A faint smile played about his lips.

My Russian improved spectacularly after Slade's arrival.

It was nearing the end of Johnny's sentence and he had been transferred to the hostel. That meant he was employed on jobs outside the prison, the theory being that it would acclimatize him gradually to the rigours of the outside world—a part of the rehabilitation process. I didn't see it would make much difference to Johnny Swift.

But it meant I didn't see him as often. Sometimes we had a few words in the exercise yard but that was as far as it went. I looked around in 'C' Hall for someone else to chum up with, someone who was a likely prospect for contacting an escape organization—if the damned thing existed. At any moment I could be transferred without notice to another nick—possibly a high security prison—and that didn't suit my book at all.

It was fifteen months to a day before anything happened. I was breathing the lovely smog-laden air in the exercise yard when I saw Johnny Swift signal that he wanted to talk. I drifted over to him and caught the football that he threw, apparently by accident. I bounced it a couple of times and took it to him and handed it over. 'You still want to get out?' he asked, and kicked the ball up the yard.

I felt my stomach muscles tense. 'Had an offer?'

'I been approached,' he admitted. 'If you're still interested it could go further.'

'I'm bloody interested. I've had enough of this.'

'Fifteen months!' he scoffed. 'That's nothing. But have you got the lolly? That's important.'

'How much?'

'Five thousand nicker—and that's just a starter,' said Johnny. 'It's to be put up before anything happens—before they even think about getting you out.'

'Christ! That's a lot of money.'

'I been told to tell you that this is the expense money—and it's non-returnable. The real payment will be more than that.'

66

'How much?'

'I dunno. That's all I been told. They want to know how soon you can spring the five thousand quid.'

'I can get it,' I said. 'I have funds tucked away in South Africa that no one knows about.' I looked along the exercise yard. Hudson was at the bottom end, making his way up slowly. 'I'll want a cheque form on the Standard Bank of South Africa, Hospital Hill Branch, Johannesburg. Got that?'

He repeated it slowly, then nodded. 'I got it.'

'I'll sign it, and they cash it. It'll have to be cashed in South Africa. That shouldn't be too difficult.'

'It'll take some time, mate,' said Johnny.

I laughed humourlessly. 'I've got nineteen years. But tell them to hurry. I'm getting nervous about being moved out of here.'

'Watch it—here's Hudson,' Johnny said. 'You'll be contacted.' He ran forward and intercepted the football and both he and I joined in the game.

The cheque form came ten days later. A new arrival brought it in and it was passed to me surreptitiously. 'I was told to give you this. Pass it to Sherwin when you've done with it.'

I knew Sherwin; he was due for release. I said quickly, 'Wait a minute; anything else?'

'I don't know nothing else,' the man muttered, and shuffled away.

That night I settled my correspondence course books on the table and started work as usual. I'd been plugging away at the Russian and I reckoned I was pretty good—my pronunciation had improved vastly since Slade's arrival although that makes no difference to the examiner's marks in a correspondence course. I carried on for half an hour and then dug out the cheque form and smoothed it out.

It had been quite a while since I'd seen that familiar sight, and I could almost smell the dust blowing off the Johannesburg mine dumps. The amount had been filled in—R10,000—Ten

Thousand Rand—and I thought the mob was laying it on a bit thick; since devaluation the value of the pound sterling had deteriorated relative to the Rand, and this cheque was for about £5,650. The payee line was blank—I wasn't supposed to know about that yet, and when I did find out it would be too late to do anything about it.

I filled in the date and added my signature—and it wasn't J. A. Rearden, either—then stuck the cheque between the pages of the Russian grammar, wondering if I was a wise man or the prize chump of all time. Someone could be conning me —it could even be Johnny Swift—and if he was I was over £5,000 in the red and all for nothing. But I had to rely on cupidity; if it was realized that there was more loot where that came from then someone would be back for more, but this time it would be payment by results—after the results had been achieved.

Next morning I passed the cheque on to Sherwin who palmed it expertly and I knew he wouldn't have any trouble in getting it out unseen. Sherwin was a card sharp and no one in 'C' Hall would dream of playing nap with him; he could make a deck of cards sit up and talk, and concealing a cheque would be no trouble at all.

Then I settled down to wait, wondering what expenses the mob would have that could run to five thousand quid.

The weeks went by and again nothing happened. I had figured out the time needed to cash the cheque and get word back to England and had estimated it at just over a week. When five long weeks had gone by without result I began to get edgy.

Then it broke very suddenly.

It was at free association time. Smeaton was giving me a minor dressing down for a small infraction; I'd not been cleaning up as well as I should have done—a sign that I was slipping. Cosgrove came up carrying a chess board. He waited until Smeaton had finished, then said, 'Cheer up, Rearden; what about a game?'

I knew Cosgrove; he'd been the brains behind a hi-jacking

mob—cigarettes and whisky mostly—and someone had squealed on him and he'd been pulled in and got ten years. He was in his sixth year and, with a bit of luck, he'd be out in another two. He was also the 'C' Hall chess champion, a very astute and intelligent man.

I said abstractedly, 'Not today, Cossie.'

He glanced sideways at Smeaton who was standing two paces away. 'Don't you want to win out?'

'Win out?' I said sharply.

'The big tournament.' He held up a box of chessmen. 'I'm sure I can give you a few tips if you play with me.'

We found a table at the other end of the Hall away from Smeaton. As we set out the pieces I said, 'Okay, what is this, Cossie?'

He put down a pawn. 'I'm your go-between. You speak to me and no one else. Understand?' I nodded briefly and he carried on. 'To begin with I'm going to talk money.'

'Then you can stop right now,' I said. 'Your mob already has over five thousand quid of mine, and I've yet to see a result.'

'You're seeing me, aren't you?' He looked around. 'Play chess—it's your first move.' I moved to QP3 and he laughed. 'You're a cautious man, Rearden; that's a piano opening.'

'Quit being subtle, Cossie. Say what you have to say.'

'I don't blame you for being cautious,' he said. 'All I'm saying is that it's going to cost you a hell of a lot more.'

'Not before I'm out of here,' I said. 'I'm not that much of a sucker.'

'I don't blame you,' said Cossie. 'It's like taking a jump in the dark. But the fact is we've got to talk money or the deal's off. We've both got to know where we stand.'

'All right. How much?'

He moved his king's knight. 'We're a bit like tax collectors—we take pro rata. You made a killing of £173,000. We want half—that's £86,500.'

'Don't be a bloody fool,' I said. 'There are too many things wrong with that calculation and you know it.'

'Such as?'

'There was only supposed to be £120,000 in that parcel. I think the owners were laying it on a bit.'

He nodded. 'Could be. Anything else?'

'Yes. Do you suppose we could sell for the full value? It's not like selling legitimate—you ought to know that more than anyone.'

'Play chess,' he said calmly. 'That screw's watching us. You could sell for full value with uncut diamonds if you were clever enough and I think you are clever. That wasn't a stupid job you pulled. You'd have got clean away if you hadn't been shopped.'

'They *weren't* uncut diamonds,' I said. 'They'd been cut in Amsterdam and were being brought back for setting. Diamonds of that value are X-rayed, photographed and registered. They've been recut and that means a hell of a drop in value. And another thing—I wasn't alone. I had a mate who's in on a fifty-fifty split. He planned it and I did it.'

'The boys were wondering about that,' said Cossie. 'They can't quite make you out. Did your mate shop you? Because if he did you've not got a bean, have you? And that means you're no good to us.'

'It wasn't my mate,' I said, hoping to make it stick.

'The buzz is going around that it was your mate.'

'The buzz couldn't have been started by a busy called Forbes—or another called Brunskill? They have their reasons, you know.'

'Could be,' he said thoughtfully. 'Who is your mate?'

'Nothing doing,' I said firmly. 'I didn't give him to the busies, and I'm not giving him to your mob. That, in itself, ought to prove he didn't shop me. My friend and I move along very quietly; we mind our business and we don't want anyone else minding it for us.'

'We'll let that one lie for a bit,' said Cossie. 'I'll put it to the boys. But that brings us back to the boodle—what was *your* take?'

'We estimated it at forty thousand nicker,' I said calmly. 'And it's out away safely. You get it through me—not my mate.'

He smiled slightly. 'In a Swiss numbered account?'

'That's right. It's quite safe.'

'So it's still half,' he said. 'Twenty years at a thousand a year —cheap at half price. We take you over the wall and deliver you *outside* the United Kingdom, and if you come back that's your trouble. But let me tell you something—you'd better not welsh on us; you'd better have the boodle for us because, if you don't, nobody will ever hear of you again. I hope that's quite clear.'

'It's very clear,' I said. 'You get me out of here and you'll get your money. I'll still be up on the deal, anyway.'

'I'll put it up to the boys,' he said. 'It's up to them whether you're accepted as a client.'

I said, 'Cossie, if your mob is as good as you say it is, what the hell are you doing in here? That puzzles me.'

'I'm just the contact man,' he said. 'I was recruited in here. Besides, I only have another two years' bird, then I'm out, anyway. Why make trouble for myself? I've got a good business waiting for me outside and I'm not going to throw that away.' He looked up. 'It'd be dicey for you if you came back to England.'

'That doesn't trouble me,' I said. 'I was only on the loose for a week in England—I know nothing about the place and I don't care to know any more.'

Cossie moved a piece. 'Check. There's another thing. You've been matey with Slade lately, haven't you? You do a lot of talking together.'

'He's helping me with my Russian,' I said, moving my king.

'That stops,' said Cossie flatly. 'You keep clear of Slade or the deal's off no matter how much money you have.'

I looked up, startled. 'What the hell . . .'

'That's the way it is,' he said equably, and moved his bishop. 'Check!'

71

'Don't tell me your mob is patriotic,' I said, and laughed. 'What's the idea?'

Cossie gave me a pained look. 'You ought to know better than to ask questions. You just do as you're told.' He turned to Smeaton who was walking past. 'What do you know?' he said. 'Rearden nearly beat me.' And that was a damned lie. 'He's got a good chance in the tournament.'

Smeaton looked at him with expressionless eyes and moved on.

3

So the game was on. I felt the tension rising in me and this time it was the tension of hope and not hopelessness. I even began to sing a bit as I scrubbed the tables in the Hall and I didn't slip up on a thing. Smeaton looked on me with approval, or as near to it as he could show. I was proving to be a model prisoner.

I obeyed Cosgrove's orders and dropped Slade who glanced at me reproachfully from time to time. I didn't know why Cossie wanted me to do that but this wasn't the time to argue it out. All the same, I felt a bit sorry for Slade; he hadn't too many friends in this nick.

I kept my eye on Cosgrove unobtrusively and watched who he talked to and who his pals were. As far as I could see he was as relaxed as usual and there were no changes in his normal pattern, but since I hadn't studied him especially before it was difficult to tell.

After a couple of weeks I went up to him during free association time. 'What about a game of chess, Cossie?'

He looked at me with blank eyes. 'Keep away from me, you silly bastard. I don't want to be involved with you.'

'You *are* involved,' I snapped. 'Smeaton was just asking if I wasn't going to enter the chess tournament, after all. He wanted to know if I'd given up my lessons. He also wanted to know if I'd given up Russian.'

Cosgrove blinked. 'Okay,' he said. 'Let's go over there.'

We set up the board. 'Any news?'

'I'll tell you when there's any news.' He was in a bad temper.

'Look, Cossie; I'm worried,' I said. 'I've just heard that the top security nick is finished—the one on Wight. I'm scared of being transferred. It could happen any time.'

He looked around the Hall. 'These things can't be rushed—it's a complicated set-up. What do you suppose you've paid five thousand quid for? Just a jump over a wall? There's a whole escape line to be laid on.' He moved a chess piece. 'I don't know much about that side of it, but I hear it's a different set-up every time. No pattern, see? You ought to know that, Rearden, of all people.'

I stared at him. 'I see someone's been checking up on me.'

He looked at me with cold eyes. 'What do you think? A part of that five thousand nicker went towards checking you out. The boys are very security-minded. You have an interesting record; I can't see why you slipped up this time.'

'It happens to all of us,' I said. 'I was shopped—same as you, Cossie.'

'But I *know* who shopped me,' he said savagely. 'And the bastard is going to regret it to his dying day once I get out of here.'

'Better have it done before you get out,' I advised. 'You have the perfect alibi—you're in the nick; and enough time has gone by so that the busies aren't likely to think of you.'

He smiled reluctantly. 'You have interesting ideas, Rearden.'

'And what makes you think I don't know who shopped *me*?' I asked. 'Trouble is I don't have contacts on the outside to arrange an accident.'

'I can arrange it,' he offered.

'Forget it. I'll be out myself soon enough if your mob comes up to scratch. So they had me investigated in South Africa, did they? I hope they were satisfied.'

'You passed. You've got some good friends out there.' Smeaton was passing close by. Cossie said, 'Not that move, stupid; it gives me mate in three moves.' He looked up at Smeaton. 'He's not as good as I thought he was; he'll never make it in the tournament.'

Smeaton sneered at him without moving a muscle of his face.

4

Cossie was right—I didn't make it in the tournament—but it wasn't because of my lousy chess. Two days later he came to me instead of *vice versa*. 'It's set up.'

'They changed my cell yesterday,' I said.

'Doesn't matter. You'll be taken out in daylight—from the exercise yard on Saturday. Three o'clock exactly—remember that.'

There was a sudden tightening in my belly. 'What's the drill?'

'Have you ever seen them putting up the Christmas lights in Regent Street?' Cossie asked. He snapped his fingers in annoyance. 'Of course, you haven't. Anyway, they have this truck, see, with a platform on a long articulated arm—to hoist up the electricians.'

'I know what you mean,' I said. 'They use them at Jan Smuts Airport at Jo'burg to service the big jets. They call them cherry-pickers.'

'Do they?' he said interestedly. 'I see why they might. Anyway, there'll be one of those coming over the wall on Saturday. I'll show you where to stand, and when it comes over you jump in quick. There'll be a bloke on the platform to help you, and you'll be out in two ticks. That's going over the wall in style.'

He turned to survey the Hall, then continued rapidly. 'There'll be a hell of a lot of other things going on at the same time, but you won't take any notice of all that. Just keep your mind on the big platform.'

'Okay,' I said.

'And I've been asked to tell you something—if you're taken out and you can't find the twenty thousand quid, then God

74

help you because no one else will. You'll not live to regret it—
and that's not a slip of the tongue. I was specially asked to tell
you that in case you want to change your mind.'

'The mob will get its money,' I said shortly.

'All right; I'll see you on Saturday then.' He turned away,
then paused and turned back. 'Oh, I nearly forgot,' he said
casually. 'Someone else is going with you, and you're going to
help him.'

'Who?'

Cosgrove looked at me blandly. 'Slade!'

CHAPTER FOUR

I

I STARED AT COSGROVE unbelievingly. 'Are you out of your mind?'

'What's the matter?' he asked. 'Don't you believe in freedom for others?'

'The matter!' My voice rose. 'The man walks with *sticks*, Cossie. He's a bloody cripple.'

'Keep your voice down,' he warned.

In a low voice I said savagely, 'How in hell is Slade supposed to make a break for it? He can't run.'

'You'll be there to help him, won't you?' said Cosgrove smoothly.

'Like hell I will.'

'Well, I'll tell you something, Rearden. Those sticks of his are a bit of a fake—he's been putting it on a bit ever since he came out of hospital. He can run well enough. Oh, I don't say he could break the four-minute mile, but he can toddle along enough for what we want.'

'Then he can bloody well toddle along by himself,' I said forcibly. 'Christ, if he obstructs my escape and I'm nabbed, I'll spend six months in solitary—and I'd certainly be sent to the new nick in Wight or to "E" Wing in Durham. I'd *never* get out of there.'

'The same applies to Slade,' said Cosgrove easily. 'And don't forget he's in for over forty years.' His voice tautened and a rasp entered into it. 'Now you listen to me, Rearden; Slade is a bloody sight more important to us than you are. You wouldn't believe how much money we have riding on him. So you'll bloody well do as you're told. As for going to Durham, you're due to be transferred there on Sunday, anyway.'

'Oh, boy!' I said. 'You play rough.'

'What's the matter? Is it that Slade is a spy? Has a sudden wave of patriotism overcome you?'

'Hell, no! I wouldn't care if he's inside for kidnapping the Queen, the Prime Minister and whole damned Cabinet. It's just that he's going to be a flaming liability.'

Cosgrove assumed a placatory tone. 'Well, now; maybe we can compensate you for that. Our agreement is that when we get you out then you pay us twenty thousand quid. Right?'

I nodded wearily. 'Right.'

'Suppose we cut that in half and make it ten thou'. With the live body of Slade as makeweight for the other ten thou'. How would you feel about that?'

'It has its points,' I conceded.

'I don't think it's at all bad considering you're going to be lumbered with Slade anyway,' said Cosgrove.

'Do you have authority for that offer?' I asked suspiciously.

'Of course I have,' he said, and smiled thinly. 'Of course, it has its converse side. If you get over the wall and Slade doesn't, then you get the chop. That's just so you remember that Slade is more important than you are.'

I said, 'This is just getting him over the wall?'

'That's it. Once the pair of you are on the other side my pals will look after you both.' He shrugged. 'It's a certainty Slade couldn't make it on his own so that's why we're doing it this way. I'll give it to you straight; he *can't* run very well. Neither could you with a stainless steel peg through each hip joint.'

'How is he at climbing?'

'His arms are strong but you might have to give him a bunk up when that platform comes over.'

'All right,' I said. 'I'd better have a talk to him.'

'No!' said Cosgrove. 'You don't go near him. That's part of the deal. He's been talked to already and he knows what to do. I'm the one who tells *you* what to do.' A bell rang stridently signifying the end of free association time. He flipped his hand at me. 'See you in the yard on Saturday.'

* * *

Saturday was a long time coming. I was in a muck sweat when they changed my cell again—two changes in three days—and I wondered if someone guessed that an escape was in the wind. It took all my will power to carry on with my studies in the evenings and my Russian suffered and I turned to the course on Eng. Lit. but found *Finnegan's Wake* hardly more relaxing in the circumstances.

I kept my eye on Slade and noted with glumness the obvious weakness of his legs. It wasn't going to be at all easy to get him over the wall, cherry-picker or no cherry-picker. Once he saw me watching him and his eyes casually swept past me without a flicker. I didn't see Cosgrove talking to him and came to the conclusion that he might have a different contact. It was possible that the whole damn prison was riddled by the hirelings of the Scarperers.

I scrubbed the tables and swept the Hall during the day and made sure I did a good job—even on the Saturday morning. I wanted no sign of abnormality to appear at all. But I hadn't much appetite for the midday meal and left most of it. At a table across the Hall I saw Slade polishing his tin plate with a slice of bread.

At two-thirty we were marched into the yard for free exercise. Some of the boys were kicking a ball about, but most strolled up and down enjoying the sun and the sky and the air. I drifted over to Cosgrove and we walked the length of the yard. He said, 'I'll tell you where it's coming over and then we walk right past, see? Then I'll take you to the place you have to wait. You stay there and you keep one eye on me and one on the wall—but don't stare at it as though expecting something to happen.'

'I'm not stupid.'

He grunted. 'That's as maybe. All right, we're coming to it now. See that chalk mark?'

'I see it,' I said, and almost laughed. It was a crudely phallic scrawl more likely to be found in a run-down public lavatory.

Cossie wasn't laughing. 'That's where it comes over. Now we

carry on to the end of the yard.' We walked on and turned in unison, just like the teachers who supervised the playground at school used to do when I was a kid. 'You might have to jump for it, but there'll be a bloke to help you.'

'Jump!' I said. 'What about Slade?'

'You give him a bunk-up first. There'll be ropes hanging from the platform. He'll be all right once he grabs those—he has strong arms.'

I saw Slade watching the football match with evident appreciation. 'He'll be leaving his sticks behind then.'

'That's obvious,' said Cosgrove impatiently. We strolled back to a point on the other side of the yard facing the chalk mark. Slade was leaning against the wall quite close to the mark and wouldn't have to move more than a few feet when the action started.

Cosgrove said, 'Now you just stay here and wait for it.' He consulted something he held in his fingers and I saw it was a very small ladies' watch. 'Nearly twenty minutes to go.'

The watch vanished. 'Where did you get that?' I asked.

'That doesn't matter,' he said with a sour grin. 'And I won't have it at all in twenty-five minutes. The screws'll act as though someone lit a fire under them when this comes off and they'll turn the whole bloody place upside down. They won't find this watch, though.'

I leaned against the wall and looked at the faint chalk mark on the other side of the yard. I could hear the traffic on the other side of that exterior wall but not much because it was Saturday afternoon with few commercial vehicles about.

Cosgrove said, 'I'll leave you now, and this is what you do. At two minutes to three a fight will start over in that corner. There'll be a lot of noise. As soon as you hear it you start walking—slowly, mind you—across the yard towards that mark. Don't make a fuss about it and, for God's sake, don't run. Slade will see you move and he'll get ready.'

'I could have done with talking to him about it myself,' I grumbled.

'Too dangerous,' said Cosgrove. 'Now, don't be surprised by anything else that happens around you, no matter what it is. Just keep your mind on your job and head for that mark. By the time you get there the platform will be coming over. You hoist Slade up on your shoulders and then you jump for it yourself. It should be easy.

'I'll be all right, Cossie.'

'Okay,' he said. 'Good luck, Rearden.' He grinned crookedly. 'Under the circumstances we won't shake hands. I'm going now; I'll be talking to Paddy Colquhoun until this thing's all over.' The watch appeared again. 'Fifteen minutes exactly.'

'Wait a minute,' I said. 'What about the closed circuit TV outside the wall?'

'That'll be taken care of,' he said patiently. 'Goodbye, Rearden.'

He walked away across the yard leaving me leaning against the wall alone. My hands were sweating and my mouth was suddenly dry as I looked at the barbed wire on top of the exterior wall. God help me if I got snagged on that. I wiped my wet hands on my trousers and squatted down on my heels.

Slade was standing next to the chalk mark and he, too, was alone. Probably everyone had been warned to keep clear of us; they wouldn't know why but they'd obey, especially if the warning had been given by the strong-arm boys. Accidents can be arranged, even in prison, and it's awfully easy to get a broken arm, or worse.

Cosgrove was talking to Paddy and they appeared to be enjoying a huge joke. I hoped the joke wasn't on me. I was taking a hell of a lot on faith, but if Cossie was conning me—if he was pulling a practical joke—I'd have his lights for a necktie. The prison wouldn't be big enough for both of us. But I looked across at Slade and knew, deep in my bones, that this was the real thing.

There were four screws in the yard, walking up and down with set, expressionless faces. And I knew there were two more watching from the high windows above my head. From there they could see into the street outside the exterior wall. God in heaven, surely they'd ring the alarm as soon as they saw that mechanical lift drive into the street. They couldn't be as stupid as all that.

The minutes went by. I found myself losing track of time. Fifteen minutes had already gone by—or was it only five? Again I could feel the sweat on the palms of my hands, and again I rubbed them dry. If I had to jump for a rope I didn't want any chance of slipping.

I looked at Cosgrove again. He was standing with his head cocked on one side listening to what Paddy had to say, and I saw him flick an eye towards me before he burst into a guffaw of laughter and slapped Paddy on the back.

I didn't see him give the signal but suddenly there were raised voices at the other end of the yard, so perhaps the slap on Paddy's back had been the signal. I got to my feet and began to walk slowly forward as though hypnotized by that distant chalk mark. Slade pushed himself away from the wall and came forward, hobbling on his sticks.

The men all around me were looking towards the disturbance which had grown noisier. Some of the prisoners were running in that direction and the screws had begun to converge on the fight. I glanced to my right and saw Hudson, the senior screw, who had apparently sprung from nowhere, making his way across the yard. He wasn't running but walking at a smart pace, and he was on a collision course with me.

Something astonishing happened behind. There was a sharp crack, like a minor explosion, and a billow of dense, white smoke erupted from the ground. I kept going but Hudson turned and stared. There were more explosions in the yard and the smoke grew thick and heavy. Somebody was being liberal with the smoke bombs that were being tossed over the wall.

Hudson was now behind me, and I heard his anguished bellow. 'Escape! Escape! Sound the alarm.'

Frantically he blew on his whistle but I kept going to where Slade was waiting. His face was set in lines of strain and as

I approached he said urgently, 'Where the hell is that damned contraption?'

I looked up and saw it coming over through the wreaths of smoke, looming over the wall like the head and neck of a prehistoric monster with slimy weeds dripping from its jaws. As it dipped down I saw that the weeds were four knotted ropes dangling from the platform on which stood a man who was, so help me, talking into a telephone.

I bent down. 'Come on, Slade; up you go!'

He dropped his sticks as I heaved him up and he made a grab at one of the ropes as it came within reach. He was no lightweight and it was not easy for me to hold him up. He caught on to the rope and I was thankful when his weight eased from me.

The man on the platform was looking down at us and when he saw that Slade had a secure hold he spoke urgently into the telephone and the platform began to rise. The only trouble about that was it was leaving me behind. I made a frantic leap and grasped the last knot on the same rope that Slade was climbing. He was going up fast but his legs were flailing about and he caught me under the jaw with the tip of his shoes. I felt dizzy and nearly let go but managed to tighten my grip at the last moment.

Then somebody grabbed my ankle and I looked down and saw it was Hudson, his face contorted with effort. The man had a grip like iron so I lifted my other leg and booted him in the face. I was learning from Slade already. He let go and tumbled to the ground which, by that time, seemed to be a long way down. I carried on up the rope, my shoulder muscles cracking, until I could grasp the edge of the platform.

Slade was sprawled on the steel floor, gasping with the effort he had made, and the man with the telephone bent down. 'Stay there,' he said. 'You'll be all right.' He spoke into the mouthpiece again.

I looked down and saw the barbed wire apparently moving away underneath as the great articulated arm swept me over the wall. Then it began to drop and the man bent down again, directing his words at both of us. 'Do exactly as I do,' he said calmly.

We were swept dizzily over the street and then stopped dead. A small open delivery truck came from nowhere and pulled up beneath the platform. The man swung over the railings of the platform and dropped lightly into the back of the truck and I thankfully let go of the rope and followed him. Slade came after and fell on top of me and I cursed him, but then he was thrown off me by a sudden surge of acceleration as the little truck took off and went round the first corner with a squeal of tyres.

I looked back along the street and saw the big cherry-picker move ponderously into view and the great arm fell forward, completely blocking the street. Men tumbled from the cab and ran, and then we turned another corner and I saw no more of that.

Slade leaned against the side of the truck with his head lolling on one side. His face was grey and he seemed thoroughly exhausted. I remembered that he had been in hospital not long before. The man with us thumped his elbow into my ribs. 'Pay attention!' he said sharply. 'You'll be transferring into a little black mini-van. Get ready to move.'

The truck was moving fast but there was little traffic to hinder us on that Saturday afternoon. Suddenly we swooped to a stop behind a mini-van which stood at the kerb with its rear doors open. 'That's it. Into there—quickly.'

I jumped out of the truck and took a header into the mini-van, and heard the doors slam shut behind. I lifted my head and, looking through the windscreen between two broad-shouldered men in the front seats, saw that the truck I had left was already on the move with Slade still in it. It turned ahead to the right and at high speed.

The mini-van took off more sedately, well within the speed limit, and turned to the left. I felt absolutely breathless. My lungs were strained and my heart was thumping as though it was going to burst in my chest. I lay there panting until I felt better and then raised myself and poked at the passenger in front with my finger. 'Why were we separated?'

He made no answer to that, so I tried again. 'Where are we going?'

'Shut up and keep down,' he said without turning. 'You'll find out soon enough.'

I relaxed as much as I could, sitting there on the hard metal floor of the van. From what I could gather from the brief glimpses I saw from the rear windows we were covering a complicated course among the streets, stopping properly at all the traffic lights and not moving fast enough to excite attention.

The van turned into a side street and swung up an alley. I leaned up on my elbow and looked forward cautiously. Ahead were two big wooden doors which were open, and inside the building was a huge moving-van with the tail-gate down. Without hesitation the driver headed right for it in low gear, bumped up the ramp formed by the tail-gate and drove right inside the pantechnicon. Behind us something came down from the roof, enclosing the van completely, and I heard the slam of the tail-gate as it was closed.

We were in complete darkness when the rear doors of the mini-van were opened. 'You can get out now.' It was a woman's voice.

I scrambled out and bumped into her, steadying myself on a soft arm. The front door of the mini-van slammed. 'For God's sake!' she said. 'Turn on a light.'

A light came on in the roof and I looked around. We were in a cramped compartment just big enough to take the van with a little space left over. The woman was a tall blonde, dressed in a white overall and looking like a doctor's reception-ist. One of the men pushed past me and bent down; I saw he was attaching a shackle to the rear bumper of the mini-van.

I heard the throb of a heavy diesel engine and the whole compartment lurched. The man straightened up and gave me a grin. He patted the side of the van. 'We don't want this to get loose, do we?'

There was another lurch and a grinding of gears. The big pantechnicon was travelling, taking me to—where?

The blonde smiled at me. 'We haven't much time,' she said practically. 'Take your clothes off.' I must have gaped at her because she said sharply, 'Strip, man! Don't be prudish—you won't be the first man I've seen ballock-naked.'

I took off the grey flannel jacket—the uniform of servitude—and watched her unpack a suitcase, producing underwear, socks, a shirt, a suit and a pair of shoes. 'You can start to get dressed in these,' she said. 'But don't put on the shirt yet.'

I took off the prison uniform and dressed in that lovely soft underwear, then balanced uneasily against the rocking motions of the moving pantechnicon to put on the socks. One of the men said, 'How does it feel to be out, chum?'

'I don't know. I'm not sure I'm out yet.'

'You are,' he assured me. 'You can bank on it.'

I put on the trousers and then the shoes. Everything was a perfect fit. 'How did you know my measurements?' I asked.

'We know *everything* about you,' the man said. 'Except maybe one thing.'

'And what's that?'

He struck a match and lit his cigarette, then blew a plume of smoke in my face. 'Where you keep your money. But you'll tell us, won't you?'

I zipped up the trousers. 'At the proper time,' I said.

'Come over here,' said the blonde. She had pulled up a stool in front of a basin set on a shelf. 'Sit down. I'm going to give you a shampoo.'

So I sat down and she lathered my hair, digging her fingers deep into my scalp. She rinsed and then shampooed again before giving a final rinse. Then she took me by the chin and tilted my head. 'That'll do. Now for the eyebrows.' She got to work on my eyebrows and when she had finished she handed me a mirror. 'How do you like yourself now?'

I looked at my reflection in the mirror. Gone was the black hair and I was now middling blond. I was surprised at the difference it made; even Mackintosh wouldn't recognize me now. I felt her fingers on my cheek. 'You'll have to shave twice a day. That dark five o'clock shadow would give you away. 'You'd better shave now—you'll find the kit in your suitcase.'

I opened the case and found it very well fitted out with everything a man would normally travel with. There was a small battery-powered shaver which I put into use immediately. As I shaved she began to lay objects on the shelf. 'Your name is Raymond Cruickshank,' she said. 'Here are your initialled cuff-links.'

'Do I have to be that kind of a man?' I asked lightly.

She wasn't amused. 'Don't be funny,' she said coldly. 'The same initials are on the suitcase. All this is your insurance, Rearden; insurance against getting caught—treat it seriously.'

'Sorry,' I said.

'You've been to Australia, Rearden. You were mixed up in something in Sydney a few years ago, so we've made you an Australian. People over here can't tell the difference between a South African and an Australian accent, so you should get away with it. Here's your passport.'

I picked it up and flipped it open. It had a photograph of a blond-haired me.

She produced a wallet and opened it for my inspection. 'This is all pure Cruickshank; you'd better check it to make sure you know what's in it.'

So I did, and was very surprised. This mob was super-efficient—no wonder Cossie had said it needed time to set up. There were membership cards of Sydney clubs, an odd Australian two-dollar note among the British currency, an Australian AA card together with an Australian driving licence and an International driving licence, a dozen business cards announcing where I lived and what I did—it seemed I was the managing director of a firm importing office machinery. All very efficient, indeed.

I held out a dog-eared photograph. 'What's this?'

'You and the wife and kids,' she said calmly.

I looked at it more closely in the dim light and, by God, she was right! At least, it was a blond-haired me with my arm around a brunette's waist and with a couple of kids in front. A nice tricky photograph.

I put it back into the wallet and felt something else at the bottom of the pocket which I dug out. It was an old theatre stub, dated two months previously—the theatre, naturally enough, was in Sydney. Apparently I had been to see *Fiddler on the Roof*.

I put it back carefully. 'Very nice,' I said admiringly. 'Very nice, indeed.' I laid down the wallet and began to put on my shirt. I was just about to fasten the sleeves with the cuff-links when she said, 'Mr Cruickshank, I said all this stuff was your insurance.'

I paused. 'Well?'

'Hold him, boys,' she said sharply, and I was grabbed from behind and held cruelly tight.

'What the hell . . . ?'

'Mr Cruickshank,' she said clearly. 'This is *our* insurance.' Her hand came from behind her back holding a hypodermic syringe which she held up to her eyes and squirted profession-ally. With one movement she rolled up the unfastened shirt sleeve. 'No hard feelings,' she said, and jabbed the needle into my arm.

There wasn't a damned thing I could do about it. I just stood there helplessly and watched her face go all swimmy. And then I didn't know any more about anything.

2

I woke up with the feeling of having been asleep for a long, long time. I didn't know why this should be, but it seemed a hundred years since I had gone to sleep in my cell, the new cell into which I had just been moved. I certainly didn't feel as though I had wakened from a normal night's sleep; after all, by now I had got used to the light being on all night.

And I had a hangover!

Hangovers I don't mind when there has been a cause for them; one takes one's pleasures and pays the consequences. But I strongly object to the consequences when the pleasure has been missed. I hadn't had a drink for eighteen months and to have an unaccountable hangover was abominable.

I lay there in bed with my eyes closed stickily. My head felt as though there was a red-hot iron bar wrapped around it and it throbbed as a blacksmith beat lustily on it with his hammer. I also had the old familiar dehydrated feeling and my mouth tasted, as a friend once inelegantly put it, like the inside of a Greek wrestler's jockstrap.

I turned over slowly and groaned involuntarily as the blacksmith gave an extra hard thump. Then I opened my eyes and looked at the ceiling vacantly. With care I traced the elegant moulding of the cornice which was picked out in gilt, being careful not to go too quickly in case my eyeballs fell out. 'Funny!' I thought. 'They've given me a nice cell this time.'

With grudging movements I leaned up on one elbow just in time to see someone leave. The door closed with a gentle click and there was the sound of a key turning in a lock. That was familiar enough, anyway, which was more than the cell was.

As I stared uncomprehendingly at the dove-grey walls and the gilt rococo panelling, at the Dolly Varden dressing table and the comfortable armchair standing on the thick-piled carpet, it hit me suddenly. My God, I made it! I got out of the nick!

I looked down at myself. I was dressed in silk pyjamas and the last time I had seen those was in the bottom of a suitcase in a moving-van.

A moving-van?

Slowly and painfully it all came back. The frantic grab at the rope; the wild swing over the barbed-wired wall; the jump into the truck; then the mini-van and the pantechnicon.

88

The pantechnicon! That was it. There was a blonde who had dyed my hair and who gave me a wallet. My name was Cruickshank and I was an Australian, she said. And then the bitch doped me. I put my hand to my arm and rubbed it where it felt sore. Now, why the hell had she done that?

I threw back the bed-clothes and swung out my legs. No sooner was I standing upright than I felt violently ill, and so I staggered to the nearest door which gave at a push and I fell into a bathroom. I lurched to my feet and over to the water-closet where I retched up my guts, but nothing came forth but a thin brown mucus. Still, when it was over I felt fractionally better, so I got to my feet and swayed towards the wash basin which I clutched hard as I stared into the mirror at the unfamiliar face.

She was right, I thought; the five o'clock shadow does give the game away. The blond hair with the black-bearded face looked incongruous and the whole ensemble wasn't improved by eyes which looked like burnt holes in a blanket. I rubbed my arm again and, on impulse, rolled up the pyjama sleeve to see *five* red pinpricks.

Five! How long had I been unconscious? I fingered my beard which rasped uncomfortably. That felt normal for about thirty-six hours, or maybe a bit longer. Unless they'd shaved me when I was dead to the world—which was a distinct possibility.

I turned on the cold tap and ran some water into the basin, then gave my face a thorough dousing, spluttering a bit. There was a clean towel at hand, and as I wiped myself dry I began to feel better, but the feeling tended to ooze away when I caught sight of the bathroom window. There were thick steel bars on the inside, and although the glass was frosted I could see the outline of similar bars on the outside.

That was going one better than the nick. Even in there they had but one set of bars to a window.

I dropped the towel on to the floor and went back into the bedroom. Sure enough the bedroom window was also barred inside and out, although here the glass was clear. I looked through the window and saw a courtyard surrounded by buildings. Nothing moved except a blackbird foraging for worms on a neatly mown lawn.

I watched the courtyard for five minutes but nothing happened, so I turned my attention to the bedroom. On the dressing table by the window was the toilet case and the shaver that the blonde had provided. I opened the case, took out a comb and combed my hair. Shaving could wait a while. I looked into the mirror and stuck out my tongue at the changed man who faced me. He did the same and I hastily pulled it in again as I saw the coating on the tongue.

Then I stiffened as I looked over his shoulder, and I whirled about to face the room. There were *two* beds; the one I had occupied had rumpled sheets, but the other bed was occupied. I strode over and found Slade breathing heavily through his mouth and totally unconscious. I slapped his cheeks and prised open his eyelids all to no avail; apart from the breathing he was a reasonable facsimile of a dead man.

So I left him to it, principally because I had seen a newspaper lying by the side of the armchair. Whoever had been waiting for me to wake up hadn't taken his *Sunday Times* with him.

We were front page news. The headlines blared in a most uncharacteristic *Sunday Times* manner, but I'd bet the *News of the World* outdid them in that respect. There was a photograph of the outside of the nick with a thick pecked line to show the course of events—there was a photograph of the cherry-picker with its neck collapsed across the entrance to a street, looking a bit like a dead Disney dinosaur from *Fantasia*; there was a photograph of someone being carried to an ambulance on a stretcher—Senior Prison Officer Hudson had unaccountably broken his leg!

The front page news story was pretty factual and they hadn't got much wrong as far as I could see. I read with interest that the exterior closed-circuit TV cameras had been rendered inoperable by having paint sprayed on to the lenses. That was a nice touch. It was also interesting to read that the small open truck had been found abandoned near Colchester, and the black mini-van near Southampton. Police had established road blocks around both areas.

Slade captured most of the limelight. What was a jewel thief compared with a master spy? But Brunskill had a go at me. 'This man is dangerous,' he said, with a straight face. 'He was convicted for a crime of violence and has a record of violence extending back for many years. The public should be wary of him and should on no account try to tackle him unaided.'

That was the most libellous thing I've ever read. Two convictions for violence over twelve years and I was being described as a Jack the Ripper. All Brunskill was trying to do was to build up the original arrest. I hoped his bosses threw the book at him for talking out of turn.

Insight had nothing to say about it, but they would, they would—I'd have to wait until next week's issue to get the inside story on how we'd escaped. But the editorial went off pop! The escape was described as a colossal piece of impudence and that if criminals were going to use such methods as mortar-fired smoke bombs then it was time that the prison authorities should also use military means to defend the integrity of the prisons.

I thought so, too.

Lord Mountbatten was not available for comment, but lots of other people were, whether they had anything relevant to say or not. One man especially fulminated about it—a Member of Parliament called Charles Wheeler who spoke bitterly about gangsterism in our English streets and swore he'd put a question to the House at the first available opportunity. I wished him luck. The mills of government grind slowly and it takes a hell of a long time to close even a stable door.

I quite enjoyed reading that Sunday paper.

I had just finished when the door clicked open and a man in a white coat wheeled in a trolley on which were several silver covered dishes. Behind him followed a tall man with a balding head fringed with silvery hair. 'Ah,' he said. 'I'm sure you would relish a light meal.'

I looked at the trolley. 'I might,' I said cautiously. 'If my stomach will stand it.'

He nodded gravely. 'You feel a little ill; that I can understand. You will find two bottles on the table. One contains aspirin and the other a stomach preparation. I had assumed you would find them.'

'I didn't,' I said, and held up the paper. 'I was more interested in this.'

He smiled. 'It does make interesting reading,' he agreed, and tapped the white-coated man on the shoulder. 'You can go now.' He turned back to me. 'You don't mind if I stay for tea?'

'Not at all,' I said magniloquently. 'Be my guest.'

White Coat had laid the table and pushed out the trolley; he closed the door behind him and again I heard the snap of the lock. They weren't taking any chances even with one of their own in the room. I looked with attention at the tall man; there was something incongruous about him which I couldn't put my finger on—and then I had it. He was tall and thin but had a curiously pudgy face, ill-suited to his build. It was as though the face of a fat man had been grafted on to a thin man's body.

He gestured. 'You'll find a dressing gown behind the bathroom door.'

I crossed to the table and found the two small bottles, then went into the bathroom. The stomach preparation I ignored but the aspirin was very welcome. I put on the dressing gown and returned to the bedroom to find Fatface in the act of pouring himself a cup of tea. 'You don't mind if I'm Mother?' he asked sardonically.

I sat down and picked up the glass of chilled tomato juice. Fatface pushed over the Worcestershire sauce. This improved it. I laced the juice liberally, added pepper, and drank it quickly. Almost immediately I felt better, but not so much better that I could face the breakfast that faced me when I

lifted the silver cover from my plate. I looked down at the
yellow eyes of eggs, with sausages for eyebrows and a bacon
moustache, and shuddered delicately. Pushing the plate away
distastefully I took a slice of toast and buttered it sparingly.

I said, 'If you're being Mother you can pour me a cup of
tea.'

'Certainly—anything to oblige.' He busied himself with the
teapot.

I crunched on the toast and said indistinctly, 'Anything?
Then perhaps you can tell me where I am.'

He shook his head regretfully. 'Then you'd know as much as
me—and that would never do. No, Mr Rearden; that is one of
the things I can't tell you. You realize, of course, that because
of that particular restriction your movements must be, shall we
say, circumscribed.'

I'd already figured that out; the double bars at the windows
weren't there for nothing. I jerked my head at the bed behind
me. 'Slade is a bit too circumscribed right now.'

'He'll be all right,' said Fatface. 'He's older than you and
takes longer to recover.' He passed me a cup of tea. 'You will
be confined to these two rooms until the time comes to move
you again.'

'And when will that be?'

'That depends entirely on you. We hope to make your stay
here as comfortable as possible. If you have any special
preferences at meals—grapefruit juice instead of tomato juice,
for instance—we will do our best to please you.' He rose to his
feet and crossed to a cabinet which he opened. It was well
stocked with bottles. 'You can help yourself to a drink at any
time. By the way, what cigarettes do you prefer?'

'Rothmans filter.'

He produced a notebook and made an entry like a con-
scientious *maître d'hôtel*. 'That we can manage easily.'

I grinned at him. 'I'd like a half-bottle of wine with lunch
and dinner. White, and on the dryish side; a hock or moselle,
preferably.'

'Very well.' He made another note. 'We try to run a top-class establishment. Of course, our expenses being what they are, our charges are high. In fact, there is a standard charge no matter how long you stay here. In your case I think it has been agreed already—twenty thousand pounds, wasn't it?'

I picked up my tea cup. 'It wasn't,' I said economically. 'Ten thousand pounds is lying on that bed over there. That was the deal.'

'Of course,' said Fatface. 'I forgot.'

'No, you didn't,' I said amiably. 'You were trying it on. Your tea is getting cold.'

He sat down again. 'We would prefer to settle the account as soon as possible. The sooner it is settled the sooner you will be able to go on the next stage of your journey.'

'To where?'

'I think you can leave that to us. I assure you it will be outside the United Kingdom.'

I frowned at that. 'I don't like buying a pig in a poke. I want a better guarantee than that, I want to know where I'm going.'

He spread his hands. 'I'm sorry, Mr Rearden; but our security arrangements preclude your knowing in advance. You must understand the importance of this. We cannot take any chances at all on the penetration of our organization by . . . er . . . undesirable elements.'

I hesitated, and he said impatiently, 'Come, Mr Rearden; you are an intelligent man. You must know that we have a reputation that rests entirely on our ability to keep our promises. Our good faith is our stock-in-trade and it would need but one dissatisfied client to do us irreparable harm.' He tapped gently on the table with his teaspoon. 'In any case, I believe you were informed of what would certainly happen to you if you did not keep your side of the bargain.'

The threat was there again—veiled but unmistakable. I had to play for time, so I said, 'All right; get me a cheque form of the *Züricher Ausführen Handelsbank*.'

Fatface looked pleased. 'And the number—the account number?'

'You'll know that when I put it on the cheque,' I said. 'I have security precautions, too, you know.' I did a quick calculation. 'Make it out for 200,000 Swiss francs. You take your share and let me have the balance in the currency of the country in which I'm being dropped.'

He nodded. 'A wise precaution. The sensible man never leaves himself short of liquid funds,' he said sententiously.

I looked down at myself. 'Do I *have* to live in pyjamas?'

He looked shocked. 'Of course not. I apologize for not telling you sooner. Your clothes are in the wardrobe.'

'Thanks.' I crossed the room and opened the wardrobe. Hanging up was a business suit and, next to it, a more sporty and informal outfit. Underwear was neatly laid out on the shelves and two pairs of highly polished shoes—black and brown—nestled in the shoe-rack.

I went through the pockets of the suits quickly and found them empty, then I clicked open the suitcase which stood at the bottom of the wardrobe and found it as empty as Mother Hubbard's cupboard. I swung on Fatface. 'No passport,' I said. 'No wallet—no identification.'

'We let you look at those to show our good faith, Mr Rearden—or should I call you Mr Cruickshank? We wanted you to see the lengths to which we would go to ensure a successful outcome of this enterprise. But there is no necessity for you to have them just yet. They will be returned to you prior to the next stage of your journey.' He wagged his finger at me solemnly. 'Security—that's the watchword here.'

That I could well believe. This mob considered all the angles.

Fatface said, 'If you want anything, all you have to do is to press this button—like this.' He waited, looking expectantly at the door, and White Coat arrived within two minutes. 'Taafe will look after you, Mr Rearden; won't you, Taafe?'

White Coat nodded, but said nothing.

'I must be going now,' said Fatface regretfully, as though he desired nothing more in the world than to stay and chat. 'We have to get on with our business.' He looked at me closely. 'I advise you to shave; you look most uncivilized. I daresay that while you are attending to your toilet Taafe will tidy up the room.' He gave me a brief nod and departed.

I looked curiously at Taafe who was busying himself with the breakfast crockery and leaving only his broad back for my inspection. He was a big man with the battered face of a small time bruiser—small time because good boxers don't get hit about like that. After a while I shrugged and went into the bathroom. It was a good idea, no matter who had suggested it.

I ran a bathful of hot water and settled down to soak and think. The mob was good—there was no doubt about that. Provided I could come up with the money I would undoubtedly be released in some foreign country with adequate, if fraudulent, identification and enough money to see me right. Of course, the converse wasn't too good—if I couldn't provide the funds required then I would probably occupy a cold hole in the ground in an isolated place and my bones would be discovered to mystify some rural copper in the distant future.

I shook my head. No—this mob was too efficient for that. They would leave no bones to be discovered. I would probably be encased in a block of concrete and tipped over the side into the deepest part of the sea available. It would be an act of charity if they killed me *before* pouring the concrete.

I shivered a little in spite of the hot water and thought glumly of the *Züricher Ausführen Handelsbank* and that cold-minded bastard, Mackintosh. I had better begin making plans to break out of this luxurious nick.

That brought me to another question. Where the hell was I? Fatface had played safe on that one, but maybe he had slipped up, after all. I thought about Taafe. That wasn't an English name at all—so could I be already out of England? It hadn't been smart of Fatface to let that name slip out.

As I mused, a little rhyme came into my head:

> *Taffy was a Welshman,*
> *Taffy was a thief;*
> *Taffy came to my house*
> *And stole a side of beef.*

I had learned that one at my mother's knee. Apart from being libellous to Welshmen did it mean that I was somewhere in Wales—still in the United Kingdom?

I sighed and splashed water. Time would tell, but time was something I hadn't much of.

CHAPTER FIVE

I

THEY LOOKED AFTER US like an international hotel looks after a couple of Greek shipping magnates. Nothing was too good for Mr Slade and Mr Rearden—nothing except immediate freedom. We asked for newspapers and we got newspapers; I asked for South African brandy and I got it—Oude Meester, too—something I had found unobtainable during my few days in London. Slade looked askance at my South African brandy; his tipple was 15-year-old Glenlivet which was also hospitably provided.

But when we asked for a television set or a radio we drew a blank. I said to Slade, 'Now why is that?'

He turned his heavy face towards me, his lips twisted with contempt for my minuscule intelligence. 'Because the programmes would tell us where we are,' he said patiently.

I acted dumb. 'But we get the newspapers regularly.'

'Oh, God!' he said, and stooped to pick up *The Times*. 'This is dated the fifth,' he said. 'Yesterday we had the issue of the fourth, and tomorrow we'll have the issue of the sixth. But it doesn't follow that today *is* the fifth. We could be in France, for example, and these newspapers are airmail editions.'

'Do you think we are in France?'

He looked from the window. 'It doesn't look like France, and neither does it . . .' He twitched his nose '. . . smell like France.' He shrugged. 'I don't know where we are.'

'And I don't suppose you care very much,' I said.

He smiled. 'Not really. All I know is that I'm going home.'

'Your people must think you're important,' I said.

'Moderately so,' he said modestly. 'I'll be glad to get home. I haven't seen Russia for twenty-eight years.'

'You must be bloody important if my help in getting you

out was worth ten thousand quid.' I turned to him and said seriously, 'As a sort of professional what do you think of this mob?'

He was affronted. 'A *sort* of professional! I'm good in my work.'

'You were caught,' I said coldly.

'After twenty-eight years,' he said. 'And then by sheer chance. I doubt if anyone could have done better.'

'Okay, you're good,' I said. 'Answer my question. What do you think of this crowd?'

'They're good,' he said judiciously. 'They're very good. Their security is first class and their organization impeccable.' He frowned. 'I didn't think ordinary criminals could retain that kind of cohesion.'

That thought had occurred to me and I didn't like it. 'You think they're in your line of work?'

'It's unlikely but just barely possible,' he said. 'To run a network takes a lot of money. The West Germans had the Gehlen *apparat* just after the war—that was more-or-less private enterprise but it was supported by American money.'

'Who would support this kind of outfit?' I asked.

He grinned at me. 'My people might.'

True enough. It seemed as though Slade was home and dry; instead of growing his beard in the nick he'd be knocking back vodka in the Kremlin with the boss of the KGB before very long, and dictating his memoirs as a highly placed member of British Intelligence. That much had come out at his trial; he'd infiltrated the British Intelligence Service and got himself into quite a high position.

He said, 'What do you think of me?'

'What am I supposed to think?'

'I spied on your country . . .'

'Not my country,' I said. 'I'm from the Republic of South Africa.' I grinned at him. 'And I come of Irish stock.'

'Ah, I had forgotten,' he said.

Taafe looked after us like Bunter looked after Lord Peter

Wimsey. The meals were on time and excellently cooked and the room kept immaculately tidy, but never a word could I get out of Taafe. He would obey instructions but when I sought to draw him into conversation he would look at me with his big blue eyes and keep his mouth tightly shut. I didn't hear him say one word the whole time I was imprisoned in that room, and I came to the conclusion he was dumb.

There was always another man outside the bedroom door. Sometimes I would catch a glimpse of him as Taafe came into the room, a dim and shadowy figure in the corridor. I never saw his face. I thought hard about him and came to a swift conclusion. It would be impossible for one man to keep up a twenty-four hour guard duty, so there would be three of them, at least. That meant at least five in the house, and maybe more.

I didn't see any women; it was a purely masculine establishment.

I checked on the bars of the windows, both in the bathroom and the bedroom, and Slade watched me with a sardonic amusement which I ignored. It seemed that to get out that way was impossible; it was the double-barred arrangement, inside and out, that was the trouble. Besides, Taafe checked them, too. I came out of the bathroom once to find him on a tour of inspection, making very thoroughly sure they hadn't been tampered with.

Fatface came to see us from time to time. He was affability itself and spent time by the hour discoursing on world affairs, the situation in Red China and the prospects for South Africa in Test Cricket. He would join us in a drink but took care not to take too much.

That gave me an idea. I took care to appear to drink a lot, both in his presence and out of it. He watched me swig the brandy and made no comment when I became maudlin. Luckily I have a hard head, harder than I allowed to appear, and I took damned good care not to drink too much in Fatface's absence, although I contrived to fool Slade as well. I didn't know that I could trust Slade very much if things came to the crunch. It was with regret that I poured many a half bottle of good hooch into the lavatory pan before pulling the chain for the night.

I've always found it good policy to appear to be what I'm not, and if Fatface and his mob thought I was a drunk then that might give me a slight edge when I needed it. There was certainly no attempt to stop me drinking. Taafe would take away the dead soldiers every morning and replace them with full bottles, and not a smile would crack his iron features. Slade, however, came to treat me with unreserved contempt.

Slade didn't play chess, but all the same I asked Fatface if he could rustle up a set of chessmen and a board as I wanted to work out chess problems. 'So you play chess,' he said interestedly. 'I'll give you a game, if you like. I'm not a bad player.'

He wasn't a bad player at all, though not as good as Cossie; but Cossie had more time to practise. He was certainly better than me and, after the first couple of games, he gave me two pawns advantage and I still had to battle to beat him.

Once, as we finished a game, he said, 'Alcohol and the type of concentration needed in chess don't mix, Rearden.'

I poured another slug of Oude Meester. 'I don't intend to take it up professionally,' I said indifferently. 'Here's to you . . . er . . . what the hell is your name, anyway?'

He kept a blank face. 'I don't think that matters.'

I giggled drunkenly. 'I think of you as Fatface.'

He was miffed at that and inclined to take umbrage. 'Well, I have to call you *something*,' I pointed out reasonably. 'What do you expect me to do? Whistle or shout "Hey, you!" '

But that crack lost me a chess partner.

The *Züricher Ausführen Handelsbank* cheque came a week after I had woken up in that room, and it was long enough for Slade and I to get on each other's nerves. I thought of the Swiss numbered account, of Mackintosh and of the slim chances of escape. What Slade thought about I don't know but he also became increasingly restless.

Once he was taken out of the room under guard, and when he returned an hour later, I said, 'What was that about?'

'A business conference,' he said enigmatically, and lapsed into silence.

My turn came the next day. I was taken downstairs and into a pleasant room which had just one fault—the curtains were drawn. The Scarperers were too bloody efficient for my own good; even here they were taking no chances of me finding out where I was.

Fatface came in and laid a cheque on the table. He unscrewed the cap of a fountain pen and put the pen down next to the cheque. 'The account number,' he said briefly.

I sat down and picked up the pen—and hesitated. Numbered accounts are funny things, and the number is something you guard as jealously as the combination of your safe.

I had to make this look good because he would be expecting it. I put down the pen, and said, 'Look, Fatface; any jiggery-pokery with this account and you'll wish you'd never been born. You take out of the account exactly the amount set out on this cheque—200,000 Swiss francs and not a centime more. If you clean out this account I'll find you and break your back.'

'Finding me might prove impossible,' he said suavely.

'Don't bank on it, buster; don't bank on it.' I stared at him. 'You've had me checked pretty thoroughly so you know my record. People have tried things on before, you know; and I have a reputation which you ought to know about by now. The word has got about that it's unprofitable to cross Rearden.' I put a lot of finality in my voice. 'You'd get found.'

If he was nervous he didn't show it, except that he swallowed before speaking. 'We have a reputation to keep up, too. There'll be no tampering with your account.'

'All right,' I said gruffly, and picked up the pen again. 'Just so we understand each other.' Carefully I wrote the number—

that long sequence of digits and letters which I had memorized at Mrs Smith's insistence—and put a stroke on the uprights of the sevens in the continental manner. 'How long will it take?'

He picked up the cheque and peered at it, then flapped it in the air to dry the ink. 'Another week.'

I watched the cheque fluttering in his hand and suddenly felt cold. Now I was totally committed.

2

Three days later they took Slade away and he didn't come back. I missed him. He had become an irritant but once he had gone I felt lonely and oddly apprehensive. I did not like at all the idea of us being separated and I had assumed that we would be going along the escape route together.

Fatface had taken a dislike to me and had stopped his social visits so I spent long hours at the window, screening my face behind the pot plants, and watched the courtyard through rain and sunshine. There wasn't much to see; just the unused gravel drive to the house and the trim lawn, much blackbird-pecked.

There was one peculiar thing that happened every morning at about the same time. I would hear the *clip-clip* of hooves; not the heavy *clip-clop* of a horse, but the lighter sound as of a pony, and accompanied by a musical clinking noise. It would stop and there would be more clinks and clanks and sometimes the faint piping whistle of a man pleased with himself. Then the *clip-clip* would begin again and fade away into the distance. And once, at this time, I saw the shadow of a man fall athwart the entrance to the courtyard, although I did not see him.

On an occasion when Fatface made a rare appearance I tried to talk my way out. 'Christ, I wish I could get some exercise,' I said. 'What about letting me stretch my legs in the courtyard?'

He shook his head.

'You can have a couple of your goons watching me,' I said, but then gave up as I saw I was making no impression. 'I should have stayed in the nick,' I grumbled. 'At least there was an exercise yard.'

Fatface laughed. 'And look what happened when you used it,' he pointed out. 'You got away. No, Rearden; if you want exercise do some physical jerks in this room.'

I shrugged and poured another drink. Fatface looked at me contemptuously. 'You'll rot your liver, Rearden. You'd better do some exercise if only to sweat the booze out of your system.'

'There's damn-all to do except drink,' I said sullenly, and took a swallow of brandy. I was glad he'd fallen for the line I was feeding him, even though it was becoming a strain to keep up. Reckoning by the dead soldiers Fatface would think I was getting through a bottle and a half a day, and when he was in the room I had to drink heavily in order to keep up the pretence. On this occasion I had drunk a quarter of a bottle in under an hour; I'm a fair drinker but my head was beginning to spin.

'What's the matter?' he asked. 'Getting edgy?' He smiled mirthlessly. 'Could it be there's nothing in that bank account? Could it be there is no bank account at all?' He stretched out his legs and looked at me thoughtfully. 'We know you were shopped, Rearden; and the story is that it was your partner who shopped you. I know you deny it, but it won't do you any good at all if your partner has skipped with all the loot leaving you holding the bag. I had my doubts about you when I heard Cosgrove's report.'

'You'll get your money,' I said. 'My mate will have seen me right.'

'I sincerely hope so,' he said. 'For your sake.'

But Fatface was right—I *was* getting edgy. I snapped at Taafe irritably when he brought my meals. It made no difference; he just looked at me with those baby blue eyes set in that battered face, said nothing and went about his business leaving me to pace the room and ignore the food.

The hours and days slipped by. Every morning I heard the *clip-clip* of the pony and the pleasantly fluting whistle; every day my chances became slimmer.

At last it happened.

Fatface came into the room. 'Well,' he said in an unusually jovial voice. 'You've surprised me, Rearden.'

'I have?'

'Yes. I rather think you've been playing fast and loose. We cashed your cheque.'

'I'm glad to hear it,' I said. 'I hope there was enough in the account to cover it.'

'Quite enough,' he said. 'You've been trying to lead me up the garden path, haven't you?'

'My God!' I said. 'I *told* you the money would be there.' I laughed a little uncertainly. 'You're like the man in Moscow who said, "Schmuel, you told me you were going to Minsk so I would think you were going to Pinsk, and you fooled me by going to Minsk, anyway. I can't believe a thing you say." '

'A very interesting illustration,' said Fatface dryly. 'Anyway, the money was there—all we needed.'

'Good!' I said. 'When do I leave?'

He gestured. 'Sit down. There's something we have to discuss.'

I walked around him to the liquor cabinet and poured a drink. This time I really needed it—I never *had* been absolutely sure of Mackintosh. I splashed water into the glass and sat down at the table. 'I'll be bloody glad to get out of this room.'

'I daresay you will,' said Fatface. He regarded me in silence for a long time, then said at last, 'There's just one snag. It's only a small detail, but it may prove to be an insuperable obstacle. Still, if you can explain it satisfactorily—and I don't mean explain it *away*—I see no reason why we can't carry on as planned.'

'I don't know what in hell you're talking about,' I said.

He lifted his eyebrows. 'Don't you? I'm sure you do. Think hard.'

'Don't play games, Fatface. If you've got anything to say, then spit it out.'

'All right,' he said. 'But *I'm* not playing games.' He leaned forward. 'Now, I know you're not Rearden but, for the record, I would like to know who the devil you are.'

It was as though a giant had gripped me hard and squeezed me in the belly, but I think I kept my face straight. 'Are you crazy?' I said.

'You know I'm not.'

I took a deep breath. 'Well, I think you are. What is this? Are you trying to welsh now you've got the loot?' I stuck my finger under his nose. 'I wouldn't try that, my friend; you'll come unstuck so bloody fast.'

'You're at a disadvantage,' said Fatface calmly. 'You're in no position to threaten anyone about anything. And I'd stop playing the innocent if I were you. You're not Rearden and we know it.'

'I'd like to see you prove it,' I said tightly.

'Don't be a damned fool—we have proved it.' He leaned back in his chair. 'You surely didn't think we pass a man on the escape line without checking him thoroughly—turning him inside out? We had you checked in South Africa and you failed the test. No police force is incorruptible—not the British police and not the South African police. If you are Rearden you must know John Vorster Square—you've been bounced in and out of there often enough.'

'But they never could prove anything,' I said.

'Yes, it's police headquarters in Johannesburg, isn't it?' He waved his hand. 'Oh, I'm sure you know the geography of Johannesburg well enough—but that doesn't prove that you are Rearden.'

'You haven't proved otherwise yet.'

'We have a friend in John Vorster Square, a brave police-man who does occasional odd jobs for us. He checked the files on Rearden and sent us a copy of Rearden's fingerprints. You've had it, chum, because they certainly don't match your dabs—and don't think we haven't tried over and over again, just to make sure.' He pointed to the glass I was holding. 'We've had plenty of chances to get your prints, you know.'

I stared at him for a long time. 'I know what a John Vorster Square dab-sheet looks like,' I said. 'I ought to—I've seen enough of them. You bring yours to me and I'll put my dabs anywhere you like for comparison.'

A veiled look filmed his eyes. 'All right,' he said abruptly. 'We'll do that. But I'll tell you something—you'll not leave this house alive until we know exactly who you are and what the hell you're doing here.'

'You know what I'm doing here,' I said tiredly. 'You bloody well brought me here. You've got your boodle, now keep your side of the bargain.'

He stood up. 'I'll be back tomorrow bright and early. That will give you plenty of time to think up a good story.' He pressed the service button. 'It had better be a true story.'

The door clicked unlocked and he stalked out.

I sat and looked at the amber liquid in the glass before me. Fatface was full of good ideas. Perhaps it would be better to think up not one story but two—the true story and a plausible false one. It would be difficult; I'm a pretty good liar when the need arises but I never was much good at sustained fiction.

3

Where does a thing like this begin? I suppose one might be logical and say it began at birth, but that's the trouble with logic—it leads to silly conclusions. Again, one might say it began in Johannesburg but it was only because of who I was— and what I was—that led to me being chosen, and so the roots go further back. Anyway, Johannesburg seemed to be a convenient point to begin, so I started to think of Jo'burg, that overgrown mining camp where the streets are paved with gold.

It was a bright sunny morning with not a cloud in the sky, something which might lighten the spirits of an Englishman but doesn't do a damn thing for a South African because most mornings are bright and sunny and clouds in winter are as rare as hens' teeth. I lived in Hillbrow in a flat in one of the towering blocks of concrete overlooking the city—the city which, at that moment, was covered with its usual layer of greasy smog. On and off, for twenty years, the City Fathers have been thinking of introducing the smokeless zone system, but they haven't got round to it yet.

A man living on his own either lives like a pig or develops certain labour-saving knacks, short-cuts like the egg in the coffee percolator. Within twenty minutes of getting up I was on my way down to the street. In the foyer I opened my personal letter box and collected the day's mail—three of those nasty envelopes with windows in them which I stuck into my pocket unopened—and a letter from Lucy.

I looked at it a little blankly. I hadn't heard from Lucy for over six years—six slow and uneventful years—and I couldn't really believe it at first. I read the letter again. It was just a quickly scrawled note really; green ink on expensive, deckle-edged writing paper.

Darling,

I'm in Johannesburg for a quick visit. Could I see you again for old time's sake? I'll be at the Zoo Lake restaurant at midday. I've changed, darling, I really have—so I'll be wearing a white gardenia. I don't want you to put your foot in it by accosting the wrong girl.

Please come, darling; I'm looking forward to seeing you so much.

Ever yours,
Lucy.

I sniffed the sheet of paper and caught a delicate fragrance. Lucy was up to her old tricks again. I put the note into my breast pocket and went back to my flat to telephone the office. I forget what excuse I used but I really couldn't tell the boss I wanted the day off to see an old girl friend. Then I took the car for servicing; it could be I would need it in a hurry and it had better be in good shape.

At a quarter to twelve I was drifting along the road towards the Zoo Lake. The expanses of winter-yellowed grass were dotted with black nannies looking after their young charges, and in the distance the lake twinkled under the hot sun. I put the car in the restaurant car park and wandered slowly down to the water's edge where people were feeding the birds.

There was nobody around who looked like Lucy. At least no one was wearing a gardenia. I looked across the lake at the people boating inexpertly then turned to go back to the restaurant where, just outside, a sand-coloured man sat on a bench fanning himself with his hat. He wore a white gardenia.

I walked over and sat beside him. 'Lucy?'

He turned and looked at me with curiously naked eyes. 'Lucy!' he said venomously. 'Ever since that Russian operation in Switzerland during the war the security clots have gone nuts on the name.' He put on his hat. 'I know who you are—I'm Mackintosh.'

'Glad to know you,' I said formally.

He cast a speculative eye at the lake. 'If I happened to be a crackerjack secret service man I'd suggest that we hire a boat and row into the middle of that bit of water so we could talk privately. But that's nonsense, of course. What I suggest is that we have an early lunch here. We'll be just as private, providing we don't shout, we'll be a bloody sight more comfortable, and I won't run the risk of making a damned fool of myself in a boat.'

'Suits me,' I said. 'I didn't have much breakfast.'

He arose and took the gardenia from his lapel to drop it into a convenient waste basket. 'Why people have this fetish for the sexual organs of vegetables is beyond me,' he said. 'Come on.'

We found a table in a corner in the outside court where a vine-covered trellis protected us from the heat of the sun. Mackintosh looked around and said appreciatively, 'This is a nice place. You South Africans know how to live well.'

I said, 'If you know who I am then you know I'm not a South African.'

'Of course,' he said, and took a notebook from his pocket. 'Let me see—ah, yes; Owen Edward Stannard, born in Hong Kong in 1934, educated in Australia.' He reeled off a string of schools. 'At university specialized in the study of Asiatic languages. Was recruited by a department that it is better not to mention while still at university. Worked in the field in Cambodia, Viet-Nam, Malaysia and Indonesia under a variety of covers. Was captured in Indonesia during the upheaval which disposed of Sukarno and cover badly blown.'

He looked up. 'I understand you had a nasty time there.'

I smiled. 'There are no scars.' That was true—no scars that were visible.

'Umph!' he said, and returned to his notebook. 'It was considered that your usefulness was at an end in the Far East so you were pulled out and sent to South Africa as a sleeper. That was seven years ago.' He snapped the notebook closed and put it back into his pocket. 'That would be while South Africa was still in the Commonwealth.'

'That's right,' I said.

'Our masters are not very trusting folk, are they? Anyway, you're here as a sleeper; you say nothing and do nothing until you're called upon—is that right?' He wagged a finger. 'Forgive the recapitulation but I'm from a different department. All this secret service stuff strikes me as being a bit comic opera, and I want to see if I've got it right.'

'You've got it right,' I assured him.

Serious conversation stopped then because a waiter came to take our order. I ordered crayfish cardinal because it wasn't often that someone stood me a lunch, while Mackintosh had something with a salad. We shared a bottle of wine.

When the dishes were on the table and it was safe to talk again Mackintosh said, 'Now I want to get this absolutely straight. Are you known to the police here—or to the security forces?'

'Not that I know of,' I said. 'I think my cover is safe.'

'So you've never had a prison sentence?'

'No.'

'What about civil cases?'

I considered. 'Just the usual things. I've had a couple of parking tickets. And a couple of years ago I had a legal barney with a man who owed me money; it came to a court case.'

'Who won?'

'He did, damn it!' I said feelingly.

Mackintosh smiled. 'I've been reading your record so I know most of these things. I just wanted to see your reactions. So what it comes to is that you have a clean record here as far as the local coppers are concerned.'

I nodded. 'That sums it up.'

'Good,' he said. 'Because you are going to be working with the South African police and it would never do if they knew you to be a British plant. I couldn't see them co-operating in those circumstances.' He nibbled on a lettuce leaf. 'Have you ever been to England?'

'Never,' I said, and hesitated. 'You ought to know that I've built up my cover with a slightly anti-British bias. It's a quite common thing here for even English-speaking people to be anti-British—especially since Rhodesia blew up. In the circumstances I thought it inadvisable to take a holiday in England.'

'I think we can forget your cover for a moment,' said Mackintosh. 'I'm authorized to pull you out if I find it necessary. The job I'm considering you for will be in England.'

It was very strange. All my adult life had been spent in the service of Britain and I'd never even seen the place. 'I'd like that,' I said.

'You might not like it when you hear what the job is,' said

Mackintosh grimly. He sampled the wine. 'Very nice,' he said appreciatively. 'If a touch acid.' He put down the glass. 'What do you know about the British prison system?'

'Nothing.'

'I'll let you have a copy of the Mountbatten Report, he said. 'You'll find it fascinating reading. But I'll give you the gist of it now. Lord Mountbatten found that the British prisons are as full of holes as a Swiss cheese. Do you know how many escapes there are each year?'

'No. There was something about it in the papers a couple of years ago, but I didn't read it up closely.'

'More than five hundred. If it's any less than that they think they've had a good year. Of course, most of the escapees are picked up quite soon, but a small percentage get clean away—and that small percentage is rising. It's a troublesome situation.'

'I can imagine it would be,' I said. I couldn't see his point, there was nothing in this to concern me.

Mackintosh wasn't a man to miss a nuance in a tone of voice. He looked me in the eye and said quietly, 'I don't give a damn how many murderers or rapists, homicidal maniacs or ordinary small time thieves get out of gaol. That's the worry of the prison officers and the police. My field is state security and, as far as I'm concerned, the situation is getting out of hand. The Prime Minister thinks likewise and he's told me to do something about it.'

'Oh!' I said uncertainly.

'Oh!' he echoed disgustedly. 'Look at it this way. We put Blake away for forty-two years, not altogether as a punishment but to keep him out of the hands of the Russians. Within five years he flies the coop and pops up in Moscow where he chirps his head off. Christ, they even gave him a medal, and that was a slap in the face.'

He looked broodingly into his glass. 'Suppose Blake hadn't got clean away—suppose he'd been picked up in a month. The police would be happy and so would the prison officers, but damn it all to hell, I wouldn't! I'd want to know what the devil he'd been doing that month—who he'd been talking to. See my point?'

I nodded. 'If that happened the major reason for gaoling him would disappear. To slap him back in chokey for another forty years would be like closing the stable door after the horse has gone.'

'The horse being the information in Blake's head—not the man himself.' Mackintosh moved restlessly. 'They're building a high security prison on the Isle of Wight. Mountbatten wants to call it Vectis which shows that, among other things, he's had a classical education. A very able man, Mountbatten. He took one look at the plans of this high class chicken-coop and demonstrated how easy it would be to get a man out.'

He looked at me expectantly as though he wanted me to say something, so I obliged. 'To *get* a man out?'

He grinned. 'I'm pleased to see you live up to the good things your dossier records of you.' He held out his glass. 'I rather like this wine.'

I gave him a refill. 'It's nice to know I'm appreciated.'

'If you read the Mountbatten Report—particularly the bits towards the end where he discusses this new prison—you'll find yourself wondering if you haven't come across a major work of science fiction. Closed-circuit television with delay lines and electronic logic circuits which trigger an alarm if anything moves in the field of vision is one nice idea—that's for the defence, of course. For the attack there are helicopters and rocket-powered jump suits, for God's sake! Very James Bondery. Do you get the drift of it?'

'Yes,' I said slowly. 'Organization.'

'Right!' said Mackintosh. 'For the first time in years someone has come up with a brand new crime. Crime is just like any other business—it's conducted only for profit—and someone has figured a way to make a profit out of getting people out of prison. I suppose it started with the Great Train Robbery; those boys were given exceptionally heavy sentences—Biggs and Wilson got thirty years each—but they had money and were able to buy an organization.'

He sighed. 'Sometimes I wonder if the judges know what the devil they're doing. A murderer can be out in ten years or less, but watch your step if you commit a crime against property. Anyway, an organization was set up, dedicated to springing long term prisoners who could pay enough, and you'd be surprised how many of those there are. And once such an organization gets going, like any other business it tends to expand, and whoever is running it has gone looking for custom—and he doesn't care where the money comes from, either.'

'The Russians?'

'Who else,' said Mackintosh sourly. 'I don't care if all the train robbers fly the coop and live the life of Riley on the Riviera, but when it comes to state security then something must be done.' He frowned. 'If I had my way such security risks would be collected together in a special prison and guarded by the army—military police empowered to kill if necessary. But our masters prefer not to do it that way.'

I said curiously, 'Where do I come into all this?'

'I haven't finished putting you in the picture,' he said irritably. 'The PM wanted something done about it—so something was done. The police had a crack at it, and so did the Special Branch and the more shady and esoteric counter-intelligence units. They all got nowhere. There was one occasion when they did get a bit close to it; a prisoner already in gaol expressed a willingness to talk. Guess what happened to him.'

I'm a realist, so I said flatly, 'He died suddenly.'

'Oh, he was killed, all right,' said Mackintosh. 'But this gang sprung him from prison to do it. Can't you see the flaming impudence of it? This organization is so bloody sure of itself that it can take a man out of one of Her Majesty's prisons who doesn't want to go. One cheep from him and he'd still be alive —but they were still able to spring him. His body was found three days later; he'd been shot through the back of the head.'

'I didn't see any reports on that,' I said.

'It was put under security wraps immediately,' said Mackintosh a little tiredly. 'Nobody wanted a thing like *that* to be aired publicly. There's a veiled reference to it in the Mountbatten Report—look at paragraph 260.'

'Where do I come in?' I asked again.

'I'll come to you when I'm good and ready. Now, my business is state security, and you can put out of your head any guff about counter-intelligence cloak-and-dagger stuff. I work on a quite different plane, at Cabinet level, in fact—responsible and reporting to only the Prime Minister. Since everybody else has fallen down on this job he has given me the sole and total responsibility of getting the job done in my own peculiar way—but not in my own time.' He rubbed the top of his head. 'Of course, time is a relative thing, as I explained to the PM and he agreed. But let's hope there are no more security escapes while I'm in charge, because it's my head that's on the block.'

He looked around and waved at a waiter. 'Let's have coffee —and I think I'll have a van der Hum; I believe in sampling the wine of the country. Will you join me?'

'I'll have a Drambuie,' I said dryly.

He ordered the coffee and the liqueurs, then said abruptly, 'Ever heard of a man called Rearden—Joseph Rearden?'

I thought about it for a while. 'No.'

'I didn't think you would. Rearden is—or was—a criminal. A very good one, too. Clever, intelligent and resourceful; somewhat like you, I'd say.'

'Thanks for the compliment.' I said. 'He's dead?'

'He was killed three weeks ago in South-West Africa. No funny business suspected—just a plain ordinary car crash. The God of Motorists sacrifices good and bad alike. The point is that no one knows he's dead, except you, me and a few highly placed South African coppers. When the PM gave me this Godawful job certain facilities were placed at my disposal, and I immediately began to look for someone like Rearden—a newly dead rotten egg whose death could be hushed up. He could have been found in Canada, Australia, New Zealand, the States or, even, South America. The fact is that he turned up in South Africa. Here's his photograph.'

I laid it face down on the table as the waiter served the coffee and only turned it up when we were alone again. Mackintosh watched me approvingly as I scanned the picture. He said, 'As soon as I had Rearden I began to look for someone who looked like Rearden, someone who could pass for a South African. Computers are marvellous gadgets—one came up with you in twenty minutes.'

'So it's going to be a substitution,' I said. 'I've done that kind of thing before, but it's risky. I could be spotted very easily.'

'I don't think so,' said Mackintosh confidently. 'To begin with, you'll be in England where Rearden has never been and, even so, you won't be moving about England much so it's unlikely you'll bump into any of his old pals.'

I said, 'What happened to Rearden's body?'

'He was buried under another name. I pulled some strings.'

'Tough luck on his family,' I said. 'Did he have a wife?'

'No wife—and his parents will get along without him.'

I looked at this spare man with the thinning sandy hair and the colourless eyelashes and thought that he was a pretty ruthless bastard. I wondered how I would get along with him in this peculiar arrangement he was planning. 'So I'm Rearden,' I said. 'And I'm in England. What then?'

'Not so fast,' said Mackintosh. 'Although Rearden was clever he lost—once only. He served a prison sentence in Pretoria a while ago. Do you know anything of South African prisons?'

'Not a thing, thank God!'

'You'd better learn. I'll have a man give you a course on prison conditions and the slang—especially the slang.' He offered me a twisted smile. 'It might be a good idea if you did time for a month to get the right idea. I can arrange that.' I could see him turning the idea over in his mind and rejecting it. He shook his head. 'No, that won't do. It's too risky.'

116

I was glad of that; I don't particularly like gaols. He drained his coffee cup. 'Let's leave here; the place is filling up and I'd like to discuss the rest of it in greater privacy.' He paid the bill and we left the restaurant and strolled into the middle distance to sit under a gum tree where there were no ears within fifty yards.

He took out a pipe and started to fill it. 'All the people who have tried to crack this organization have failed. They've tried it from the outside and failed, and they've tried penetration and failed. They've tried to ring in fake gaolbirds—and failed. The organization has fantastically good security because we know as much now as we did at the beginning—and that's only one thing. The organization is known to the underworld as the Scarperers, and that doesn't get us very far.'

He struck a match. 'Stannard, this is a volunteer's job, and I'll have to ask you to make up your mind now. I can't tell you anything more—I've already told you too much. I suppose I must tell you that if anything goes wrong it'll go badly for you —and your death may not be the worst thing that can happen. Not in my book, at any rate. It's a tricky and dangerous task and, I don't mind telling you, I wouldn't volunteer for it myself. I can't be more honest than that.'

I lay back on the grass and looked up at the sky, leaf-dappled through the branches of the gum tree. My life in South Africa had been calm and uneventful. Seven years before I had been in pretty bad shape and I'd sworn I'd never do that kind of thing again. I suppose my bosses had seen that frame of mind and had given me the job of a sleeper in South Africa as a sort of sinecure—a reward for past services. God knows, I had done nothing to earn the retainer that was piling up quite nicely in that British bank account and which I had never touched.

But time heals everything and of late I had been restless, wishing that something would happen—an earthquake— anything. And here was my earthquake in the person of this insignificant-looking man, Mackintosh—a man who hob-nobbed with the Cabinet, who chit-chatted about security with the Prime Minister. I had a vague idea of what he was getting at and it didn't seem difficult. Risky, perhaps; but not too difficult. I wasn't afraid of a gang of English crooks; they couldn't be worse than the boys I'd been up against in Indonesia. I'd seen whole towns full of corpses there.

I sat up. 'All right; I volunteer.'

Mackintosh looked at me a little sadly and thumped me gently on the arm. 'You're a lunatic,' he said. 'But I'm glad to have you. Perhaps we need a little lunacy on this job; orthodox methods haven't got us anywhere.'

He pointed at me with the stem of his pipe. 'This is top-secret. From now on only three people will know about it; you me and one other—not even the PM knows.' He chuckled sardonically. 'I tried to tell him but he didn't want to know. He knows how my mind works and he said he wanted to keep his hands clean—he said he might have to answer questions in the House and he didn't want to be put in the position of lying.'

I said, 'What about the South African police?'

'They know nothing,' said Mackintosh flatly. 'It's a *quid pro quo*—a favour returned. They might do a bit of digging into your background, though. Can it stand it?'

'It should,' I said. 'It was designed by experts.'

Mackintosh drew gently on his pipe and blew out a plume of smoke. 'Other people have tried to penetrate this damned organization and they've failed—so we start from there and ask, "Why did they fail?" One of the more promising gambits was to ring in a fake prisoner and wait for advances to be made. At one time there were no less than eight of these decoys scattered through the British prisons. Not one of them was contacted. What does that suggest to you?'

'The Scarperers have a good intelligence service,' I said. 'I'll bet they do a preliminary check before contact.'

'I agree—and that means that our bait, which is Rearden, must stand up to rigorous scrutiny. There must be no cracks in the cover at all. Anything else?'

'Not that I can think of off-hand.'

'Use your loaf,' said Mackintosh with an air of disgust. 'The crime, man; the crime! Rearden—or, rather, you—is going to commit a crime in England. You'll be caught—I'll see to that —you'll be tried and you'll be jugged. And it has to be a particular form of crime; a crime which involves a lot of money and where the money isn't recovered. The Scarperers have to be convinced that you can pay hard cash for your escape. Now, what does that suggest to you—in view of what I've already told you?'

'Nothing much,' I said. 'It shouldn't be too difficult to arrange.'

'No, it shouldn't be too difficult,' said Mackintosh in an odd voice. 'Look here, Stannard; this is going to be a genuine crime—don't you understand that? Nothing else will do. I am going to plan, and you are going to execute, a crime of some magnitude. We are going to steal a considerable sum of money from some inoffensive British citizen who will scream to high heaven. There's going to be no fake about it because . . .' He spaced his words very distinctly. '. . . I . . . will . . . not . . . risk . . . breaking . . . security.'

He turned and said very earnestly, 'If this is so then when you are tried and gaoled you will be in the jug for a perfectly genuine crime, and if anything goes wrong there will be nothing that I, or anyone else, can do about it. If you get fourteen years then you'll rot in prison for your sentence if the Scarperers don't contact you. And the reason for that is because I *cannot* compromise security on this operation. Are you willing to risk it?'

I took a deep breath. 'Christ! You're asking a hell of a lot, aren't you?'

'It's the way it's got to be,' he said doggedly. 'A trained man like you should be able to get out of any leaky British prison without half trying. But you won't, damn you! You'll sit on your backside and wait for the Scarperers to get you, no matter how long they take to make up their minds. You'll bloody well wait, do you hear?'

I looked into his fanatical eyes and said very gently, 'I hear. Don't worry; I'm not going to back out now. I gave you my word.'

He took a deep breath and relaxed. 'Thanks, Stannard.' He grinned at me. 'I wasn't worried about you—not *too* worried.'

'I've been wondering about something,' I said. 'Mountbatten investigated the prisons when Blake flew the coop. That was quite a long time ago. Why all the sudden rush now?'

Mackintosh reached out and knocked out his pipe on the trunk of the tree. 'A good question,' he agreed. 'Well, for one thing, the effect of Mountbatten is wearing off. When the Report came out and the prisons tightened security every sociologist and prison reformer in Britain let out an outraged howl—and I'm not saying they were wrong, either. There are two ways of regarding prisons—as places of punishment and as places of rehabilitation. The suddenly tightened security knocked rehabilitation right out of the window and the penal reformers say it did ten years of damage in six months.'

He shrugged. 'They're probably right, but that's outside my field. I'm not interested in civil prisoners—it's the Blakes and Lonsdales of this world who are my meat. When you catch them you can either put them up against a wall and shoot them, or you can put them in chokey. But you imprison them not to punish and not to rehabilitate, but to keep them out of circulation because of what they know.'

There was nothing in this to explain the question I had asked, so I prompted him. 'So what now?'

'There's a big fish coming down the line,' he said. 'The biggest we've caught yet. God knows, Blake was big enough, but this man is a shark to Blake's tiddler—and he must not escape. I've pleaded with the PM to establish a special prison for this type of prisoner but he says it's against policy, and so Slade goes into the general prison system, admittedly as a high risk man.'

'Slade!' I said thoughtfully. 'Never heard of him.'

'He's in hospital,' said Mackintosh. 'He was shot through

the hips when he was caught. When he's fit he'll stand trial, and if we handed out sentences like the Texans he'd get five thousand years. As it is, we must keep him secure for the next twenty—after that it won't matter very much.'

'Twenty years! He must know a hell of a lot.'

Mackintosh turned a disgusted face towards me. 'Can you imagine that a Russian—and Slade is a Russian—could get to be second-in-command of an important department of British Intelligence concerned with counter-espionage in Scandinavia? Well, it happened, and Sir David Taggart, the damned fool who put him there, has been kicked upstairs—he's now Lord Taggart with a life peerage.' He snorted. 'But he won't be making any speeches or doing any voting. If he knows what's good for him he'll keep his mouth permanently shut.'

He blinked his colourless eyelashes and said in a passionately suppressed voice, 'The man who caught Slade was a man whom Taggart had fired for inefficiency, for God's sake!' He rapped his pipe against the tree with such force that I thought it would break. 'Amateurs!' he said in a scathing voice. 'These bloody amateurs running their piddling private armies. They make me sick.'

'How do I relate to Slade?' I asked.

'I'm going to try to put you next to him,' he said. 'And that will mean breaking the law. What Slade knows is sheer dynamite and I'd break every law in Britain, from sodomy upwards, to keep that bastard inside where he belongs.' He chuckled and thumped my arm. 'We're not just going to bend the laws of England, Stannard; we're going to smash them.'

I said a little shakily, 'Now I *know* why the Prime Minister wouldn't listen to you.'

'Oh, yes,' said Mackintosh matter-of-factly. 'It would make him accessory to the crime, and he's too much the gentleman to get his hands dirty. Besides, it would lie heavily on his conscience.' He looked up at the sky and said musingly, 'Funny animals, politicians.'

I said, 'Do you know what kind of a tree this is?'

He turned and looked at it. 'No, I don't.'

'It's a gum tree,' I said. 'The thing I'll be up if this operation doesn't pan out. Take a good look at it.'

4

I suppose you could call Mackintosh a patriot—of sorts. There don't seem to be many avowed patriots around these days; it has become the fashion to sneer at patriotism—the TV satire programmes jeer at it, and to the with-it, swinging set it's a dead issue. So with patriots so few on the ground you can't pick and choose too freely. Certainly, to a casual eye Mackintosh bore a remarkable resemblance to a dyed-in-the-wool fascist; his God was Britain—not the Britain of green fields and pleasant country lanes, of stately buildings and busy towns, but the *idea* of Britain incorporated in the State. He took his views directly from Plato, Machiavelli and Cromwell who, if you think about it, aren't all that different from Mussolini, Hitler and Stalin.

But there was more to him than that as I found out later—much later.

There was a lot of work to be done and not a great deal of time in which to do it. I studied South African prison conditions with a prison officer, temporarily donning the guise of a sociologist for the occasion. He advised me to read the works of Herman Charles Bosman which was a superfluity as I had already done so. Bosman, possibly the best writer in English South Africa has produced, knew all about prison conditions —he had done a stretch for killing his step-brother and he wrote illuminatingly about his experiences in Pretoria Central Prison—Pretoria Tronk, in the vernacular—which conveniently was where Rearden had served his sentence.

I also studied Rearden's record, culled from the files of John Vorster Square. There was not much fact and a hell of a lot of conjecture in that file. Rearden had been imprisoned only once and that for a comparatively minor offence, but the conjecture was lurid. He was suspected of practically every crime in the book from burglary to drug-smuggling, from armed robbery to illicit gold buying. He was a many-faceted character, all nerve and intelligence, whose erratic and unexpected switches in criminal activity had kept him out of trouble. He would have made a good intelligence agent.

I smiled at that. Perhaps Mackintosh had been right when he said that Rearden was like me. I had no illusions about myself or my job. It was a dirty business with no holds barred and precious little honour, and I was good at it, as would have been Rearden if anyone had had the sense to recruit him. So there we were—birds of a feather—Mackintosh, Rearden and Stannard.

Mackintosh was busy on the upper levels of the job in South Africa—pulling strings. From the way people danced to his tune like marionettes I judged he had been right when he said the Prime Minister had given him 'certain facilities'. This was counter-espionage work at diplomatic level and I wondered what was the *quid pro quo*—what the hell had we done for the South Africans that we should be given this VIP treatment with no questions asked?

Gradually I was transformed into Rearden. A different style of haircut made a lot of difference and I took much trouble with the Transvaal accent, the accent of the Reef towns. I studied photographs of Rearden and copied his way of dress and his stance. It was a pity we had no films of him in action; the way a man moves means a lot. But that I would have to chance.

I said to Mackintosh once, 'You say I'm not likely to run into any of Rearden's pals in England because I'm not going to be at large for very long. That's all very well, but I'm a hell of a lot more likely to run into his mates when I'm in the nick than when I'm walking up Oxford Street.'

Mackintosh looked thoughtful. 'That's true. What I can do is this; I'll have a check done on the inhabitants of the prison you're in, and any that have been to South Africa I'll have transferred. There shouldn't be too many and it will minimize your risk. The reason for transfer shouldn't become apparent —prisoners are being transferred all the time.'

He drilled me unmercifully.

'What's your father's name?'

'Joseph Rearden.'

'Occupation?'

'Miner—retired.'

'Mother's name?'

'Magrit.'

'Maiden name?'

'Van der Oosthuizen.'

'Where were you born?'

'Brakpan.'

'The date?'

'28th May, 1944.'

'Where were you in June, 1968?'

'. . . er . . . in Cape Town.'

'Which hotel did you use?'

'Arthur's Seat.'

Mackintosh stuck his finger under my nose. 'Wrong! That was in November of the same year. You'll have to do better than that.'

'I could get away with it if I had to,' I said.

'Maybe. But this has to be a seamless job—no cracks which need papering over. You'd better get down to studying a bit more.'

Again I pushed my nose into the files, if a little resentfully. My God, a man wasn't supposed to remember and account for every minute of his life. But I knew Mackintosh was right. The more I knew about Rearden, the safer I'd be.

At last it was over and Mackintosh was due to return to England. He said, 'The local coppers are a bit worried about you; they're wondering why you've been picked for this job. They're wondering how I was able to lay my hands on an

Australian immigrant to impersonate Rearden. I don't think you'll be able to come back here.'

'Will they talk?'

'There'll be no talk,' he said positively. 'There are only a few of the top brass who know about you, and they don't know *why*—that's why they're becoming curious. But it's all top-secret, diplomatic-level, hush-hush stuff and that's something the South Africans are good at. They understand security. As far as the middle and lower levels of the police are concerned —well, they'll be a bit surprised when Rearden gets nabbed in England, but they'll just heave a sigh of relief and cross him off the books for a few years.'

I said, 'If you're right about the Scarperers they'll be doing some extensive checking here in South Africa.'

'It'll stand up,' he said with certainty. 'You've done a good job on this, Stannard.' He smiled. 'When it's all over you'll probably get a medal. There'll be a few private words with the people concerned—insurance company, whoever we rob, and so on. The Home Secretary will probably issue a free pardon and you won't have a stain on your character.'

'If it comes off,' I said. 'If it doesn't, I'll be up that bloody gum tree.' I looked straight at him. 'I want a bit of insurance on this. I know you're nuts on security—and rightly so. As you've organized it there'll be only three people who know about this operation—you, me and one other. I'd like to know who this "other" is, just in case anything happens to you. I'd be in a hell of a mess if you got run over by a bus.'

He thought about that. 'Fair enough,' he said. 'It's my secretary.'

'Your secretary,' I said expressionlessly.

'Oh, Mrs Smith is a very good secretary,' he said. 'Very efficient. She's hard at work on this case now.'

I nodded. 'There's something else,' I said. 'I've been going over possible eventualities. What happens if I'm sprung and Slade isn't?'

'Then you go for the Scarperers, of course.'

'And if Slade is sprung and I'm not?'

Mackintosh shrugged. 'That wouldn't be your fault. We'd have to leave it to the ordinary authorities. Not that I'd like it very much.'

'Try this on for size,' I said. 'Supposing both Slade and I are sprung. What then?'

'Ah,' he said. 'I see what you mean.'

'Yes; I thought you would. Which is the more important? To smash the Scarperers or to take Slade back to the jug?'

He was silent for a moment. 'Slade is obviously the more important, although ideally I'd like you to pull off both jobs should that eventuality arise. As far as taking Slade back to prison goes you may use your own discretion. If he turned up dead I wouldn't shed a single tear. The important thing about Slade is that he must not get loose—he must not communicate any information to a third party.' He flicked his pale blue eyes in my direction. 'Dead men tell no tales.'

So that was it. Orders to kill Slade—at my discretion. I began to understand the Prime Minister's reservations about Mackintosh. A tame hatchet man must be an uncomfortable asset to have around the house. He went to England next day and I followed two months later in response to another letter from Lucy. The crime had been set up.

CHAPTER SIX

I

I STARED at the brandy in the glass. I had been thinking for a long time and I hadn't touched a drop. The time for drinking had gone and the time for thinking had arrived. And I had a hell of a lot to think about.

Everything had gone as Mackintosh had planned. The crime, the trial, the nick, Slade—and the Scarperers. Then things turned sour. They were a clever mob and as keen on security as any professional espionage ring. Here I was injected into their organization like a drug, and I was no nearer to cracking it than I had been in South Africa.

It was that damned hypodermic syringe in the moving-van that had turned the trick in their favour. I hadn't expected that, nor had I expected this imprisonment. Still, I could see their point; they worked on the 'need to know' principle, and an escapee didn't need to know how he had escaped—just that he'd done so. They were too bloody professional to be true.

And I had lost Slade.

That was the worst bit, and Mackintosh would rip open my guts for it if ever I got past Fatface. His instructions had been oblique but clear; if there was any possibility of Slade getting clear then I was to kill him. I could have cut his throat with a blunt table knife while he slept, or strangled him with a length of electrical wire from the table lamp. I had done neither.

Of course, if I had killed Slade one night then next morning I would have been a dead man, but that wasn't why I'd refrained. I had weighed the odds and made a number of assumptions—that Slade and I would be going out together; that I still had a chance of escape, taking Slade with me; that my cover was still secure. Not one of those assumptions had proved valid and now things were in one hell of a mess.

I lay on the bed with my hands clasped behind my head and wondered how they had tumbled to the substitution. Fatface was trying to convince me that he knew I wasn't Rearden because of Rearden's fingerprints extracted from his file at John Vorster Square. I knew that to be a damned lie because I had personally substituted my own fingerprints for Rearden's in that very file, with Mackintosh looking on, and any prints coming from that file would match mine.

If Fatface knew I wasn't Rearden it certainly wasn't on account of fingerprints—so why in hell was he trying to kid me?

I thought hard, trying one hypothesis after another. For instance supposing Fatface only suspected I wasn't Rearden—he might try to pull a bluff in the hope that I'd crack. I hadn't cracked, and I'd put him in the position of having to produce those fingerprints which I knew damned well he hadn't got or, if he had, would certainly match mine.

That was one hypothesis among many, but they all boiled down to the same thing—that either Fatface knew for a certainty I wasn't Rearden, or he merely suspected it. And in both cases the problem was how the devil had he done it? Where had I slipped up?

I went back over my actions since my arrival in England and found no flaw. I had done nothing, in either word or deed, to break my cover, and that led me to the nasty suspicion that there had been a leak—a flaw in security.

I thought about Mackintosh. Now there was a tough, ruthless, conniving bastard who would sell his grandmother to boil down for soap if that soap would grease the runway of the Ship of State. I shook my head irritably. That was straining a metaphor pretty far which showed I was tired—but it was true, all the same. If Mackintosh thought it would serve his purpose to break security on me he would do it without hesitation.

I thought about it hard then rejected the possibility for the time being because I could see no purpose to it. And that left the super-efficient Lucy Smith whom Mackintosh trusted so much and about whom I knew damn-all. There were other possibilities, of course; either of them could have inadvertently broken security, his office could have been bugged by an interested third party, and so on.

I went into the bathroom and doused my face in cold water. To hell with Mackintosh's devious ways! What I had to do now was to find a way out of this trap. There must be less thinking of how I had got into it and more on how to get out.

I wiped my face dry, went back into the bedroom, and sat at the table to review my armoury of weapons. A trained man in my position assembles his weapons as and when he can from the materials at hand. For instance, I had three meals a day at which pepper was on the table. In my pocket was a twist of paper containing enough pepper to blind a man, which could come in useful on an appropriate occasion.

After a few minutes' thought I went to the wardrobe and took out a sock which I half-filled with earth from the row of pot plants on the window ledge, taking a little from each. I hefted the sock, whirled it, and swung it against the palm of my hand. It made a satisfying thump. It wasn't as good as a sandbag—it wasn't all that heavy—but it would do.

There are many ways of getting out of a locked room. You can shoot your way out—if you have a gun. You can set fire to the place, but that's risky; there's no guarantee you'll get out, and it can have disastrous consequences—I've always kept in mind Charles Lamb's story of burnt pig. You can use deception in its many forms but I didn't think these boys would be deceived easily; I'd already tried to con Fatface into letting me walk in the courtyard and he hadn't fallen for it.

That led me to think of Fatface and what he did when he came into the room. He was very careful; the door would click open and he would walk in, closing it behind him and always facing into the room with his back to the door. The man outside would then lock it. Fatface always kept his front to me. I had experimented a bit—trying to get behind him—but he'd never let me. He also carried a gun. When your life may depend on it you notice little details like that, and, no matter how carefully tailored the suit, the bulge shows.

So I had to get behind Fatface and club him with a sockful of wet leaf mould. And that involved a conjuror's trick—he had to believe I was in front of him when I was really behind him. Short of hypnosis I didn't see how I could do it but I tackled the problem.

Presently I went into the bathroom and flushed the water closet. It had no chain being one of those low cistern contraptions operated by a short lever. Then I hunted around for a cord. What I really needed was a ball of string, but that I hadn't got, so I had to improvise.

The light switch in the bathroom was operated, as good building regulations insist, by a ceiling pull-switch from which a strong cord hung to a convenient hand level. That gave me four feet. The bedside lamp was wired to a plug on the skirting board behind the bed, and the wire was two-strand, plastic coated, the strands spiralling around each other. When I separated the strands I had a good bit more cord.

There was another lamp on the dressing table which contributed more, but still not enough, so I was forced to consider other sources. My dressing gown was of terry-towelling and had a cord which went around the waist. This cord unravelled into several strands which I plaited and, at last, I had enough. In fact, there was enough wire to make a garrotting loop—not as efficient as piano wire, it's true—but I was in no position to complain.

I made a loop on the end of my long cord and slipped it over the lever of the cistern, then ran the cord from the bathroom, around the walls of the bedroom and right up to the door. I could have done with some small pulleys but, instead, I used the insulated staples which had held down the electric wiring and hoped they would hold.

They didn't.

A gentle tug and nothing happened. A harder tug gave the

same result. A very hard tug and a staple sprang from the skirting board.

This wasn't working at all.

I went back to the bathroom and flushed the water closet again, using as little pressure on the lever as possible. It was obviously too stiff to be pulled down by my improvised cord, so I had to think of something else. I studied the cistern for a while, and then removed the top, revealing its guts—the ball valve and associated gimmickry invented by that unsung genius, Thomas Crapper. The action of the lever downwards resulted in the movement of a plunger upwards, and I figured it was the friction involved in this mechanism that stiffened the lever action. If I could disconnect the lever and work on the plunger directly I thought I could do it.

Half an hour later I was ready to try again. I had lengthened my cord by means of a strip torn from the sheet; it would show, but that didn't matter in the bathroom. I left the bathroom door ajar and returned to my post at the other end of the cord. I picked it up, crossed my fingers, and pulled steadily.

The toilet flushed with a welcome and loud squirt of water.

I dropped the cord and carefully surveyed the room, making sure that nothing was out of place, that nothing would give the game away to Fatface when he entered. Everything was neat and tidy except for the bed I had stripped. I took the sheet I had ripped and tore it into long lengths. I would have a use for those. Then I remade the bed.

There still remained a few things to do. I opened the wardrobe and considered the contents. There was a suit of a decent dark grey, and there was a sports coat with non-matching trousers and brown shoes. I didn't know where I was—country or town—and if I emerged into a town then the suit would be more appropriate; but if I was in the heart of the country the suit would stick out a mile whereas the more informal dress would not be out of place in a town. So I plumped for the sports coat and associated trimmings. I'd also take the hat and the raincoat.

I'd been on the run before and I knew that one of the most difficult things to do is the apparently simple act of washing and the general idea of keeping clean. If my beard grew out a different colour from my hair I'd be an object of attention—that blonde had warned me to shave twice a day. This question of cleanliness is something of which the police are well aware, and in searching for a man on the run a check is routinely made on all public washrooms in railway stations and large hotels.

So I was taking the shaver, a tablet of soap, a face cloth and a hand towel—all of which would fit conveniently into the pockets of the raincoat without bulging too much. I coiled my garrotting wire loosely and fitted it into the sweatband of the hat. Any copper worthy of the name knows one of those when he sees it, and if I was searched I didn't want it to be obvious —I'd be thrown in the nick immediately if it were found.

That also went for the gun—if I could get hold of Fatface's artillery. Which brought me to another question. How far was I justified in using a gun if the occasion arose?

The cult of James Bond has given rise to a lot of nonsense. There are no double-o numbers and there is no 'licence to kill'. As far as I knew I didn't have a number at all, except perhaps a file number like any other employee; certainly no one ever referred to me as number 56, or whatever it was—or even 0056. And agents don't kill just for the hell of it. That doesn't mean that agents never kill, but they kill strictly to order under carefully specified conditions. Elimination by death is regarded with distaste; it's messy and irretrievable, and there are usually other ways of silencing a man which are almost as effective.

Yet sometimes it has to be done and an agent is detailed to do it. Whether this constitutes a licence to kill I wouldn't know; it certainly doesn't grant a general licence to commit un-restricted mayhem. You leave too many unexplained bodies lying around and the secret service stops being secret.

Now, Mackintosh hadn't told me to kill anyone apart from

Slade and that meant, generally speaking, no killing. Such unordered deaths are known in the trade as 'accidental' and any agent who is crass enough to cause such an accidental death quickly gets the chop as being unreliable and inept. For an agent to leave a trail of corpses in his wake would cause untold consternation in those little hole-in-the-corner offices in Whitehall which have the innocuous and deceptive names on the doors.

In fact, it came back to the old moral problem—when is a man justified in killing another man? I resolved it by quoting the phrase—'Kill or be killed!' If I were in danger of being killed then I would kill in self-defence—and not until then. I had killed only one man in my life and that had made me sick to my stomach for two days afterwards.

That settled in my mind I began planning arson. An inspection of the liquor cabinet showed a bottle and a half of South African brandy, the best part of a bottle of Scotch, ditto gin, and a half bottle of Drambuie. A few tests showed the brandy and the Drambuie as being most flammable, although not as fiery as I would have wished. I was sorry I hadn't developed a taste for rum—there's some nice 100° stuff on the market which would have suited me fine—although God knows what it does to the lining of the stomach.

Then I went to bed and slept the sleep of the morally just.

2

There was no breakfast next morning. Instead of Taafe trundling his trolley before him he came in empty-handed and jerked his thumb at the door. I shrugged and walked out. It seemed as though the party was over.

I was taken downstairs and across the hall into the closely curtained room where I had signed the cheque. In the hall I passed an elderly couple, Darby and Joan types, who were sitting nervously on the edges of their chairs as though they thought it was a dentist's waiting room. They looked at me incuriously as I walked past them into the room where Fatface was waiting for me.

There was a bleak look on his face. 'You've had a night to think about it,' he said. 'Your story had better be very good Mr Whoever-you-are.'

I went on the attack. 'Where's that dab-sheet?'

'We don't keep it here,' he said shortly. 'In any case, it isn't necessary.'

'I still don't know what you're talking about,' I said. 'And if you think I've spent all night cooking up a cock-and-bull story just to satisfy you then you're crazy. I don't have much to do with my time, but I've better things to do than that.' I was telling him the exact truth.

He made a noise expressive of disgust. 'You're a liar. Can't you get it into your thick skull that the gaff has been blown? There's just one little detail missing—your identity.' He shook his head pityingly. 'We *know* you're not Rearden. All we want to know is who the devil you really are.'

Now, why did he want to know that? I had a fair idea, and I didn't like it at all. If I wasn't Rearden then he'd want to know if I'd be seriously missed. That's an important thing to know if you're contemplating murdering anyone. Was I important? Did I have important connections? For whom was I working? And why? All those were questions he would want answering.

And he was too damned certain that I wasn't Rearden, which was faintly alarming. I heaved a deep sigh. 'I'm Joseph Rearden. From what Cosgrove told me before you got me out of the nick you've done a thorough check on me. Why this sudden switch, Fatface? Are you trying to slip out of your obligations?'

'Don't call me Fatface,' he snapped. 'I don't need finger-prints to tell me you're not Rearden because you've just proved it yourself. Out there in the hall you passed a couple of old people, Mr and Mrs Rearden from Brakpan, South Africa. Your dear old father and your sainted old mother, you son of a bitch. You didn't recognize them and they didn't recognize you.'

There wasn't much to say to that, so I kept my mouth shut. But my stomach did a back flip.

Fatface showed his teeth in a savage grin. 'I said the gaff has been blown, and I meant it. We know about Mackintosh, and there's no point in you denying you know him. We know all about that tricky little set-up, so you'd better get ready to tell the truth for a change.'

This time I really was jolted—and badly. I felt as though I'd just grabbed a live wire and I hoped it didn't show on my face. For my cover to be blown could have meant any number of things; for Mackintosh's cover to be blown sky-high was bloody serious.

I said, 'For God's sake—who is Mackintosh?'

'Very funny,' said Fatface acidly. He looked at his watch. 'I can see we'll have to take stronger measures, but unfortunately I have an appointment and I don't have the time now. I'll give you two hours to think about those stronger measures; I can assure you they will be most unpleasant.'

Depressed as I was I nearly laughed in his face. He was acting like the villain in a 'B' picture. He had no appointment and the two hours were intended to break me down thinking of very imaginable tortures. And he wouldn't be away for two hours, either; he'd be back in an hour, or possibly three hours. It was supposed to add to the uncertainty of the situation. Fatface was an amateur who seemed to get his ideas from watching TV. I think he was too soft-centred to get down to the torture bit and he was hoping I'd break down more-or-less spontaneously.

'All right,' I said. 'If you want me to cook up a story, then I'll cook up a story. It will take me two hours to think it up.'

'We don't want a story—as you put it. We want the truth.'

'But you've got the truth, damn it!'

He merely shrugged and waved to the man behind me who took me upstairs again. The Reardens—if that's who they were—had vanished from the hall. It struck me that Fatface might very well have been bluffing about them. But he still knew about Mackintosh.

Once locked in the bedroom I got on with what I had to do. I shaved quickly and put the shaver and the rest of the stuff into the pockets of the raincoat. I dressed and put on the tweed sports coat, grabbed my weighted sock and took up position behind the door, the end of the improvised cord held in my fingers.

It was a long wait and it seemed to be hours, but I had to stay there, exactly in that place, because in this thing timing was everything. I looked about the bedroom, checking to see that all was in order, and found it good. The bathroom door was ajar, but looked closed; the cord going around the room was invisible and wouldn't be noticed by the casual eye. All I had to do was to stay behind that door and wait.

Although it seemed a long time he was back on the hour—I'd been right in predicting that. I heard the murmur of voices on the other side of the door and tightened my fingers on the cord. As soon as I heard the key in the lock I began to pull, exerting a steady and growing pressure on the piston in the cistern.

As the door opened the cistern flushed noisily.

Fatface came into the room alone and cautiously, but relaxed visibly as he heard the noise from the bathroom. He took a step forward, pushing the door closed behind him, and I heard the key turn as the outside guard locked it. He took another step forward without looking behind him. He could easily have seen me by a half turn of his head but the thought never came to him. After all, wasn't I in the bathroom?

I wasn't! I hit him with the weighted sock very hard, much harder than I'd hit the postman in the Kiddykar office. He gasped and his knees buckled but he kept his feet and he twisted his head slightly so that I could see his mouth was open and he was gasping for air and struggling to shout. I knew the sock wasn't too efficient—not like a proper sandbag—so I hit him even harder, and then again, pounding unconsciousness into his skull.

I caught him as he fell. I didn't want him thumping on the floor with a noise which might be heard outside. Even then, the repeated thud of the sock hitting his head had seemed to echo around the room and I paused for a moment, holding him in my arms, and waited to see if anything would happen.

Nothing did, so with a sigh of relief I lowered him to the floor. The first thing I did was to go for his gun. It was a neat flat automatic with nine rounds in the magazine but nothing in the chamber. I had been right; the man was an amateur, after all! To carry a gun with nothing up the spout is to carry a piece of junk metal. What's the use of a gun which can't be fired at a split second's notice?

I put back the magazine, worked the action to jump a round into the breech, saw the gun was on safety, and put it into my pocket. And all the time I was talking aloud. The guard outside must not hear dead silence.

I stripped off Fatface's jacket and took off the shoulder holster he wore. Then I trussed him like a fowl, using the strips of sheeting I had prepared, and not forgetting to stuff his mouth with a gag. He was breathing heavily through his mouth and I wondered for a moment if the gag would suffocate him, but he began to breathe through his nose rather noisily and I knew I hadn't hit him too hard. Apart from the moral aspects of murder I wanted him alive. I had a use for him.

Swiftly, I went through the pockets of his jacket. There was a wallet, which, when flicked open briefly, displayed the edges of many bank notes. That was very good—I'd need money. I didn't investigate it further, but stowed it away, together with a small notebook I found, and got on with the search. I found a handful of loose change which went into my pocket and a couple of spare magazines for the pistol, also well worth confiscating. Everything else I left, except for a penknife and a fountain pen, both of which could prove handy to have.

Then I went about the next part of the plan. I tossed the

mattress on to the floor just by the door and ripped open the ticking, using Fatface's useful penknife. There was a lot of beautifully inflammable cotton wadding which I piled in a heap ready for the conflagration, and I set the bottles of brandy and Drambuie close to hand.

Then I turned my attention to Fatface who was just coming round. He stirred a little and a heavy snoring noise came from his nose which would have been a groan if he hadn't been gagged. I went into the bathroom, filled the tooth glass with cold water, went back and dumped the lot on his face. He snorted again and his eyes flickered open.

It must have been quite a shock for him to see the muzzle of his own gun held not a foot from his head. I waited until full comprehension came to him, then said casually, 'If you think there isn't one up the spout, you're wrong. If I want to blow your brains out all I have to do is pull the trigger.'

He flinched and arched his neck, trying to pull his head away, while muffled noises came from behind the gag. 'Take it easy,' I counselled. 'That way you won't get hurt.' I could see the muscles of his arms working as he tested the bindings on his wrists which were pinioned behind his back. When he had finished struggling, I said, 'I'm going out of here—and you are going to help me. You can help voluntarily or involuntarily; take your pick. I have to warn you that one mistaken move on your part might mean your death. You'll be in the middle and if any shooting starts you'll probably stop a bullet.'

I didn't wait to see his reaction to that—it didn't really matter—but took the raincoat and hat and put them on, and checked the pockets to see if I had everything. Then I doused the mattress wadding with the spirits, pouring liberally until the room smelled like a distillery.

I returned to Fatface and cut his ankles free. 'Get up— slowly!'

He staggered to his feet, hampered by the bonds on his arms. He stood quite passively, just looking at me, and I could read no expression in his eyes. I jerked the gun. 'Walk forward to the door and stop a yard in front of it. I wouldn't kick it, though; that could be fatal.'

He shuffled forward obediently, and I took his jacket and draped it across his shoulders so that the empty sleeves hung loose. Apart from the gag and the lack of hands he looked quite normal—normal enough to give me a fraction of a second's advantage when that door opened. The trick is to keep the opposition off balance, and the guard would have other things to do with his eyes just at that moment.

I struck a match and dropped it on the pile of wadding, and blue flames ran over the surface. It wasn't much of a fire but it was the best I could do under the circumstances. I kept an eye on it until the first yellow flames appeared, then pressed the bell push—the signal that Fatface wanted to be let out.

When the lock snapped I was right behind him, prodding him with the pistol to make sure he understood the spot he was in. The door swung open and I pushed him forward, the flat of my hand in the middle of his back, and yelled at the top of my voice, 'Fire!'

I followed up fast as he staggered into the corridor and, over his shoulder, saw the startled face of the guard who was slow in reacting. He had some kind of a weapon in his hand, but he dithered as he saw Fatface lurch towards him and the flickering glow of the flames from the room. With the opening of the door a draught had swept into the bedroom and the fire really got going. I don't think the guard saw me at all.

I gave Fatface another mighty push so that he collided heavily with the guard and they both went down in a tangled heap. A gun went off and someone screamed; it must have been the guard because Fatface had a gag in his mouth.

I jumped over the sprawl of wriggling bodies and ran down the corridor, the pistol in my hand with the safety catch off. The corridor was wood-panelled with doors on either side which I ignored. At the end was a stair landing with stairs going both up and down. I went *up*. I had made my decision on that one the previous evening. It's a curious thing, but people escaping from a house always try to get immediately to the ground floor—which is why they're usually caught. I suppose it's an instinctive reaction, but the department that trained me worked hard to eradicate it.

The floor above was not so fancy—no wood-panelled walls —so I figured I was in the servants' quarters, which meant I had to look out for Taafe, if he was that kind of servant, which I doubted. I moved fast, trying to make no noise, and heard an increasing uproar from downstairs. It was becoming too dangerous to stay in the corridors so I ducked into the nearest room—gun first.

It was empty of occupants, thank God, and I'd done it just in time because someone ran down the corridor with a heavy thumping tread. I shot the bolt and crossed to the window and found I was on the other side of the house away from the courtyard. For the first time I could see the surrounding country and it was very pleasant to view—rolling fields and areas of woodland with blue-green mountains beyond. About half a mile away a car sped along a road. There lay freedom.

For over a year and a half I had seen nothing but stone walls and my eyes had focused on nothing further away than a few yards. This glimpse of countryside caused a sudden lump to come to my throat and my heart thumped in my chest. It didn't matter that dark clouds were lowering and that a sudden shift of wind sent a spatter of raindrops against the window. Out there I would be free and nobody was going to stop me.

I returned to the door and listened. There was a slice of chaos downstairs and it seemed that the fire I had started had got out of hand. I unbolted the door and opened it a crack, to hear Fatface shout, 'To hell with the fire—I want Rearden. Taafe, get downstairs to the front door; Dillon, you take the back door. The rest of us will search the house.'

A deep voice said, 'He's not upstairs. I've just come down.'
'All right,' said Fatface impatiently. 'That leaves just this

floor. Taafe was at the bottom of the stairs and didn't see him. Get moving.'

Someone else said, 'Mother of God, will you look at it! It'll burn the house down.'

'Let it burn. We're done for here, anyway, if Rearden escapes.'

I stepped out into the corridor and hastened away from the staircase and, turning a corner, came upon the back stairs. I trotted down quickly, depending on speed to get to the ground floor before the searchers spread out. And I made it, too, only to find the back door wide open and a man standing before it. That would be Dillon.

Fortunately, he was not looking in my direction as I came down the back stairs, but was staring up the wide passage which led to the front of the house. I oozed my way into a side passage and out of his line of sight and then let out my breath inaudibly. No doubt I could have overcome Dillon, but not without noise, and noise would have brought the lot on top of me.

The first door I opened led into a broom closet—useless because it had no window. But the second door led into a well-stocked larder and there was a sash window. I closed the door gently and tackled the window which evidently hadn't been opened for years because it was very tight. As I forced it open it groaned and rattled alarmingly and I stopped to see if Dillon had heard it. But there was no sound apart from a few heavy thumps upstairs.

I attacked the window again and got it open at last, a mere nine inches or so, but enough to take me. I went through head first and landed in a bed of nettles, but fortunately screened from the back door by a large water-butt. As I rubbed my stinging hands I looked about and felt a bit depressed as I noted the high stone wall which seemed to encircle the house. The only gate within view was directly opposite the open back door and if I tried to leave that way Dillon would certainly spot me.

A trickle of water ran down my neck. It was beginning to rain really hard, which was in my favour. The wind was strong and blowing sheets of rain across the kitchen garden. If I could get into the open countryside I stood a chance of getting clean away because the low visibility was in my favour. But it wasn't as low as that—Dillon could certainly see from the back door to the garden gate.

The water-butt wasn't going to collect much rain; it was rotten and useless, and a stave had come away from the hoops. I picked it up and hefted it thoughtfully. No one, least of all Dillon, would expect me to go back *into* the house, and one of the major arts of warfare is the attack from the unexpected direction. I grasped the stave in both hands, sidled up to the back door, and then stepped through boldly.

Dillon heard me coming and must have noticed the dimming of the light as I blocked the entrance. But he was very slow in turning his head. 'Found him?' he asked, and then his eyes widened as he saw who it was. He didn't have time to do much about it because I swung the stave at him and caught him on the side of the head. His head was harder than the stave which, rotten as it was, splintered in two—but it was hard enough to lay Dillon out.

Even as he fell I turned and ran for the gate, dropping the remnant of the stave as I went. The gate wasn't locked and within seconds I was through and walking in a dampish country lane. That wasn't good enough because it was too open, so I ran to the left until I found a gate leading into a field, over which I jumped and then sheltered in the lee of a hedgerow.

Rain dripped on to my face from the brim of my hat as I looked across the field, trying to remember the layout of the land as I had seen it from that upstairs window. If I went across that field I would come to a wood beyond which was the road I had seen. I set off at a brisk pace and didn't look back.

Only when I was sheltered in the wood did I stop to check

on my tracks. There was no sign of pursuit and, over the house, I thought I saw an eddying streamer of black smoke, although I could have been wrong because of the wind-driven rain.

I reached the other side of the wood and left by a gate and came out on to the road. But before I got to the gate I heard again the light *clip-clip* of hooves, together with a clinking sound and that pleasant fluting whistle. I opened the gate and looked up the road. A flat cart was just passing, drawn by a donkey, and a man was sitting holding the reins and whistling like a blackbird. A couple of cans which might have held milk clinked behind him on the cart.

I watched it go and tried to figure out which country I was in. The donkey cart looked as though it could be Spanish but, surely to God, it never rained like this in Spain except, maybe, in the plain. I watched the cart recede into the distance and found I couldn't even tell which side of the road he was supposed to be on because he drove dead centre.

I turned and looked up the road the other way. In the distance I could see an approaching bus, and on the other side a man was waiting by a bus stop. I noted that the bus was coming up on the left of the road so it was pretty certain I was still in England. I was surer of it still when I crossed the road and the man turned a shining red countryman's face towards me, and said, ''Tis a grand, soft morning.'

I nodded, and the rain dripped from the brim of my hat. 'Yes.'

Then my self-confidence received a sudden jolt because when I looked up at the sign above my head I found it was written in two languages, English and another, and the second wasn't even in Roman script but in some weird characters I had never seen before, although they were vaguely familiar.

The bus was coming along the road very slowly. From where I was standing I could see the roof and the top storey of the house, from which a column of black smoke was rising. I switched my gaze back to the bus and wished the bloody thing would get a move on. I felt terribly vulnerable.

On impulse I put my hand into my pocket and fished out some of the loose change I had looted from Fatface. The first coin I examined was apparently a penny, but certainly not an English one. It depicted a hen and chickens and underneath was a single word in that odd script—a word I couldn't even read. I turned the coin over in my fingers and nearly dropped it in surprise.

On this side was a harp and the inscription in the strange script, but this time it was readable. It said: 'Eire—1964.'

My God, I was in Ireland!

CHAPTER SEVEN

I

THE BUS DREW UP, and because I was now screened from the house some of the tension left me. However, so pre-occupied had I been with my discovery, I had neglected to look at the destination board of the bus. Damn silly omissions of that kind can be the death of one, and I felt a bit of a fool as I sat down. I took Fatface's wallet from my breast pocket and riffled through the bank notes. Most of them were British Bank of England fivers but there were some Irish pound notes, so I took one of those as I didn't know if British currency was acceptable in Ireland.

The conductor came up and I held out a pound note. 'All the way,' I said casually.

'Right you are,' he said. 'That'll be two-and-tuppence.' He gave me the ticket and counted the change into my hand. I hung on to it until he had moved away and then examined it. It was interesting to see that half the coinage was British, so it seemed as though all the currency in Fatface's wallet would be readily negotiable.

So here I was, going 'all the way' and with not a notion in my head about where I was going. It was bloody ridiculous! I looked at the passing scene and found nothing to tell me where the devil I was. Ireland! What did I know about Ireland?

The answer came without much thought—practically nothing! Ireland was a page in the atlas I hadn't bothered to study, and Irishmen were comic characters given to fighting. There were also vague ideas of revolution and civil war—the Black and Tans and armed insurrection—but that had been a long time ago, although I had read of recent trouble in Northern Ireland.

The bus stopped to take on passengers and before it started again a fire engine went by with a clanging bell, going the other way at a hell of a clip. Necks were craned to follow its passage and I smiled. During my getaway a gun had gone off and someone had screamed, so there was probably someone in the house with a gunshot wound, a circumstance which Fatface might have difficulty in explaining away.

The bus trundled on, going God knows where. We passed a place called Cratloe which didn't sound particularly Irish, but there was a sign pointing the other way to Bunratty, which did. A big jet came over—a commercial air liner, not a military job—and circled widely, losing altitude and obviously intending to land somewhere nearby. From nowhere a name clicked in my mind—*Shannon Airport*. That was the Irish international airport, but I hadn't a clue where in Ireland it was.

I mentally added an item to the list of things urgently required—maps.

We pressed on and the sun came out, shining through the rain to make a rainbow. There were more houses here, and a racecourse—and then a magic word—Limerick. So that's where I was! It didn't make a great deal of difference; all I knew of Limerick was the one about the girl from Khartoum. But it was a big, busy city and that was something to be thankful for; I could get lost in a town of this size.

I got off the bus before it reached the centre of town and the conductor looked at me in a puzzled way—but that might have been my imagination. The reason I dropped off was that I had seen a biggish bookshop which could give me what I wanted most of all—information. I walked back the hundred yards to the shop and went inside, drifting casually from counter to counter until I found what I wanted.

It was there in plenty. There were a score of guidebooks to choose from, and any number of maps from folded sheets to bound volumes. I disregarded the antiquarian and literary guides and settled for a closely printed compendium of information. I also bought a single sheet motoring map which would fold for the pocket, a writing pad, a packet of envelopes and a newspaper, paying with one of Fatface's fivers. I took this booty into a tea-shop next door and settled to examine it over a pot of weak tea and a few stale buns—it was that kind of tea-shop.

The map told me that Limerick was at the head of the Shannon estuary and, as I had suspected, not very far from Shannon Airport. The house from which I had escaped was to the north of Limerick, somewhere between Sixmilebridge and Cratloe, very handily placed for Fatface and his crew, a mere fifteen minutes' drive from the airport.

I poured another cup of lukewarm tea and opened the newspaper to find that Slade and Rearden were still very much in the news and even on the front page, but that might have been because Detective-Inspector Brunskill had arrived in Dublin which would make for local interest. There was a photograph showing him getting off the aircraft and when questioned about what he expected to find, he said, tight-lipped, 'No comment.' Detective-Inspector Forbes was just back in London from Brussels where he reported, 'No joy!'

Of course, Slade made the running in the newspaper much more than I did; a spy has more glamour than a jewel thief. But, from the way Brunskill and Forbes were running around, I wasn't being neglected. Those two had been picked because they could identify me by sight, and it seemed they had a lot of travelling still to do because Rearden had been seen in the Isle of Man, Jersey, the Côte d'Azure, Ostend, Manchester, Wolverhampton, Regent Street, Bergen and Middle Wallop. I wondered if Detective-Sergeant Jervis was just as busy.

The tea-shop was empty so I pulled out the wallet and opened it. First I counted the money; it was important and I couldn't get far without it. There was a total of £78, mostly in British fivers, which was most welcome. There was also a British driving licence which was even more welcome. I wanted to be mobile which meant hiring a car, something I couldn't do without producing a driving licence. It was made out in the name of Richard Allen Jones, which sounded phoney on the face of it, although the name could have been genuine. There *are* a few Joneses around; there must be for the rest of us to keep up with.

There was a letter which made no sense at all because it was written in an unknown language. I tasted the words on my tongue and thought I detected faintly slavic overtones but I could have been wrong; eastern languages are my strong point. I pondered over it for some time then carefully put it away without becoming any the wiser.

The thin notebook was of more interest because it contained a few addresses scattered through the pages—some in Ireland, some in England and others in France, Italy and Spain. It gave me a jolt to find the address of Anglo-Scottish Holdings Ltd, in London; Mackintosh's cover was blown wide open.

There were two Irish addresses, one in the Irish Republic at a place called Clonglass in Connemara, and the other in Belfast. Both places were a hell of a long way from Limerick, and Belfast was across the frontier in Northern Ireland. It was thin stuff to work on but it was all I had and it would have to do.

I paid for the tea and asked for, and got, a handful of loose change; then I went to look for a telephone box, which I found difficult until I discovered that the Irish paint them green. I didn't make a call from the first box I found but took a note of the number and then went in search of another from which I put a call through to Anglo-Scottish in London. It was only a few minutes before I heard the voice of Mrs Smith: 'Anglo-Scottish Holdings Ltd.' Her voice was warm and friendly, but that might have been an illusion on my part—I hadn't spoken to a woman for a year and a half, apart from the one who doped me.

I said, 'Your telephone might be tapped—I think it is. Find a safe phone and ring this number as soon as possible.' I gave her the number of the other box and rang off before she could answer.

148

Ultra-cautious maybe, but I'm still around to prove it's the best method. Besides, if she rang me I wouldn't have to keep stuffing small coins in the slot during what might be a lengthy conversation. I trudged back to the first telephone kiosk and found it occupied, so I sneered at the woman through the glass until she went away, then I went inside and fiddled with the directory while waiting for the ring.

All things considered she was prompt; the bell rang within ten minutes. I picked up the telephone, and said, 'Stannard.'

'What are you doing in Limerick?' Her voice wasn't as warm as it had been.

'What the hell do you think I'm doing?' I said grumpily. 'I want to speak to Mackintosh.'

'He's not available.'

'Make him available,' I snapped.

There was a pause. 'He's in hospital,' she said. 'He was in a car accident.'

'Oh! How serious?'

'The doctors don't expect him to live,' she said flatly.

A yawning cavity opened in the pit of my stomach. 'Christ!' I said. 'That's bad. When did it happen?'

'The day before yesterday. It was a hit-and-run.'

Bits of a deadly jigsaw began to fall into place. That was about the time that Fatface Jones had become so certain I wasn't Rearden—and he'd had Mackintosh's address in his notebook. 'That was no accident,' I said. 'His cover was blown!'

Mrs Smith's voice sharpened. 'Impossible!'

'What's so impossible about it?' I demanded.

'Only the three of us knew.'

'That's not so,' I contradicted. 'I've just hammered one of the Scarperers and he had the Anglo-Scottish address written down in a notebook. That's why I thought you might have a tap on your phone.' I took a deep breath. 'Take very good care of yourself, Mrs Smith.'

I had every reason for saying that, even apart from natural

humanity. If Mackintosh died and the Scarperers also killed Mrs Smith then I'd be well and truly up that gum tree. The very best that could happen was that I'd be taken back to gaol to serve the rest of the twenty-year sentence, and escapees don't get any remission for good conduct neither are they allowed parole.

And there would be more. Curiously enough, it's not a crime to escape from prison but they would nail me for an assault on a prison officer; I had kicked the Chief Screw in the face and caused him to break his leg and they'd put me away for another five years because of that.

With Mackintosh and Mrs Smith gone I wouldn't have a hope of proving anything. Mackintosh's tight security system had just blown up in my face. I had lowered the telephone and a quacking noise came from the earpiece. I raised it again, and said, 'What was that?'

'How *could* they have known the address?'

'That doesn't matter right now,' I said. 'This whole operation has gone sour on us and the best we can do is to cut our losses.'

Her voice sharpened. 'What happened to Slade?'

'He got away,' I said wearily. 'God knows where he is now. Probably stowed away in the hold of a Russian freighter bound for Leningrad. It's a bust, Mrs Smith.'

'Wait a minute,' she said, and there was an abrupt silence which lasted a full five minutes. I became aware of a man standing outside the kiosk tapping his foot impatiently and glaring at me. I gave him the stony stare and turned my back on him.

Mrs Smith came back on the line. 'I can be at Shannon Airport within three hours. Is there anything you need.'

'By God there is,' I said. 'I need money—lots of it; and a new identity.'

'There's no reason why you shouldn't resume your real identity,' she said. 'I have your suitcase here with your clothing and passport. I'll bring them with me.'

'Stay away from the Anglo-Scottish office,' I warned her. 'And watch out for strange men on your tail. Do you know how to shake surveillance?'

Her voice was cold. 'I wasn't born yesterday. Meet me at Shannon in three hours.'

'That's not on. Airports aren't for men on the run. They're apt to be full of men in my own line of business. Don't forget I'm on the run from the police and that Brunskill has just arrived in Ireland.' I turned and looked past the queue that was forming. 'Take a taxi to the Hotel St George—I'll meet you outside. I might even have a car.'

'All right—and I'll bring the money. How much do you want?'

'As much as you can lay your hands on conveniently. Can you really make it in three hours?'

'If I'm not held up talking to you,' she said acidly, and rang off.

I put down the telephone and pushed open the door. The first man in the queue said sarcastically, 'And where would it be you'd be telephoning to? Australia?'

'No,' I assured him blandly. 'Peking.' I pushed past him and walked up the street.

2

Hiring a car proved to be easy—the British licence was good enough. A hired car is not notoriously speedy but I managed to get a Cortina 1500 which would be enough to get me out of trouble—or into it—reasonably quickly.

I arrived at the St George Hotel early and parked on the other side of the road and about a hundred yards along. Several taxis drew up but no Mrs Smith appeared but finally she arrived and only fifteen minutes late. She stood on the pavement when the taxi departed with two suitcases at her side and the hall porter from the hotel dashed out to succour her. I saw her shake her head and he went back into the hotel, a disappointed man, while she looked uncertainly about her. I let her stew for a while because I was more than curious to see if anyone was taking an undue interest in her.

After ten minutes I came to the conclusion that if I didn't pick her up then someone else would because she looked too damned fetching in stretch pants, open-neck shirt and short jacket, so I entered the traffic stream and swung around to pull up in front of the hotel. I wound down the nearside window, and said, 'Give you a lift, ma'am?'

She leaned down to look into the car, and her green eyes were snapping. 'Where have you been?' she said curtly. 'I've been standing here like a fool. I've already slapped down three passes.'

'It's the Irish,' I said. 'They can't resist a pretty girl. Get in; I'll put the bags into the boot.'

Three minutes later we were rolling on our way out of Limerick and towards Cratloe. I said, 'You made good time. You must have just caught the plane at the right moment.'

She stared ahead through the windscreen. 'I flew in my own plane.'

'Well, well!' I said. 'The intrepid aviatrix. That might prove useful—but for what, I don't know.'

'I didn't like something you said on the telephone,' she said.

'What was that?'

'You were talking about cutting losses. I didn't like that at all.'

'I don't like it much,' I said. 'But there are precious few leads to follow and I have no great hopes.'

'Why did you let Slade get away?'

'I didn't,' I said. 'He was taken.'

'There must have been *something* you could have done.'

I glanced sideways at her. 'Would you have relished cutting his throat while he slept?'

She gave me a startled glance. 'Why, I . . .' She fell into silence.

I said, 'It's easy criticizing from the sidelines. These

152

Scarperers are efficient—more efficient than any of us realized. Slade thought they might be a Russian outfit—Russian subsidized, anyway; possibly Russian trained. One thing is certain; they're no gang of ordinary criminals.'

'You'd better tell me about it,' she said. 'But first tell me where we're going now.'

'I want to have a look at the house in which we were incarcerated. We may be able to pick up something, but I doubt it; the last I heard the boss man was shouting about abandoning the place. Anyway, this is the way it went.'

One thing about Irish roads is that they're traffic free and we made good time, so much so that I was only half-way through my tale of woe by the time I saw the first fire engine. 'This is it,' I said, and pulled off the road well away from the scene of action.

It was a shambles. Mrs Smith took one look at the smoking shell of the house, and said, 'I don't know about the boss abandoning the house, it looks as though it abandoned him. Why should he burn it down?'

'He didn't,' I said immodestly. 'I did.' I stuck my head out of the window and hailed a passing cyclist coming from the scene of the crime. 'What's happened here?'

The cyclist, a gnarled old man, wobbled across the road and lurched to a halt. 'A wee bit of a fire,' he said, and gave me a gap-toothed grin. 'Reminds me of the Troubles, it does.'

'Anyone hurt?'

'Indeed there was. They found a poor gentleman in the middle of it all—burnt to a crisp.'

'That's dreadful,' I said.

The old man leaned forward and peered at me. 'A friend of yours, could he be?'

'Oh, no,' I said. 'I was just passing and saw the fire engines.'

'A natural curiosity,' he agreed. 'But there's a mystery going on, there is. There were other men in that house and they've all run away. The *garda* are wondering why.'

'The *garda*?'

'The natural enemies of good men,' said the ancient. 'The men in blue.' He pointed up the road. 'In England you call them the police.'

About a hundred yards away was a police car—they're unmistakable—with a policeman walking towards it. I glanced at Mrs Smith. 'Should we be on our way, darling? We have to be in Roscommon tonight.'

'Roscommon, is it?' said the old man. 'But it's on the wrong road you are.'

'We're calling in to see friends in Ennis,' I said. The man was as sharp as a tack.

'Ah, then it's straight ahead.' He took his hand from the side of the car. 'May you have luck in Ireland—you and your beautiful lady.'

I smiled at him and let out the clutch and we drove slowly past the police car. I looked at the mirror and checked that it showed no inclination to follow before I said, 'If they do a thorough autopsy of that corpse they're likely to find a bullet.'

'Did you kill him?' asked Mrs Smith. Her voice was as cool and level as though she had asked if I had slept well.

'Not me. It was an accident, more or less; he shot himself in a scuffle.' I checked the mirror again. 'He was right, you know.'

'Who was?'

'The old man. You *are* beautiful.' I gave her no time to worry about it but went straight on. 'How's Mackintosh?'

'I telephoned the hospital just before I left London,' she said. 'There was no change.' She turned to me. 'You don't think it was an accident?'

'How did it happen?'

'He was crossing a street in the City late at night. A man found him by the roadside. Whoever hit him didn't stop.'

'The man Jones knew I wasn't Rearden about the same time,' I said. 'I don't think it was an accident.'

'But how did they know?'

'I didn't tell them so it must have been either you or Mackintosh,' I said.

'It wasn't me,' she said quickly. 'And why should it have been him?' I shrugged and she was silent for a while before she said slowly, 'He's always been a good judge of men but . . .' She stopped.

'But what?'

'But there was £40,000 in that Swiss numbered account and you had the number.'

I glanced at her. She was staring straight ahead, her body held rigid, and a pink spot glowed on her cheek. 'That's all we need,' I said. 'So you think I sold out to the Scarperers, is that it?'

'Can you think of any other explanation?'

'Not many,' I admitted. 'Talking about money—how much did you bring?'

'You're taking this too damned coolly.' Her voice had an edge to it.

I sighed and drew the car to a halt by the roadside. I put my hand beneath my jacket and brought out the gun I had taken from Jones—butt first. I offered it to her on the palm of my hand. 'If you're so certain I sold out then we may as well get it over with quickly,' I said. 'So take this and let me have it.'

Her face whitened when she first saw the pistol, but now she flushed pink and lowered her eyelids to avoid my gaze. 'I'm sorry,' she said quietly. 'I shouldn't have said that.'

'It's just as well you did,' I said. 'Or you might be still thinking it. There are only the two of us, and if we can't trust each other we'll get nowhere. Now, you're sure you couldn't have let fall even a hint of the operation?'

'I'm positive,' she said.

I put away the gun. 'I didn't,' I said. 'So that leaves Mackintosh.'

'I don't believe it,' she said.

'Who did he see just before this so-called accident?'

She thought about it. 'He saw the Prime Minister and the Leader of the Opposition. They were both worried about the lack of news of Slade. There's an election coming up and the PM thought the Leader of the Opposition should be informed of developments.'

'Or the lack of them,' I said. 'I suppose he might do that—it's not a party issue. Anyone else?'

'Yes; Lord Taggart and Charles Wheeler. Wheeler is a Member of Parliament.'

'I know of Taggart,' I said. 'He was Slade's boss at one time.' The name, Wheeler, rang a faint bell. 'What did he talk to Wheeler about?'

'I don't know,' she said.

'If Mackintosh were to tell anyone of the operation would you expect him to inform you?'

'He never kept anything from me that I know of,' she said. 'But he had the accident before he could get to me.'

I mulled it over and got nowhere. I sighed, and said, 'I'm damned if I'm going to keep calling you Mrs Smith and neither am I going to call you Lucy. What *is* your name?'

'All right,' she said resignedly. 'You may call me Alison.'

'What do we do now, Alison?'

She said decisively, 'We check on the Irish addresses you found in Jones's notebook. First, at Clonglass, and then at Belfast if necessary.'

'That might not be too easy. The Clonglass reference wasn't as much an address as a mention—just a scribbled memorandum: "Send Taafe to the House at Clonglass".'

'We'll try it anyway,' she said. 'It's not far.'

3

We booked in for the night at a hotel in Galway, but pushed on immediately to Clonglass which was about 25 miles further west along the coast. From the bare look of the map there didn't seem to be any likelihood of finding an hotel west of Galway, especially late at night, so we played safe.

Clonglass proved to be a wide place in the road overlooking

a small inlet from the main bay. The houses were scattered, each with its thatched roof tied down against the advent of the western gales, and each with its peat stack handy to the door. It didn't look too promising.

I drew the car to a halt. 'What do we do now? I wouldn't know where to start in a place like this.'

She smiled. 'I do,' she said, and got out of the car. An old woman was toiling up the road, swathed in black from head to foot and with a face like a frost-bitten crab apple. Alison hailed her and damned if she didn't proceed to jabber away in a strange language.

As always when one eavesdrops on a conversation in a foreign language it seemed as though they were discussing everything from the current price of potatoes to the state of the war in Viet-Nam and it seemed to go on interminably, but presently Alison stepped back and the old woman resumed her trudge up the road.

I said, 'I didn't know you could speak Irish.'

'Oh, yes, I have the Gaelic,' she said casually. 'Come on.'

I fell into step. 'Where are we going?'

'To the place where the gossip is,' she said. 'The local shop.'

The shop was instantly familiar. I had seen many like it in the back-blocks of Australia and the more remote parts of the African veld. It was what I used to call as a child an 'anything shop' selling anything and everything in minute quantities to a small population. This shop had an added attraction; it had a bar. Alison went into her Irish routine again and the words washed around my ears without penetrating and then she turned to me, and asked, 'Do you drink whiskey?'

'Indeed I do.'

I watched with fascination as the bartender did his best to empty the bottle into a glass. In Ireland a glass of whiskey is a tenth of a bottle and the men are noble drinkers. Alison said, 'One of them is for him—his name is Sean O'Donovan. You talk to him and I'll join the ladies at the other end of the shop. Men can talk to each other better over a drink.'

'Talk to him!' I said. 'That's easy, but what do I do when he talks back?'

'Oh, Sean O'Donovan speaks English,' she said, and drifted away.

'Yes,' said O'Donovan in a soft voice. 'I have the English. I was in the British army during the war.' He put the glasses on the counter. 'You'll be here for a bit of a holiday?'

'Yes,' I said. 'Having a look around—a travelling holiday. You have a beautiful country, Mr O'Donovan.'

He cracked a grin. 'You English have always shown a fancy for it,' he said sardonically. He lifted his glass and said something in Irish which I didn't catch but the action was obvious so I returned the toast in English.

We talked for a while about the things a man talks about to a bartender in bars, and finally I got down to the meat of it. 'All over Ireland I've been crossing the tracks of a friend of mine,' I said casually. 'But I haven't caught up with him. I was wondering if he's been here. His names is Jones.' That sounded silly, but I said it all the same.

'Would he be a Welshman?' asked O'Donovan.

I smiled. 'I doubt it. He's English.'

O'Donovan shook his head. 'I have not heard of the man. He may be at the Big House, but they keep to themselves entirely.' He shook his head. 'They buy their provisions in Dublin and not a thought do they give to the local trader. My father, now, who had this place before me, supplied the Big House all his days.'

That sounded promising. I said sympathetically, 'Stand-offish, are they?'

He shrugged. 'Not that Himself is here often. He comes only once or twice a year—from the Other Island, you know.'

It took me a good twenty seconds to realize that O'Donovan meant England. 'So the owner is English?'

O'Donovan gave me a sidelong glance. 'It would seem he is another Englishman who has taken a fancy to a piece of Ireland.' I looked at O'Donovan's tough face and wondered if he was an active member of the IRA; he appeared to like Englishmen only in so far as they stayed in England, although he chatted pleasantly enough to me.

He held up his hand. 'I said "seems" and that is what I meant, for I was reading in the paper only the other day that the man is not English at all.'

'So he gets his name into the newspapers?'

'And why wouldn't he? He speaks in the Parliament of the Other Island. Now isn't that a strange thing, and him not an Englishman.'

'It is, indeed,' I said. My acquaintanceship with members of the British Parliament was limited, to say the least of it, and I didn't know the rules of entry. 'So what is he if he isn't English?'

'Ah, now; that I forget entirely. Some small place far away in Europe he comes from. But it's a rich man he is. He has all the money in the world that the American Kennedys haven't laid their fists on already. He comes here in his big yacht which is now anchored in the bay and it's as big as the British royal yacht, if not bigger. Such a pleasure boat has never been seen in these waters before.'

A wealthy and foreign Member of Parliament! It wasn't as promising as I had thought, although it had its curiosity value.

O'Donovan shook his head. 'Maybe Mr Wheeler is richer than the Kennedys, after all.'

Wheeler!

Every nerve cell in my cerebrum sprang to attention simultaneously. That was the name of the MP Mackintosh had seen, the day before being hit by the car. I put down my glass slowly. 'I think we'll have another, Mr O'Donovan.'

'And that's a kindly thought,' he said. 'I'm thinking you'll be from the newspapers yourself.' I opened my mouth to speak, and he winked at me. 'Hush, now; you've no need to fear I'll give you away. We've had other London reporters here—ay, and one American—all trying to find out things about the Wheeler man to publish in their papers but not one of them had the wit that you have—to bring an Irish girl with you to do a bit talking in the Gaelic.'

'I thought it might smooth the way,' I said prevaricatingly.

He leaned over the counter and looked into the shop where Alison was talking animatedly to a group of black-shawled women. 'Ah, but she did not learn her tongue in the West; in Waterford, maybe.'

'I believe she mentioned that she lived there,' I said guardedly. 'But she lives in Dublin now.'

O'Donovan nodded in satisfaction, pleased to have been proved right. He picked up the glasses, and then paused, looking over my shoulder. 'Look, now; here comes Seamas Lynch from the Big House. I'll not tell him what you are.'

I turned and looked at the man who was walking up to the bar. He was a black Irishman, dark as a Spaniard, and tall, lean and muscular. O'Donovan put our whiskey on the counter, and said, 'And what will you have, Seamas?'

'I'll have a half,' said Lynch.

O'Donovan picked up a glass and turned to fill it, throwing a question over his shoulder. 'Seamas, when is Himself leaving in his big boat?'

Lynch shrugged. 'When he takes it into his head to do so, Sean O'Donovan.'

O'Donovan put the glass in front of Lynch. I observed that half an Irish single whiskey was about as big as an English double. 'Ah, it's nice to be rich,' he said. 'And have all the time in the world.'

I said, 'Maybe the House of Commons isn't sitting.'

'Then he should be talking to his constituents—and he has none here,' said O'Donovan. He turned to Lynch. 'This gentleman is having a fine time seeing Ireland.'

Lynch looked at me. 'So you think Ireland is a fine place, do you?'

It wasn't what he said but the way he said it that made my hackles rise; his tone of voice held a thinly veiled contempt. I said, 'Yes; I think it's very nice country.'

'And where are you going next?' asked O'Donovan.

I had an inspiration and told a true story. 'I believe my grandfather on my mother's side was harbour master at Sligo many years ago. I'm going up there to see if I can trace the family.'

'Ach,' said Lynch. 'Every Englishman I meet tells me of his Irish ancestry.' His contempt was now open. 'And they all claim to be proud of it. You'd think from the way of it that the British Parliament ought to be in Dublin.'

I nearly lost my temper but kept my voice even. 'Maybe it's true. Maybe it's because your Irish girls can't find good husbands at home so they have to cross the Irish Sea,' I said coolly.

Lynch's face darkened and his hand tightened on his glass. As he straightened up from leaning on the counter O'Donovan said sharply, 'Seamas, that's enough, now. You've got as good as you've given, which does not happen too often, so put your glass back in your mouth or on to the counter. I'll have no breakages in my house unless it's your head with a bottle I'll be holding.'

Lynch sneered at me and turned his back. O'Donovan said, not very apologetically, 'You'll understand the English are not well liked hereabouts.'

I nodded. 'And with good reason, from some of the things I've heard. As it happens, I'm not English—I'm Australian.'

O'Donovan's face lightened. 'Are you, now? I ought to have know from your pleasant ways and your good manners in the face of provocation. That's a great country—it is, indeed.'

I finished my drink as I saw Alison giving me a come-hither look. O'Donovan watched approvingly as I sank the full Irish measure in four seconds flat. I put down the empty glass. 'It's been nice talking to you, Mr O'Donovan,' I said. 'I'll be back.'

'And you'll be welcome,' he said.

I went to join Alison at the door. As I passed Lynch he stuck his foot out backwards but I neatly evaded it and carried on. I wasn't looking for a fight. Alison opened the door and went outside. I was about to follow her but stood aside as a big man entered. He walked past me and then paused uncertainly.

I ran for it. It was Taafe, and while his thought processes might have been slow they hadn't stopped altogether. While he was making up his minuscule mind about what action to take I dashed outside and grabbed Alison's arm. 'Run for the car! I said urgently. 'We've found trouble.'

What I liked about Alison was her quick comprehension. She wasted no time insisting on having an explanation, but immediately took to her heels and ran. She must have been in superb physical condition because she could cover the ground faster than I, and within a hundred yards she was ten yards ahead.

Behind I heard boots thumping the ground as someone chased behind and I reckoned the someone was Taafe. It was now dusk and the light was ebbing from the western sky which is why I didn't see the fishing net spread out to dry about twenty yards from where we had left the car. I got my feet tangled in the netting and pitched forward to the ground.

That made it easy for Taafe. I heard the crunch of his boots as he ran up, and then the rasp of the engine as Alison started the car. The next thing I knew was Taafe had put the boot into me good and solid. He had boots like a skinhead, probably steel-tipped, and one of them crunched into my side with terrifying force. He made no sound apart from a heavy breathing.

I rolled over, desperately trying to free my feet, and his foot whistled past my head so closely that I felt the draught. If he kicked me in the head it would be lights-out for Stannard—maybe permanently. The engine of the car roared and then we were illuminated as Alison switched on the headlights.

I looked up and saw Taafe loom over me, his teeth drawn back over his lips in a snarl as he manœuvred for another kick. I rolled frantically and saw a stab of light from the direction of the car, and heard a report as from a dud firecracker. Taafe made a gargling sound in his throat and suddenly collapsed on top of me. He made horrible noises as I heaved him off and then he writhed on the ground clutching his left knee.

I ripped the netting from my feet and ran to the car. The passenger door was open and Alison was revving the engine impatiently. As I tumbled in she was putting a small pistol into the glove compartment and, before I got the door closed, she was away, swinging the car around and barely avoiding Taafe who still wriggled on the ground.

I gasped, 'Where did you shoot him?'

'In the kneecap,' she said. Her voice was as steady and cool as though she was discussing a shot on the target range. 'It seemed the best thing to do. He was going to kill you.'

I turned and looked back. Although it was dark I could see someone bending over Taafe. It was someone tall and lean and it could very well have been Seamas Lynch.

4

'Wheeler,' I said thoughtfully. 'What do you know of him?'

It was next morning and we were having breakfast in my bedroom. If the management thought this an irregular procedure they showed no sign of it, and, in view of the previous evening's brouhaha I didn't feel like being pinned down to a static and open position in the public dining room.

She spread marmalade on toast. 'MP for Harlingsdon East, very wealthy, not too popular with fellow Commons members, so I understand.'

'And a foreigner?'

She wrinkled her brow. 'I believe he is. But he must have arrived in England a long time ago. He'll be naturalized, of course.'

'Can a foreign-born person become an MP?'

'Oh, yes; there have been quite a few,' Alison said indistinctly past the toast.

'An American President must be American born,' I said. 'What about an English Prime Minister?'

'I don't think there's any rule about it,' she said. 'We'd have to look it up in Erskine May.'

'What's his standing? In politics, I mean? Is he a Minister or anything like that?'

'He's a very vociferous back-bencher.'

I snapped my fingers. 'That's where I saw his name before. He was blowing off steam after Slade and I escaped. Going on about "gangsters in our English streets". I read about him in the *Sunday Times*.'

'Yes,' said Alison. 'He made quite a noise about it in the House. The PM put him down quite firmly.'

I said, 'If what I'm thinking is correct then he's got a hell of a nerve. Try this on for size. Mackintosh sees Wheeler and he's hit by a car—a hit-and-run car. I take a notebook from Jones which mentioned Clonglass. In Clonglass we run across Wheeler; we also run into Taafe—and too bloody hard, if I might say so—and I know that Taafe is one of the Scarperers. Wouldn't you think it would be too much of a coincidence for Wheeler *not* to be implicated with the Scarperers?'

Alison buttered another piece of toast; the girl had a healthy appetite. 'I'd say he's in it up to his neck,' she said concisely. She paused. 'What I don't understand is why Taafe didn't shout; he didn't make a sound even when I shot him.'

'I don't think he *can* shout,' I said. 'I think he's dumb. I've never heard him speak. Let me have a look at that pistol.'

She leaned over, picked up her bag, and produced the pistol. It was a very natty little weapon, only ·22 in calibre and with a total length of less than four inches—hardly the gun for accurate shooting in uncertain light at any range over twenty feet. I said, 'Did you intend to hit Taafe in the kneecap?'

'Well,' she said. 'He had one foot off the ground but even then these bullets are so small that if I'd hit him anywhere else it wouldn't bring him down. I could have gone for a head shot, of course, but I didn't want to kill him.'

I looked at her with respect. As I had thought, Mackintosh gathered around him people with talents.

'So you *did* intend to hit him where you did.'

'Oh, yes,' she said, and put the ridiculous little gun away.

I said, 'Let's get back to Wheeler. What kind of a foreigner is he? Or was he? Where did he come from?'

'I don't know. I haven't taken much interest in him. But the details ought to be in *Who's Who.*'

'I'm thinking of Slade,' I said. 'He was taken out of the house near Limerick four days ago. That yacht is very convenient. If it has been anchored at Clonglass for more than four days *and* Wheeler decides to take off on a Baltic cruise this summer then there'll be a bloody good chance that Slade is on board. It's just a hypothesis, mind you.'

'I like it.'

'I've got a few more. What about this one? Let's say there's a man called X who's either a Russian or favours the Russian philosophy; and let's say he devotes his time to springing Russian spies from British gaols. He'd need assistance and where would he get it?' Alison opened her mouth to answer but I ploughed on. 'There's a fair amount of anti-British feeling in Ireland, especially now that Northern Ireland has blown up, and the IRA is still an active force. I detected a bit of that ill feeling last night.'

'Was that the man you were talking to at the bar?'

'He was Seamas Lynch and he seemed to hate my guts on principle. What's more, he works for Wheeler and I think I saw him helping Taafe when we left last night. But I digress. Let's say Mr X organizes the Scarperers from elements of the IRA. He has the money to get it started but from then on it's self-financing because the Scarperers don't confine their attention to spies. The IRA need the money and it's a better way of getting it than holding up banks, so they're happy. Mr X is also happy because the IRA are doing a good job for him. How does that strike you?'

She raised her eyebrows. 'Mr X being Wheeler?' She shook her head sadly. 'Self-made millionaires aren't usually enthusiastic communists.'

'How did he make his money?'

'I think he made his first fortune in the property boom of the 1950s and early '60s. Then he got into the property market in the United States and made another fortune. *Time* had a front cover article about him; they called him "Wheeler-Dealer". Since then he's diversified into nearly everything you can think of that makes money.'

'And he still has time to be a Member of Parliament! He's a busy little man.'

'Too busy to be a Russian spy,' said Alison.

'Maybe.' I had my own reservations about that. I said, 'I'd like to know how Mackintosh is getting on. Will you telephone?'

'I was going to,' she said. 'I think we ought to get rid of the car. It will have been seen at Clonglass.' She hesitated. 'I'll go out and get another. I don't think you ought to walk the streets of Galway just now.'

'But . . .'

'They're not likely to know much about me yet,' she said. 'We weren't conspicuously together last night.'

'Provided Sean O'Donovan has kept his mouth shut.'

'I'll have to chance it,' she said, and picked up the telephone.

She put a call through to London and talked to someone at the hospital. Her words were brief and she did more listening than talking but I knew what was happening by the expression of her face. She put down the handset and said bleakly, 'Still no change. He's fighting hard—but he would.'

I lit a cigarette. 'Have you known him long?'

'All my life,' she said. 'He's my father.'

5

That led to an argument. My immediate reaction was to say that I'd get on with the job myself while she went back to London. 'Damn it!' I said. 'You *ought* to be there. You'll never forgive yourself if he dies in your absence.'

'And he'd never forgive me if Slade gets away because I'm too damned sentimental,' she said. 'You don't know my father very well, Owen, if you think he'd want that. He's a hard man.'

'And you're a hard woman,' I said. 'A chip off the old block.'

She said tautly, 'An unnatural daughter?'

'I think you ought to go back,' I said stubbornly.

'And I'm staying,' she said, equally stubbornly. 'I have two jobs to do here. One is to help you to get Slade. You can't run up against this crowd by yourself.'

'And the other?'

'To stop you getting yourself killed, you damned fool!'

I was turning that over in my mind while she opened her suitcase and impatiently ripped open a brown-paper parcel, revealing more money than I've seen anywhere outside a bank. For a moment that diverted me. 'How much have you got there, for God's sake?'

'Five thousand pounds,' she said, and tossed me a bundle of fivers. 'There's five hundred. We might get separated and you'll need the money.'

I said dryly, 'Her Majesty's Treasury is becoming unreasonably reckless. Do I sign a receipt?'

'I'm going to find out what I can about Wheeler,' she said. 'Don't move out of this room.'

She stuffed the rest of the money into one of those oversized bags women carry and stormed out of the room before I could say another word. I sat down bonelessly on the bed and looked at the bundle of notes, one hundred sheets thick, and the only thought in my head was the irrelevancy that she had called me by my given name for the first time.

She was away for two hours and came back with news— Wheeler's yacht was on the move, heading south. She didn't know if Wheeler was on board or not.

She pulled a piece of paper from her pocket, a printed page from a book. 'I bought an old copy of *Who's Who*. It was a bit too big to lug around so I tore out the relevant page.'

She passed it to me and pointed out the paragraph. Charles George Wheeler, aged 46, was born in Argyrokastro, Albania. *Albania!* He was a Member of Parliament with three honorary doctorates, a member of this, an associate of that, a fellow of the other. A flat in London, a country house in Herefordshire; clubs so-and-so and such-and-such—my eye skipped down the page until I was suddenly arrested by an entry—Interests— penal reform, for God's sake!

I said, 'How does he come by the name of Charles George Wheeler?'

'He probably changed it by deed poll.'

'Do you know when he arrived in England from Albania?'

'I know nothing about him,' said Alison. 'I've had no occasion to study him.'

'And his yacht has gone south. I'd have thought he'd have gone north—to the Baltic.'

'You're still assuming that Slade is aboard.'

'I have to,' I said grimly.

Alison frowned. 'He might be going to the Mediterranean. If so, he'll refuel somewhere in the south, perhaps Cork. I have a friend in Cork: an old lady—an honorary aunt. We can fly to Cork from Shannon.'

'There'll be more coppers than tourists at Shannon Airport,' I said. 'I can't risk it.'

'Airports are big places. I can get you through,' Alison said confidently.

'And how will you account for me to your old aunt?'

Alison smiled. 'I could always twist Maeve O'Sullivan around my little finger.'

6

We sneaked into Shannon Airport quite easily and un-obtrusively. It seemed to me that their security was lousy, but the places are so big and the perimeters so extensive that to make them leakproof would swallow all the profits. Within fifteen minutes, after a bit of radio natter, we were in the air heading for Cork while I watched Alison's expert handling of the controls. She flew the plane—a Piper Apache—like she did everything else—with an economy of movement and a total lack of showmanship. I wondered what it was like to have Mackintosh as a father. Some girls might have found it a traumatic experience.

Maeve O'Sullivan lived in Glanmire on the outskirts of Cork. She was very old, but still quick and sharp-eyed and shrewd as the proverbial barrel-load of monkeys. She crowed with delight as she saw Alison and gave me a glance which stripped me to the bone in two seconds. 'You've been away too long, Alison Mackintosh.'

Alison smiled. 'Smith,' she said.

'And so it is—so it is. A sassenach name for a Celt, more's the pity.'

'This is Owen Stannard,' said Alison. 'He's working for my father.'

The wise old eyes regarded me with renewed interest. 'Is he, now? And what devil's business is that young rip up to now?'

The idea of a man as hard-bitten as Mackintosh being referred to as a young rip made me want to smile, but I manfully repressed it. Alison gave me a warning glance. 'Nothing that should concern you,' she said tartly. 'He sends you his love.' I mentally agreed with her that it would not be a kindness to tell the old lady of his condition.

'You're just in time for your tea,' said Mrs O'Sullivan, and went off in a bustle into the kitchen with Alison close behind her. I sat down in a big armchair which swallowed me in comfort and looked at my watch. It was six-thirty—early evening—less than twenty-four hours had passed since Alison had punctured Taafe in the kneecap.

'Tea' proved to be an enormous meal with many dishes thrust upon us interspersed with brisk and depreciatory comments on the poor appetites of young folk these days. When I called the old lady Mrs O'Sullivan she laughed and said, 'You call me by my name, young man, and I'll feel easier,' so I called her Maeve, but Alison called her Aunt Maeve.

'There's something I must tell you, Aunt Maeve,' said Alison. 'Owen, here, is wanted by the *garda*, so no one must know he's here.'

'The *garda*, is it?' cried Maeve. 'It'll not be dishonest, I know; but is this Alec's doing?'

'In a way,' said Alison. 'It *is* important.'

'I've held my tongue about more things than you've ever spoken in your life, girl,' said Maeve. 'You don't know what it was like here in the old days, and now the crazy men are at it again in the North.' She looked up with sharp black-button eyes. 'It's nothing to do with that, is it, now?'

'No,' I said. 'Nothing to do with Ireland at all, really.'

'Then I'll keep my peace,' she said. 'You are welcome in this house, Owen Stannard.'

After tea we washed up and Maeve said, 'I'm an old woman and I'm wanting my bed. Make yourselves easy, the pair of you.'

'I'd like to use the telephone,' said Alison.

'It's there when you want it. Put your sixpences in the box— I'm saving up for my old age.' Maeve shouted with laughter.

'It'll be more than sixpences, Aunt Maeve,' said Alison. 'I'll be telephoning to England and more than once.'

'Rest easy, girl. If you talk to Alec, ask him why he never comes to Ireland these days.'

'He's a busy man, Aunt Maeve.'

'Aye,' said Maeve. 'And when men like Alec Mackintosh get busy it's time for normal folk to find a deep hole. But give him my love, and tell him he doesn't deserve it.'

She went off and I said, 'She's quite a character.'

'I could tell you stories about Maeve O'Sullivan that would make your hair curl,' said Alison. 'She was very active during the Troubles.' She picked up the telephone. 'Let's hear what the Harbourmaster has to say.'

The Harbourmaster was most obliging. Yes, *Artina* was

expected. Mr Wheeler had arranged for refuelling. No, he didn't really know when she would arrive but if previous visits by Mr Wheeler were anything to go by then *Artina* would be staying in Cork for a couple of days.

As Alison put down the telephone I said, 'Now I have to think of a way of getting aboard. I wish I knew more about Wheeler's craft.'

'Give me a few hours and I'll have all you need to know,' said Alison. 'The telephone is a wonderful invention. But first I must ring the hospital.'

It was a time for rejoicing because Alec Mackintosh was fighting his way through to life again. Alison was radiant. 'He's better! The doctor said he was better! His condition has improved and they think there's a chance now.'

'Is he conscious? Is he able to speak?'

'No, he's still unconscious.'

I thought back. If Mackintosh had been unconscious all this time it would be quite a while before the doctors let him speak to anyone, even if he was able and willing. I'd have given a lot to be able to hear what he'd said to Wheeler the day before the hit-and-run.

'I'm glad he's better,' I said sincerely.

Alison picked up the telephone again, suddenly all business-like. 'And now to work.'

I left her to it, only answering her questions from time to time. I was busily engaged in developing my hypothesis which was beginning to blossom into a very strange shape indeed. If I was right then Wheeler was a most odd fish, and a very dangerous man—more dangerous to State security, even, than Slade.

I was deep in thought when Alison said, 'I've done all I can now; the rest will have to wait for morning.'

She flipped open the notebook which was full of shorthand notes, page after page. 'What do you want first—Wheeler or the yacht?'

'Let's have the yacht.'

She leafed through the pages. 'Here we are. Name—*Artina*; designed by Parker, built by Clelands on the Tyneside; she was two years' old when Wheeler bought her. She's a standard design known as a Parker-Clelands which is important for reasons I'll come to later. Overall length—111 feet, beam—22 feet, cruising speed—12 knots, speed flat out—13 knots. She has two Rolls-Royce diesel engines of 350 horse-power each. Is this the sort of stuff you want?'

'Just right.' I could begin to build up a picture. 'What's her range?'

'I haven't got that yet, but it's coming. A crew of seven—skipper, engineer, cook, steward and three seamen. Accommodation for a maximum of eight passengers.'

'How is the accommodation arranged?'

'That will be coming tomorrow. The plans of her sister ship were published a few years ago. They're being photographed and sent by wire to the Cork *Examiner* where we can pick them up tomorrow, together with some photographs of the ship.'

I regarded Alison with admiration. 'Wow! Now that's something I wouldn't have thought of doing.'

'The newspaper is a very efficient information gatherer and transmitter. I told you I could pull strings.'

'What about Wheeler?'

'There's a detailed account coming to the *Examiner* on the telex, but this is the meat of it. He fought the Italians when they moved into Albania before the war.' She looked up. 'He'd be about 14 years old then. He fled with his family into Jugoslavia and again fought against the Italians and the Germans during the war both in Jugoslavia and Albania towards the end of the war. He left Albania in 1946 when he was somewhere in his early twenties and settled in England. Was naturalized in 1950. Started to deal in property just about that time and that was the beginning of his fortune.'

'What kind of property?'

'Offices. That was about the time they first began to put up the big office blocks.' She wrinkled her brow. 'I talked to a financial editor; he said there was something funny about the first deals Wheeler made.'

'That's interesting,' I said. 'Tell me more.'

'According to this editor it wasn't easy to see how Wheeler had made a profit. He evidently had made a profit because he suddenly had the money to go bigger and better, and he never looked back right from the early days.'

'I wonder how he paid his taxes,' I said. 'It's a pity we can't subpoena his tax inspector. I'm beginning to see the light. Tell me, when he was fighting in the war—did he fight for the Cetniks or the Partisans? Nationalists or Communists?'

'I don't have that here,' said Alison. 'It will be coming by telex, if it's known at all.'

'When did he enter politics?'

She consulted her notes. 'He fought a by-election in 1962 and lost. He fought in the general election of 1964 and got in by a fair margin.'

'And I suppose he lashed out generously for party funds,' I said. 'He'd do that, of course. Any known connections at present with Albania?'

'Nothing known.'

'Russia? Any communist country?'

Alison shook her head. 'He's a dinkum capitalist, mate. I don't see it, Owen. He's always popping off with anti-communist speeches in the House.'

'He's also against prisoners escaping from gaol, if you remember. What about this prison reform bit?'

'He used to be a prison visitor, but I suppose he's got too big for that now. He's generous in his subscriptions to various prison reform societies, and he's a member of a House Committee studying prison reform.'

'My God, that would come in useful,' I said. 'Did he visit prisons in that capacity?'

'I suppose he might.' She put down the notebook. 'Owen, you're building up quite a structure on a weak foundation.'

'I know.' I stood up and paced the room restlessly. 'But I'll add another layer on my hypothesis. I once talked to a multi-millionaire, one of the South African variety; he told me that the first quarter-million is the hardest. It took him fifteen years to make £250,000, three years to bring it up to the round million, and in the next six years he reached the five million mark. The mathematicians would say he was riding an exponential curve.'

Alison was getting a little impatient. 'So what?'

'The first quarter million is hardest because our potential millionaire has to make all his own decisions and has to do his own research, but once he has money he can afford to hire regiments of accountants and platoons of lawyers and that makes decision-making a lot easier. It's the starting of the process that's the snag. Go back to your financial editor—the one who smelled something funny in Wheeler's first deals.'

Alison picked up her notes again. 'I haven't anything more than I've already told you.'

'Let's take our man X,' I said. 'He's not a Russian—let's call him an Albanian—but he still favours the Russians. He comes to England in 1946 and is naturalized in 1950. About that time he starts dealing in property and makes money at it, but at least one man can't see how he did it. Let's assume the money was fed to him from outside—perhaps as much as half a million. X is a sharp boy—as sharp as any other potential millionaire—and money makes money. So he begins to roll in the time-honoured capitalistic way.'

I swung around. 'In 1964 he entered politics and got himself a seat in the Commons where he's now an enthusiastic and keen back-bencher. He's 46 years old and still has another 25 years of political life in him.'

I stared at Alison. 'What would happen if he were to attain high position in the Government? Say, Chancellor or Minister of Defence—or even Prime Minister—in 1984, which seems to me to be an appropriate date? The boys in the Kremlin would be laughing their heads off!'

CHAPTER EIGHT

I

I SLEPT BADLY THAT NIGHT. In the dark hours my hypothesis began to seem damned silly and more and more unlikely. A millionaire and an MP could not possibly be associated with the Russians—it was a contradiction in terms. Certainly Alison found she could not accept it. And yet Wheeler was associated with the Scarperers, unless the whole series of assumed links was pure coincidence—and that possibility could not be eliminated. I had seen too many cases of apparent cause and effect which turned out to be coincidence.

I turned over restlessly in bed. Yet assume it was so—that Wheeler actually was controlling the Scarperers. Why would he do it? Certainly not to make money; he had plenty of that. The answer came out again that it was political, which again led to Wheeler as a Member of Parliament and the dangers inherent in that situation.

I fell asleep and had dire dreams full of looming menace.

At breakfast I was still tired and a shade bad-tempered. My temper worsened rapidly when Alison made the first phone call of the day and was told by the Harbourmaster that *Artina* had arrived during the night, refuelled quickly, and left for Gibraltar in the early hours.

'We've lost the bastard again,' I said.

'We know where he is,' said Alison consolingly. 'And we know where he'll be in four days.'

'There are too many things wrong with that,' I said glumly. 'Just because he has clearance for Gibraltar doesn't mean he's going there, for one thing. For another, what's to prevent him from transferring Slade to a Russian trawler heading the other way through the Baltic? He could do it easily once he's over the horizon. And we don't even know if Slade is aboard *Artina*. We're just guessing.'

After breakfast Alison went out to collect the stuff from the *Examiner*. I didn't go with her; I wasn't going anywhere near a newspaper office—those reporters had filled up their columns with too much about Rearden and too many photographs. A sharp-eyed reporter was the last person I wanted to encounter.

So I stayed in the house while Maeve tactfully busied herself with the housework and left me alone to brood. Alison was away for an hour and a half, and she brought back a large envelope. 'Photographs and telex sheets,' she said, as she plopped the envelope in front of me.

I looked at the photographs first. There were three of Wheeler, one an official photograph for publicity use and the others news shots of him caught with his mouth open as the news photographers like to catch politicians. In one of them he looked like a predatory shark and I'd bet some editor had chortled over that one.

He was a big man, broad-shouldered and tall, with fair hair. The photographs were black-and-white so it was difficult to judge, but I'd say his hair was ash-blond. His nose was prominent and had a twist in it as though it had been thumped at some time or other, and the cartoonists would have no trouble taking the mickey if he ever attained a position of eminence. I put the photographs of Wheeler aside—I would recognize him if I saw him.

The other photographs were of the *Artina*, and one was a reproduction of the plans of her sister ship. Sean O'Donovan had exaggerated—she was not nearly as big as the royal yacht, but she was a fair size for all that, and it would take a millionaire to buy her and to run her. There was an owner's double cabin forward of the engine room and aft were three double cabins for six guests. The crew lived forward, excepting the skipper who had the master's cabin just behind the wheel-house.

I studied the plan until I had memorized every passage and door. If I had to board her I would want to know my way around and to know the best places to hide. I checked off the aft peak and the room which held the air conditioning equipment as likely places for a stowaway.

Alison was immersed in reading the telex sheets.

'Any joy there?'

She looked up. 'There's not much more than I told you last night. It's expanded a bit, that's all. Wheeler fought for the Partisans in Jugoslavia.'

'The communists,' I said. 'Another strand in the web.'

I began to read and found that Alison was right; there wasn't much more solid information. The picture was of a bright young man who became a tycoon by the usual clapper-clawing methods and who now had a solid base in society built up by saying the right things at the right times and by contributing largely to the right causes. The picture of a successful man now looking for new worlds to conquer—hence the politics.

'He's not married,' I said. 'He must be the most eligible bachelor in England.'

Alison smiled wryly. 'I've heard a couple of rumours. He runs a mistress who is changed regularly, and the story goes that he's bisexual. But no one in his right mind would put that on the telex—that would be publishing a libel.'

'If Wheeler knew what was in my mind libel would be the least of his worries,' I said.

Alison shrugged unenthusiastically. 'What do we do?'

'We go to Gibraltar,' I said. 'Will your plane take us there?'

'Of course.'

'Then let's chase the wild goose. There's nothing else to do.'

2

We had time to spare and in plenty. An inspection of the plans of *Artina*'s sister ship and a reading of the description that went with it made it quite certain that she was no high speed craft and she certainly couldn't get to Gibraltar in less than four days. We decided to play it safe and to be in Gibraltar in three days so we would be there when she came in.

That gave Alison time to fly back to London to see how Mackintosh was managing to survive and to dig up more dirt on Wheeler. We decided it would be most unwise for me to go back to London. Ducking in and out of Cork airport was one thing—Gatwick or Heathrow was quite another. Every time I smuggled myself incognito through the airport barriers I took an added risk.

So I spent two days cooped up in a suburban house in Cork with no one to speak to but an old Irishwoman. I must say that Maeve was most tactful; she didn't push and she didn't question, and she respected my silences. Once she said, 'Och, I know how it is with you, Owen. I went through it myself in 1918. It's a terrible thing to have the hand of every man against you, and you hiding like an animal. But you'll rest easy in this house.'

I said, 'So you had your excitement in the Troubles.'

'I had,' she said. 'And I didn't like it much. But there are always troubles—if not here then somewhere else—and there'll always be men running and men chasing.' She gave me a sidelong glance. 'Especially men like Alec Mackintosh and whoever concerns himself with that man.'

I smiled. 'Don't you approve of him?'

She lifted her chin. 'Who am I to approve or disapprove? I know nothing of his business other than that it is hard and dangerous. More dangerous for the men he orders than for him, I'm thinking.'

I thought of Mackintosh lying in hospital. That was enough to disprove that particular statement. I said, 'What about the women he commands?'

Maeve looked at me sharply. 'You'll be thinking of Alison,' she said flatly. 'Now that's a bad thing. He wanted a son and he got Alison, so he did the best with what he had and made her to his pattern; and it's a strong pattern and a hard pattern, enough to make a girl break under the burden of it.'

'He's a hard man,' I said. 'What about Alison's mother? Didn't she have a say in the matter?'

Maeve's tone was a little scornful, but the scorn was inter-mingled with pity. 'That poor woman! She married the wrong man. She didn't understand a man the like of Alec Mackin-tosh. The marriage never went well and she left Alec before Alison was born and came to live here in Ireland. She died in Waterford when Alison was ten.'

'And that's when Mackintosh took over Alison's education.'

'It is so,' said Maeve.

I said, 'What about Smith?'

'Has Alison not told you about him?'

'No,' I said.

'Then I'll not be telling,' said Maeve decidedly. 'I've gossiped enough already. When—and if—Alison wants you to know, then she'll tell you herself.' She turned away, and then paused, looking back. 'I'm thinking you're a hard man your-self, Owen Stannard. I doubt if you'll be the one for Alison.'

And I was left to make of that what I could.

Alison rang up late the first night. 'I flew out to sea when I left,' she said. '*Artina* was on course for Gibraltar.'

'You didn't make the inspection too obvious, I hope.'

'I overtook her flying at five thousand feet and climbing. I didn't turn until I was out of sight.'

'How is Mackintosh?' I still called him that, even to her.

'He's better, but still unconscious. I was allowed to see him for two minutes.'

That wasn't too good. I could have done with Mackintosh being awake and talkative; he wasn't alive enough yet for my liking. Which brought me to another and delicate subject. 'You might be under observation in London.'

'No one followed me. I didn't see anyone I know, either, except one man.'

'Who was that?'

'The Prime Minister sent his secretary to the hospital. I saw him there. He said the PM is worried.'

I thought of Wheeler and the man who had been taken out of prison to be killed, and then I thought of Mackintosh lying helpless in a hospital bed. 'You'd better do something,' I said. 'Ring the secretary chap and ask him to spread it around that Mackintosh is dying—that he's cashing in his chips.'

She caught on. 'You think they might attack Father in hospital?'

'They might if they think he's going to recover. Ask the PM's secretary to drop the unobtrusive word, especially to any of Wheeler's known associates in the House. If Wheeler rings London to have a chat with one of his mates the news might get through—and that could save your father's life.'

'I'll do that,' she said.

'Anything on Wheeler?'

'Not yet; not what we want, anyway. He lives a blameless public life.'

'It's not his public life we're interested in,' I said. 'But do your best.'

Alison came back two days later, arriving in a taxi in mid-afternoon. She looked tired as though she had not had much sleep, and Maeve clucked at the sight of her but relaxed as Alison said, 'Too much damned night-clubbing.'

Maeve went away and I raised my eyebrows. 'Been living it up?'

She shrugged. 'I had to talk to people and the kind of people I had to talk to are in the night club set.' She sighed. 'But it was a waste of time.'

'No further dirt?'

'Nothing of consequence, except maybe one thing. I checked the servant situation.'

'The *what* situation!'

She smiled tiredly. 'I checked on Wheeler's servants. The days of glory are past and servants are hard to come by, but

Wheeler does all right even though he needs a large staff.' She took her notebook from her pocket. 'All his staff are British and have British passports excepting the chauffeur who is an Irish national. Do you find that interesting?'

'His contact with Ireland,' I said. 'It's very interesting.'

'It gets better,' she said. 'As I said, the rest of his servants are British, but every last one of them is naturalized and they've all had their names changed by deed poll. And what do you think was their country of origin?'

I grinned. 'Albania.'

'You've just won a cigar. But there's an exception here too. One of them didn't take a British name because it would be peculiar if he did. Wheeler has taken a fancy to Chinese cooking and has a Chinese cook on the premises. His name is Chang Pi-wu.'

'I see what you mean,' I said. 'It would seem bloody funny if he changed his name to McTavish. Where does he hail from?'

'Hong Kong.'

A Hong Kong Chinese! It didn't mean much. I suppose it was quite reasonable that if a multi-millionaire had a taste for Chinese food then he'd have a Chinese cook; millionaires think differently from the common ruck of folk and that would be part of the small change of his life. But I felt a tickle at the back of my mind.

I said carefully, 'It may be that Wheeler is doing the charitable bit. Maybe all these British Albanians are his cousins and his cousins' cousins, nieces and nephews he's supporting in a tactful sort of way.'

Alison looked up at the ceiling. 'The problem with servants is keeping them. They want four nights a week off, television in their rooms, and a lie-in every morning, otherwise they become mobile and leave. The turnover is high, and Wheeler's turnover in servants is just as high as anyone else's.'

'Is it, by God?' I leaned forward and peered at Alison closely. 'You've got something, damn it! Spit it out.'

She grinned cheerfully and opened her notebook. 'He has thirteen British Albanians working for him—gardeners, butler, housekeeper, maids and so on. Not one has been with him longer than three years. The last one to arrive pitched up last month. They come and go just like ordinary servants.'

'And they take holidays in Albania,' I said. 'He's got a courier service.'

'Not only that,' said Alison. 'But someone is supplying him with a regular intake.' She consulted her notebook again. 'I did a check with the local branch of the Ministry of Social Security in Herefordshire; in the last ten years he's had fifty of them through his hands. I can't prove they were all Albanian because they had British names, but I'll take a bet they were.'

'Jesus!' I said. 'Hasn't anyone tumbled to it? What the hell is the Special Branch doing?'

Alison spread her hands. 'They're all British. If it's come to anyone's attention—which I doubt—then he's doing the charitable bit, as you said—rescuing his compatriots from the communist oppressors.'

'Fifty!' I said. 'Where do they all go when he's done with them?'

'I don't know about the fifty—I've only had time to check on two. Both are now in the service of other MPs.'

I began to laugh because I couldn't help it. 'The cheek of it,' I said. 'The brazen nerve! Don't you see what he's doing? He's getting these fellows in, giving them a crash course on British *mores* and customs as well as the finer points of being a gentleman's gentleman, and then planting them as spies. Can't you imagine him talking to one of his mates in the Commons? "Having servant trouble, dear boy? It just happens that one of mine is leaving. Oh, no trouble like that—he just wants to live in Town. Perhaps I can persuade . . ." It beats anything I've ever heard.'

'It certainly shows he has present connections with Albania,' said Alison. 'I wasn't convinced before—it seemed too ridiculous. But I am now.'

I said, 'Do you remember the Cicero case during the war. The valet of the British Ambassador to Turkey was a German spy. Wheeler has been in the money for twenty years—he could have planted a hundred Ciceros. And not only at the political end. I wonder how many of our industrial chieftains have Wheeler-trained servants in their households?'

'All with English names and all speaking impeccable English,' said Alison. 'Wheeler would see to that.' She ticked off the steps on her fingers. 'They come to England and while they're waiting for naturalization they learn the language thoroughly and study the British in their native habitat. When they're British they go to Wheeler for a final gloss and then he plants them.' She shook her head. 'It's a long term project.'

'Wheeler himself is a long term project. I don't see him packing his bags and returning to his native land. Look at Slade, for God's sake! He was worming his way in for *twenty-eight* years! These people take the long view.' I paused. 'When do we leave for Gibraltar?'

'Tomorrow morning.'

'Good,' I said. 'I want to catch up with this incredible bastard.'

3

I went into Cork airport the hard way, as usual. I was beginning to forget what it was like to use the front door. Maeve O'Sullivan had been uncharacteristically emotional when we left. 'Come back soon, girl,' she said to Alison. 'It's an old woman I am, and there's no telling.' There were tears in her eyes but she rubbed them away as she turned to me. 'And you, Owen Stannard; take care of yourself and Alec Mackintosh's daughter.'

I grinned. 'She's been taking care of me so far.'

'Then you're not the man I thought you were to let her,' replied Maeve with asperity. 'But go carefully, and watch for the *garda*.'

So we went carefully and it was with relief that I watched the city of Cork pass under the wings of the Apache as we circled to find our course south. Alison snapped switches and set dials, then took her hands from the control column. 'It will be nearly six hours,' she said. 'Depending on the wind and the rain.'

'You're not expecting bad weather?'

She smiled. 'It was just a manner of speaking. As a matter of fact, the weather report is good. The wind is northerly at 24,000 feet.'

'Will we be flying that high? I didn't think these things did that.'

'The engines are supercharged, so it's more economical to fly high. But this cabin isn't pressurized, so we'll have to go on oxygen soon—as soon as we reach 10,000 feet. You'll find the mask by your side.'

The last time I had seen the Apache it had been a six-seater but in Alison's absence in London the two rearmost seats had been removed and had been replaced by a big plastic box. I jerked my thumb over my shoulder, and said, 'What's that?'

'An extra fuel tank—another seventy gallons of spirit. It increases the range to 2,000 miles at the most economical flying speed. I thought we might need it.'

The capable Alison Smith thought of everything. I remembered what Maeve had said: *Made to a hard pattern, enough to break a girl under the burden of it.* I studied Alison; her face was calm as she checked the instruments and then tested the oxygen flow, and there were no lines of stress to substantiate Maeve's remark. Alison glanced sideways and caught me looking at her. 'What's the matter?'

'A cat may look at a king,' I said. 'So a dog may look at a queen. I was just thinking that you're lovely, that's all.'

She grinned and jerked her thumb backwards. 'The Blarney Stone is back there, and I know for a fact you never went near it. You must have Irish in your ancestry.'

'And Welsh,' I said. 'Hence the Owen. It's the Celt coming out in me.'

'Put on your mask,' she said. 'Then you'll look as beautiful as me.'

It was a long and boring flight. Although the masks had built-in microphones we didn't do much talking, and presently I put down the back of the seat to a reclining position. We flew south at 200 miles an hour—fifteen times faster than Wheeler in *Artina*—and I slept.

Or, rather, I dozed. I woke up from time to time and found Alison alert, scanning the sky or checking the instruments or making a fine adjustment. I would touch her shoulder and she would turn with a smile in her eyes and then resume her work. After nearly four hours had passed she nudged me and pointed ahead. 'The Spanish coast.'

There was a haze of heat below and a crinkled sea, and ahead the white line of surf. 'We won't overfly Spain,' she said. 'Not if we're landing at Gibraltar. It's politically in-advisable. We'll fly down the Portuguese coast.'

She took out a map on a board and worked out the new course, handling the protractor with smoothly efficient movements, then switched off the auto-pilot and swung the aircraft around gently. 'That's Cape Ortegal,' she said. 'When we sight Finisterre I'll alter course again.'

'When did you learn to fly?' I asked.

'When I was sixteen.'

'And to shoot a pistol?'

She paused before answering. 'When I was fourteen—pistol and rifle and shotgun. Why?'

'Just wondering.' Mackintosh believed in teaching them young. I found it hard to imagine a little girl of fourteen looking past the sights of a rifle. I bet she knew the Morse code, too, and all the flag semaphore signals, to say nothing of programming a computer and lighting a fire without matches. 'Were you a Girl Guide?'

She shook her head. 'I was too busy.'

Too busy to be a Girl Guide! She'd have her head down at her books studying languages when she wasn't practising in

185

the air or banging away on the target range. I wouldn't have put it past Mackintosh to make certain that she was at home in a submarine. What a hell of a life!

'Did you have any friends in those days?' I asked. 'Girls of your own age?'

'Not many.' She twisted in her seat. 'What are you getting at, Owen?'

I shrugged. 'Just the idle thoughts of an idle man.'

'Has Maeve O'Sullivan been filling you up with horror stories? Is that it? I might have known.'

'She didn't say a word out of place,' I said. 'But you can't help a man thinking.'

'Then you'd do better to keep your thoughts to yourself.' She turned back to the controls and lapsed into silence, and I thought it would be as well if I kept my big mouth shut, too.

As we turned the corner and flew up the Strait of Gibraltar Alison took the controls and we began to descend. At 10,000 feet she took off her oxygen mask and I was glad to do the same. And then, in the distance, I saw the Rock for the first time, rising sheer from the blue water. We circled and I saw the artificial harbour and the airstrip jutting into Algeciras Bay like the deck of an aircraft carrier. Apparently, to Alison who was busy on the radio, it was all old hat.

We landed from the east and our small aircraft did not need all that enormous runway. We rolled to a halt and then taxied to the airport buildings. I looked at the military aircraft parked all around, and said grimly, 'This is one airport which will have good security.' How was I going to smuggle myself through this one?

'I have something for you,' said Alison, and took a folder from the map pocket from which she extracted a passport. I flicked it open and saw my own face staring up from the page. It was a diplomatic passport. She said, 'It will get us through customs in a hurry, but it won't save you if you are recognized as Rearden.'

'It's good enough.' Even if I was recognized as Rearden the

sight of that diplomatic passport would be enough to give my challenger cause to wonder if he could possibly be right. I said, 'My God, you must have pull.'

'Just enough,' she said calmly.

The passport officer smiled as he took the passport, and the civilian with the hard face who was standing next to him ceased to study me and relaxed. We went right through within three minutes of entering the hall. Alison said, 'We're staying at the Rock Hotel; whistle up a taxi, will you?'

If Wheeler's trained Albanians made the perfect servants then Alison Smith was a God-given secretary. I hadn't thought for one moment of where we were going to lay our heads that night, but she had. Alec Mackintosh was a lucky man—but, perhaps, it wasn't luck. He'd trained her, hadn't he?

We had adjoining rooms at the Rock Hotel and agreed to meet in the bar after cleaning up. I was down first. Alison Smith was no different in that respect from any other woman, I was glad to observe; the female takes fifty per cent longer to prink than the male. It *is* only fifty per cent even though it seems twice as long. I had sunk my first cold beer by the time she joined me.

I ordered her a dry Martini and another beer for myself. She said, 'What will you do when Wheeler arrives?'

'I have to find if Slade is aboard *Artina* and that will mean a bit of pirate work.' I grinned. 'I promise not to have a knife in my teeth when I go over the bulwarks.'

'And if he is on board?'

'I do my best to bring him off.'

'And if you can't?'

I shrugged. 'I have orders covering that eventuality.'

She nodded coolly, and I wondered briefly if Mackintosh had ever given his own daughter similar instructions. She said, 'Wheeler being what he is and who he is will probably anchor off the Royal Gibraltar Yacht Club. I wouldn't be surprised if he's a member—he comes here often enough.'

'Where is it?'

187

'About half a mile from here.

'We'd better take a look at it.'

We finished our drinks and strolled into the sunshine. The yacht basin was full of craft, sail and power, big and small. I stood looking at the boats and then turned. 'There's a convenient terrace over there where they serve cooling drinks. That will be a nice place to wait.'

'I'm just going to make a telephone call,' said Alison, and slipped away. I looked at the yachts and the sea and tried to figure how I could get aboard *Artina* but without much success because I didn't know where she would be lying. Alison came back. 'Wheeler is expected at eleven tomorrow morning. He radioed through.'

'That's nice,' I said, and turned my face up to the sun. 'What do we do until then?'

She said unexpectedly, 'What about a swim?'

'I forgot to pack trunks; I didn't expect a semi-tropical holiday.'

'There *are* shops,' she said gently. So we went shopping and I bought trunks and a towel, and a pair of German duty-free binoculars, smooth, sleek and powerful.

We went across the peninsula and swam at Catalan Bay which was very nice. That night we went night-clubbing, which was even nicer. Mrs Smith seemed to be human and made of the same mortal clay as the rest of us.

4

At ten o'clock next morning we were sitting on the terrace overlooking the yacht basin and imbibing something long, cold and not too alcoholic. We both wore sun-glasses, not as much to shade our eyes as to join the anonymous throng just as the film stars do. The binoculars were to hand and all that was lacking was *Artina* and Wheeler and, possibly, Slade.

We didn't talk much because there wasn't anything to talk about; we couldn't plot and plan in the absence of *Artina*. And

Alison had loosened the strings of her personality the previous night, as near as she had ever got to letting her hair down, and possibly she was regretting it. Not that she had let me get too close; I had made the expected pass and she evaded it with ease. But now she had returned to her habitual wariness—we were working and personal relationships didn't matter.

I soaked up the sun. It was the thing I had missed in England, especially in prison, and now I let it penetrate to warm my bones. Time went on and presently Alison picked up the binoculars and focused them on a boat making its way to harbour between the North Mole and the Detached Mole. 'I think this is *Artina*.'

I had a glass to my lips when she said it, and I swallowed the wrong way and came up for air spluttering and choking. Alison looked at me with alarm. 'What's the matter?'

'The impudence of it!' I gasped with laughter. '*Artina* is an anagram of Tirana—and that's the capital of Albania. The bastard's laughing at us all. It just clicked when you said it.'

Alison smiled and proffered the binoculars. I looked at the boat coming in with the dying bow wave at her forefoot and compared what I saw with the drawings and photographs of her sister ship. 'She could be *Artina*,' I said. 'We'll know for sure within the next five minutes.'

The big motor yacht came closer and I saw the man standing at the stern—big and with blond hair. '*Artina* it is—and Wheeler.' I swept the glasses over her length. 'No sign of Slade, but that's to be expected. He wouldn't parade himself.'

She anchored off-shore and lay quietly in the water and I checked every man who walked on deck, identifying five for certain without Wheeler. There was a crew of seven apart from an unknown number of guests, but the men I saw didn't seem to be guests. Two were on the foredeck by a winch and another was watching the anchor chain. Two more were lowering a boat into the water.

I said, 'Count the number of men who come ashore. That might be useful to know.'

The two men by the winch moved amidships and unshipped the folding companionway and rigged it at the side of the yacht. One of them went down the steps and tethered the boat. Presently Wheeler appeared with a man in a peaked cap and they both descended the companionway into the waiting boat. The engine started and it took off in a wide curve and then straightened, heading for the yacht club.

Alison said, 'Wheeler and the skipper, I think. The man at the wheel is a crewman.'

They stepped ashore at the club and then the tender took off again and returned to *Artina* where the crewman tethered it to the bottom of the companionway and climbed up on board again.

Alison nudged me. 'Look!'

I turned my head in the direction her finger indicated. A big work boat was ploughing across the water towards *Artina*. 'So!'

'It's a fueller,' she said. '*Artina* is taking on diesel fuel and water already. It seems that Wheeler isn't going to waste much time here.'

'Damn!' I said. 'I was hoping he'd stay the night. I'd much rather go aboard in darkness.'

'He doesn't seem to have any guests,' she said. 'And he's in a hurry. From our point of view those are encouraging signs. Slade might very well be on board.'

'And a fat lot of use that is if I can't go aboard to find him. How long do you think refuelling will take?'

'An hour, maybe.'

'Time enough to hire a boat,' I said. 'Let's go.'

We dickered with a Gibraltan longshoreman for the hire of a motor launch and got away with him charging not more than twice the normal rate, and then launched out into the harbour. The fueller and *Artina* were now close-coupled on the port side, with hoses linking them. Another crew member in a peak cap was supervising—that could be the engineer.

I throttled down as we approached and we drifted by about fifty yards from the starboard side. Someone came into view,

190

looked at us incuriously and then lifted his head to look up at the Rock. He was Chinese.

I said, 'That, presumably, is Chang Pi-wu. Wheeler must like Chinese cooking if he takes his Chinese chef to sea. I hope the crew like Chinese food.'

'Maybe they have their own cook.'

'Maybe.' I studied the Chinese covertly. Many occidentals claim that all Chinese look alike. They're wrong—the Chinese physiognomy is as varied as any other and I knew I'd recognize this man if I saw him again. But I'd had practice; I'd lived in the East.

We drifted to the stern of *Artina*. The ports of the rearmost guest cabin were curtained in broad daylight, and I had a good idea of where Slade was lying low. It was exasperating to be so close and not be able to get at him.

Even as I opened the throttle and headed back to the shore I saw a crewman drop into the boat moored at the bottom of *Artina*'s companionway and take off. He was faster than we were and as we handed our launch to the owner I looked out and saw him returning with Wheeler and the skipper. They climbed aboard and the companionway was unshipped and stowed.

An hour later I was burning with a sense of futility as *Artina* moved off and headed out to sea. 'Where the hell is she going now?' I demanded.

'If he's going east into the Mediterranean to the Greek islands he'll refuel at Malta,' said Alison. 'It would be the logical thing to do. Let's go and find out where he's cleared for.'

So we did, and Alison was right—not that it made me feel any better. 'Another four days?' I asked despondently.

'Another four days,' she agreed. 'But we might have better luck at Valletta.'

'I'd like that yacht to have an accident,' I said. 'Just enough to delay her for one night. You don't happen to have any limpet mines about you?'

'Sorry.'

I stared moodily at the white speck disappearing into the distance. 'That Chinese worries me,' I said. 'He ought to worry Slade even more.'

'Why ever should he?'

'Communist Albania has ceased to hew to the Moscow line. Enver Hoxha, the Albanian party boss, has read the Little Red Book and thinks the thoughts of Mao. I wonder if Slade knows he's in the hands of an Albanian?'

Alison wore a half-smile. 'I was wondering when you'd get there,' she said.

'I got there a long time ago—probably before you did. It would be very nice for the Chinese if they could get hold of Slade—a top British intelligence man and a top Russian intelligence man in the same package. They'd squeeze him dry in a month and they wouldn't care how they did it.'

I shrugged. 'And the damned fool thinks he's going home to Moscow.'

CHAPTER NINE

I

LIMPET MINES we didn't have but, in the event, I got hold of something just as good and a lot simpler. That was in the Grand Harbour of Valletta and four days later. In the meantime we paid the bill at the Rock Hotel and flew to Malta where that diplomatic passport got me though the barriers at Luqa Airport just as easily as it had done at Gibraltar.

With nearly four days to wait we suddenly found ourselves in holiday mood. The sky was blue, the sun was hot and the sea inviting, and there were cafés with seafood and cool wine for the days, and moderately good restaurants with dance floors for the nights. Alison unbent more than she had ever done.

I found there was something I could do better than she, which did my mauled ego a bit of good. We hired scuba equipment and went diving in the clear water of the Mediterranean and I found I could out-perform her at that. Probably it was because I had lived in Australia and South Africa where the ambient waters are warmer and skin-diving is a luxury and not a penance as it is in England.

We swam and lazed the days away and danced the nights away for three days and three nights until, on the morrow, Wheeler was due to arrive. It was nearly midnight when I brought up the subject of Mr Smith. Alison took no umbrage this time but, perhaps, it was because I had been plying her with the demon alcohol. Had it been the opposition tipping the bottle she would have been wary but the hand that filled her glass was the hand of a friend and she was taken unaware. Sneaky!

She held up the wine glass and smiled at me through liquid amber. 'What do you want to know about him?'

'Is he still around?'

She put down the glass and a little wine spilled. 'No,' she said. 'He's not around any more.' She seemed sad.

I lit a cigarette and said through the smoke, 'Divorce?'

She shook her head violently and her long hair flowed in heavy waves. 'Nothing like that. Give me a cigarette.'

I lit her cigarette and she said, 'I married a man called John Smith. There *are* people called John Smith, you know. Was he an intelligence agent? No. Was he even a policeman? No. He was an accountant and a very nice man—and Alec was horrified. It seemed I hadn't been designed to marry an accountant.' Her voice was bitter.

'Go on,' I said gently.

'But I married him, anyway; and we were very happy.'

'Had you been with your father before then?'

'With Alec? Where else? But I didn't stay on—I couldn't, could I? John and I lived in a house near Maidenhead—in the Stockbroker Belt—and we were very happy. I was happy just being married to John, and happy being a housewife and doing all the things which housewives do, and not having to think about things I didn't want to think about. Alec was disappointed, of course; he'd lost his robot secretary.'

I thought of John Smith, the accountant; the nine-to-fiver who had married Alison Mackintosh. I wondered how he had regarded the situation—if he ever knew about it. I couldn't see Alison cuddling up on his knee, and saying, 'Darling, you're married to a girl who can shoot a man in the kneecap in impossible light, who can drive a car and fly a plane and kill a man with one karate chop. Don't you think we're going to have a delightful married life? Look how handy it will be when we're bringing up the children.'

I said, 'And then?'

'And then—nothing. Just a stupid, silly motorway accident on the M4.' Her face was still and unsmiling and she spoke through stiff lips. 'I thought I'd die, too; I really did. I loved John, you see.'

'I'm sorry,' I said inadequately.

She shrugged and held out her glass for more wine. 'Wanting to die didn't help, of course. I brooded and moped for a while, then I went back to Alec. There wasn't anything else to do.' She sipped the wine and looked at me. 'Was there, Owen?'

I said very carefully and non-committally, 'Perhaps not.'

She gave me a wry look, and said, 'You're pussyfooting, Owen. You don't want to hurt my feelings by saying what you think. Well, that's commendable, I suppose.'

'I'm not one to make casual judgments.'

'Without knowing the facts—is that it? I'll give you some. Alec and my mother never got on very well. I suppose they were basically incompatible, but he was away so often, and she didn't understand his work.'

'Was he in the same work as now?'

'Always, Owen; always. So there was a legal separation just before I was born, and I was born in Waterford where I lived until I was ten when my mother died.'

'Were you happy in Waterford?'

Alison became pensive. 'I don't really know. I can't seem to remember much about those days; there has been so much overlaid on top since.' She stubbed out her cigarette. 'I don't know if anyone would ever call Alec an ideal father. Unorthodox, maybe, but not ideal. I was a bit of a tomboy— never one for frilly frocks and playing with dolls—and I suppose he took advantage.'

I said slowly, 'You're a woman now.'

'I sometimes wonder about that.' She plucked at the table-cloth with tapering fingers. 'So Alec trained me to be—I didn't know what. It was fun at the time. I learned to ride a horse, to ski on snow and water, to shoot, to fly—I'm qualified on jets, did you know that?'

I shook my head.

'It was damned good fun, every bit of it—even grinding at the languages and mathematics—until he took me into the office. When I learned what it was for, it wasn't fun any more.'

'Did he send you out on field jobs?'

'I've been on three,' she said evenly. 'All very successful—and most of the time I was sick to my stomach. But that wasn't the worst of it. The worst was being in the office and sending others out into the field, and watching what happened to them. I planned too many operations, Owen. I planned yours.'

'I know,' I said. 'Mackintosh . . . Alec told me.'

'I became the one person whom he could trust absolutely,' she said. 'A very valuable consideration in the profession.'

I took her hand. 'Alison,' I said. 'What do you really think of Alec?'

'I love him,' she said. 'And I hate him. It's as simple as that.' Her fingers tightened on mine. 'Let's dance, Owen.' There was a hint of desperation in her voice. 'Let's dance.'

So we went on to the dimly lit floor and danced to the sort of music that's usually played in the early hours of the morning. She came very close and rested her head on my shoulder so that her lips were by my ear. 'Do you know what I am, Owen?'

'You're a lovely woman, Alison.'

'No, I'm a Venus Fly Trap. Vegetables—like women—are supposed to be placid; they're not supposed to be equipped with snapping jaws and sharp teeth. Have you ever watched a fly alight on a Venus Fly Trap? The poor beastie thinks it's just another vegetable plant until the jaws snap closed. Most unnatural, don't you think?'

I tightened my arm about her. 'Take it easy.'

She danced two more steps and then a deep shudder went through her body. 'Oh, God!' she said. 'Let's go back to the hotel.'

I paid the bill and joined her at the door of the restaurant and we walked the two hundred yards to our hotel. We were both silent as we went up in the lift and along the corridor, but she held my hand tightly as we came to the door of her room. She was trembling a little as she held out her key.

She made love like a maniac, like a savage, and I had the deep scratches on my back to prove it next morning. It seemed

196

as though all the pent-up frustrations of a warped life were loosed on that night-time bed. But when it was over she was relaxed and calm, and we talked for a long time—maybe two hours. What we talked about I'll never remember; just inconsequentialities too meaningless to take note of—she had had time for few trivialities in her serious life.

The second time was better and she was all woman, and when it was over she fell asleep. I had sense enough to go to my own room before she woke; I thought she would not be too pleased with herself in the sober light of day.

Wheeler was due that morning and we had plans to make. When she came down to breakfast I was on my first cup of coffee and rose from the table to greet her. She was a little self-conscious as she came up and tended to avoid my eye. I sat down, and said, 'What do we use instead of a limpet?'

When I leaned against the back of the chair I felt the pain as the pressure impinged on the scratches she had inflicted. Hastily I leaned forward again and took a piece of toast.

I looked up and saw she had snapped back into professionalism as she took in what I said; personal relationships were one thing and the job was quite another. 'I'll check with the Port Captain when *Artina* is due.'

'We don't want to have a repetition of Gibraltar,' I said. 'One jump from here and Wheeler and Slade will be in Albania—home and dry. What do we do if *Artina* arrives in daylight and leaves in daylight?'

'I don't know,' she said.

'There's one thing certain,' I said. 'I can't invade her in the middle of the Grand Harbour in daylight and take Slade off. So what remains?' I answered the question myself. 'We have to make sure she stays all night.'

'But how?'

'I've thought of a way. We'll go shopping after breakfast.'

So the pair of us ate a hearty breakfast and sallied forth into the hot streets of Valletta, a heat seemingly intensified by the warm golden limestone of the buildings. The Port Captain expected *Artina* at midday and that was sad news. Sadder still was the information that the fuelling ship had been booked in advance and was to go alongside as soon as *Artina* anchored.

We went away, and I said, 'That does it. Let's do my bit of shopping.'

We found a ship's chandlery and went inside to find all the usual expensive bits and pieces that go towards the upkeep of a yacht. I found what I was looking for—some light, tough nylon line with a high breaking strain. I bought two hundred feet of it and had it coiled and parcelled.

Alison said, 'I suppose you know what you're doing.'

'It was the scuba gear we've been using that gave me the idea.' I pointed towards the harbour. 'How would you get to the middle of there without being seen?'

She nodded. 'Underwater. That's all very well, but doesn't help you to get aboard.'

'It will—eventually. You're included in this operation. Come and get the gear. We want to be back on the spot when *Artina* arrives.'

We went to the place we had hired the scuba gear and I made absolutely certain we were issued with full bottles. Then, after a brief test in the swimming pool of the hotel, we went back to the harbour. At the swimming pool Alison suddenly drew in her breath and I turned to find that she was blushing deeply. She was looking at my back.

I chuckled. 'They ought to issue a bottle of Dettol with you,' I said. 'You're quite a woman.'

Unaccountably she became angry. 'Stannard you're a . . . a . . .'

'Buck up,' I said sharply. 'We have a job to do.'

That brought her back fast and the awkward moment was over. We went down to the harbour and settled down to wait for *Artina*. Alison said, 'What's the plan?'

'If you've read my record you'll know I was in Indonesia,' I said. 'One of the diciest moments I ever had out there was when I was in a small launch being chased by a fast patrol boat which was popping off with a 20 mm cannon. There was a mangrove swamp nearby so I nipped in there for shelter—that was a big mistake. There was too much seaweed and it got wrapped around the propeller shaft and the launch came to a dead stop. That seaweed was nearly the end of me.'

'What happened then?'

'That doesn't matter.' I nodded towards the harbour. '*Artina* is a lot bigger than the launch I had, but this nylon line is a hell of a lot stronger than strands of seaweed. When she comes in we're going to swim out and wrap the lot around both propeller shafts. It might immobilize her and it might not, but I'm betting it will. And the beauty of it is that even when they find it there'll be no suggestion of foul play. It's something that could happen to any boat. Anyway, they'll have a devil of a job freeing it once the engines have tightened it up, and I'm hoping it will take all night.'

'It could work,' agreed Alison, and then continued evenly, 'I'll do something for those scratches. This water is dirty and they might become infected.'

I looked at her and she met my eye without a tremor. 'Good enough,' I said, and took great pains not to laugh.

She went away briefly and returned with a bottle of something-or-other which she applied to my back. Then we sat and waited patiently for *Artina* to show up.

It was a long hot day. *Artina* was late and I began to wonder if she hadn't by-passed Malta and headed straight for Albania. She came in at two-thirty and dropped anchor well off shore. Again she lowered a boat but this time only the skipper came ashore. Wheeler wasn't to be seen.

I stubbed out my cigarette. 'This is it,' I said, and tightened the straps of the scuba gear. 'Can you swim as far as that?'

Alison splashed water into her mask. 'Easily.'

'Just stick close to me.' I pointed. 'We're not going to swim right for it. We'll pass by about twenty yards from the stern and then come in from the other side. The fueller might be there—I hope it is—so keep your head down.'

I had the skein of nylon rope strapped to my thigh; I tested to see if it was secure and then slipped into the water. I doubt if skin divers are encouraged in the Grand Harbour, not that they would want to make a habit of swimming there—the water is none too clean and decapitation by the churning propellers of passing traffic a constant hazard. I had chosen a quiet spot where we could go into the water unobserved.

We went deep right from the start, going down to about twenty-five feet before heading on course. I knew my speed and I had estimated the distance so I kept a steady count of the seconds and minutes. The problem on this sort of exercise was to keep swimming in a straight line. Occasionally I looked back and saw Alison swimming strongly in echelon, behind and to the left.

When I estimated we had arrived at the point I had chosen I waved Alison to a halt and we swam lazily in circles while I looked about. There was an oncoming rumble and a shadow overhead as a vessel passed, her propellers flailing the water and causing eddies which jerked us about. The propellers stopped and presently there was an audible clang transmitted through the water. That would be the fueller coupling to *Artina*.

I waved to Alison and we went on in the new direction. As we went on towards the two boats I hoped that no one was looking over the side to see the line of bubbles breaking on the surface. But we were coming in at the side of the fueller and all the action would be where they were coupling up the fuel and water lines. If anyone had time to look over the side then that fueller was over-manned.

The light diminished as we swam underneath the two boats and I paused again before heading aft and rising to trail my fingers along *Artina*'s keel. We came to the stern and I stopped with my left hand on one blade of the port phosphor-bronze propeller, hoping that no damned fool in the engine room would punch the wrong button and start the engine. If those three blades started to move I'd be chopped into bloody mince-meat.

Alison swam up on the starboard side as I fumbled with the strap holding the rope to my thigh. I got it free and began to uncoil it with care. The propeller was about four feet in diameter, and the shaft was supported by struts before it entered the stern gland in the hull. I slipped the end of the rope in between the strut and the hull and coiled it around the shaft and then passed a loop around the shaft in between the propeller and the strut. When I tugged gently it held firm, so that was a start.

That rope was the damnedest stuff. At times it was like wrestling with a sea serpent—the coils floated around in the water dangerously, threatening to strangle us or bind our legs, and Alison and I must have closely resembled that remarkable piece of antique statuary, the Laocoön.

But we finally did it. We entangled those two propellers in such a cat's cradle that when the engines started and the ropes began to tighten all hell would break loose. Most probably everything would grind to a sudden halt, but a shaft could bend and, at worst, one of the engines might slam a piston through the cylinder casing. It was a good job.

We slipped away and swam back to shore, emerging from the water quite a distance from where we had gone in. My sense of direction had become warped, but then it always does underwater. An unshaven character leaning on the rail of a tramp steamer looked at us with some astonishment as we climbed up to the quay but I ignored him, and Alison and I walked away, our back packs bumping heavily.

We went back to our original position and I lit a cigarette and looked across at *Artina*. The fueller had finished and was just casting off, and the skipper was returning in the tender. It seemed as though they intended a faster turnaround than Gibraltar. I wondered where the skipper had cleared for—it wouldn't be Durazzo, the port for Tirana, although I'd be willing to bet that was where he intended to go.

The skipper climbed aboard and the companionway was unshipped immediately. There was a lot of movement on deck and even as the tender was hoisted clear of the water someone was at the winch on the foredeck ready to lift anchor.

Alison said, 'They're very much in a hurry.'

'It seems so.'

'I wonder why.'

'I don't know—but I expect they'll be very annoyed within the next few minutes.'

The anchor came up and *Artina* moved off slowly. I hadn't expected her to move at all and it came as a shock. Apparently 700 horse-power was more than a match for a few coils of nylon line. Alison drew in her breath. 'It isn't working!'

Artina turned and headed for the open sea, picking up speed so that a bow wave showed white. I lowered the binoculars, and said, 'It was a good try.' I felt gloomy. Albania was only 450 miles away and *Artina* could be there in less than two days. The only way I could think of stopping her was by a kamekazi attack in the Apache.

Alison was still watching through her monocular. 'Wait!' she said urgently. 'Look now!'

Artina had swerved suddenly and unnaturally as though someone had spun the wheel fast, and she was now heading straight for the shore. She slowed and water boiled at her stern as the engines were put into reverse. Then the bubble of white water stopped and she drifted helplessly, right into the path of a big Italian cruise liner which was leaving harbour.

There was a deep *booom* as the liner peremptorily demanded right of way but *Artina* did not react. The liner altered course fractionally at the last moment and her sheer side might have scraped *Artina*'s paintwork. From the bridge of the liner an officer in whites was looking down and I guessed that a string of choice Italian imprecations was being directed down at the hapless skipper of *Artina*.

202

The liner went on her way and *Artina* bobbed inertly in the waves raised by her wake. Presently a little tug put out and went to her aid and she was towed back to where she had come from and dropped anchor again.

I grinned at Alison. 'For a moment there I thought. . . . Well, it's done and she'll be staying the night. When they find out what's happened they'll be cursing the idiot who carelessly dropped a line in the water.'

'There's no chance they'll guess it was done deliberately?'

'I shouldn't think so.' I looked over the water at *Artina*. The skipper was at the stern looking down. 'They'll soon find out what it is, and they'll send down a diver to cut it free. It'll take a hell of a lot longer for him to free it than it did for us to tangle it—those engines will have tightened the tangle considerably.' I laughed. 'It'll be like trying to unscramble an omelette.'

Alison picked up her gear. 'And what now?'

'Now we wait for nightfall. I'm going to board her.'

3

We went into Marsamxett Harbour from Ta'Xbiex to where *Artina* was anchored in Lazzaretto Creek. A tug had moved her during the afternoon and put her with the rest of the yachts. We went out in a fibreglass object that resembled a bathtub more than a boat, but Alison seemed to find no difficulty in handling it and she used the oars as though she'd been trained as stroke for Oxford. More of Mackintosh's training coming to the surface.

It was a moonless night but the sky was clear so that it was not absolutely pitch-black. Ahead loomed Manoel Island and beyond a light flashed at Dragutt Point. To our left Valletta rose, cliff-like and impregnable, festooned with lights. There were no lights on *Artina*, though, apart from the obligatory riding lights; since it was 2.30 a.m. this was not surprising. I hoped everyone on board was in the habit of sleeping soundly.

Alison stopped sculling as we approached and we drifted silently to *Artina*'s stern. The rope ladder which the diver had been using was not there but I hadn't been counting on it even though it was nine feet from the water to the stern rail. What I wanted was a grapnel, but those are hard to come by at a moment's notice, so I had improvised. A shark hook is shaped like a grapnel, being three big fish-hooks welded together. I had wrapped it in many layers of insulating tape, not only to prevent myself from being nastily hooked but also for the sake of silence.

I looked up and saw the ensign-staff silhouetted against the sky and used that to mark the position of the rail. Holding a coil of the rope I threw up my grapnel so it went over the rail. There was a soft thud as it landed on the deck and, as I drew the line back, I hoped it would hold. It did; it caught on the rail and a steady pull told me it would be not unreasonable to climb the rope.

I bent down and whispered, 'Well, this is it. I may come back with Slade or I may not. I may come over the side in a bloody hurry so stick around to fish me out of the drink.' I paused. 'If I don't come back then you're on your own and the best of British luck to you.'

I swarmed up the rope and managed to hook my arm round the ensign-staff, taking the strain off the shark hook. The pistol thrust into the waist of my trousers didn't help much; as I twisted like a contortionist to get a foot on deck the muzzle dug into my groin agonizingly and I was thankful that I'd made sure there wasn't a bullet in front of the firing pin.

I made it at last and in silence. At least nobody took a shot at me as I looked back at the water. Alison was nowhere to be seen and there was just a suspicious looking ripple where no ripple should have been. I stayed there quietly for a moment and strained my ears listening to the loud silence.

If there was a man on watch he was being quiet in his watching. I hazarded a guess that anyone on watch would stay up forward, perhaps in the wheelhouse or comfortably in the dining saloon. To get to the stern cabins I didn't have to go forward; the entrance to the cabin deck was by a staircase in the deck lounge, and the door to the lounge was just in front of me if the ship plans I had studied were correct.

I took out a pen-light and risked a flash. It was lucky I did so because the deck immediately in front of me was cluttered with diver's gear—I could have made a Godawful clatter if I hadn't seen that. I managed to navigate the booby traps safely until I got to the deck lounge door and was thankful to find it unlocked; which was just as expected because who locks doors on a ship?

The lounge was in darkness but I saw light gleaming through a glass-panelled door on the starboard side. There was just enough light spilling through to illumine the hazards of furniture so I stepped over to look through the door and I froze as I saw movement at the end of a long passage. A man came out of the dining saloon and turned into the galley and out of sight. I opened the door gently and listened; there was the slam of something heavy followed by the clink of crockery. The man on watch was enlivening the night hours by raiding the refrigerator, which suited me very well.

I crossed the lounge again and went below to the cabin deck. There were three cabins down there, all for guests. Wheeler's master cabin was 'midships, the other side of the engine room, so I didn't have to worry about him. The problem that faced me was if he had any guests, apart from Slade, occupying any of the three guest cabins.

The cabin that had been curtained in broad daylight at Gibraltar was the big stern cabin, and that was my first objective. This time the door *was* locked, and this raised my hopes because Slade would certainly be kept under lock and key. I inspected the lock with a guarded flash of the light. It wasn't much of a problem; no one installs Chubb triple-throw locks on a cabin door and I could have opened one of those if I had to—it would have taken longer, that's all.

As it was I was inside the cabin inside two minutes and with

205

the door locked again behind me. I heard the heavy breathing of a sleeping man and flicked my light towards the port side, hoping to God it was Slade. If it wasn't I was well and truly up that gum tree I had shown Mackintosh.

I needn't have worried because it was Slade all right and I cheered internally at the sight of that heavy face with the slightly yellowish skin. I took the gun from my waist and pushed a bullet up the spout. At the metallic sound Slade stirred and moaned slightly in his sleep. I stepped forward and, keeping the light on him, I pressed gently with my finger at the corner of his jaw just below the ear. It's the best way to awaken a man quietly.

He moaned again and his eyelids flickered open, and he screwed up his eyes at the sudden flood of light. I moved the pen-light so that it illumined the gun I held. 'If you shout it'll be the last sound you make on earth,' I said quietly.

He shuddered violently and his adam's apple bobbed convulsively as he swallowed. At last he managed to whisper, 'Who the hell are you?'

'Your old pal, Rearden,' I said. 'I've come to take you home.'

It took some time to sink in, and then he said, 'You're mad.'

'Probably,' I admitted. 'Anyone who wants to save your life must be mad.'

He was getting over the shock. The blood was returning to his face and the self-possession to his soul—if he had one. 'How did you get here?' he demanded.

I let the light wander to the nearest port. It wasn't curtained, after all; plates of sheet metal had been roughly welded over the oval scuttles so that it was absolutely impossible for Slade to see outside—more security expertise on the part of the Scarperers. I grinned at Slade, and asked softly, 'Where is here?'

'Why—on board this ship,' he said, but his voice was uncertain.

'I've been following you.' I watched with interest as his eyes shifted sideways to look at a bell-push by the side of his berth, and I hefted the gun so that it came into prominence again. 'I wouldn't,' I warned. 'Not if you value your health.'

'Who are you?' he whispered.

'I suppose you could say that I'm in the same business as yourself, but in the other corner. I'm in counter-espionage.'

The breath came from him in a long, wavering sigh. 'The executioner,' he said flatly. He nodded towards the gun. 'You won't get away with it. You have no silencer. Kill me with that thing and you're dead, too.'

'I'm expendable,' I said lightly, and hoped I wouldn't have to make that statement stick. 'Use your brains, Slade. I could have slid into this cabin and cut your throat in your sleep. It would have been messy, but silent. A better way would have been to stick a steel knitting needle through the nape of your neck and into the medulla oblongata—there's not much blood. The fact that we're talking now means I want you alive.'

He frowned slightly and I could almost see the wheels spinning as he thought it out. I said, 'But don't have any misconceptions. I either take you out alive or you stay here dead. It's your choice.'

He had recovered enough to smile slightly. 'You're taking a big chance. You can't keep me under the gun all the time. I could win yet.'

'You won't want to,' I said. 'Not when you've heard what I have to say. My guess is that you were taken from that room we shared, given a shot of dope, and woke up in this cabin where you've been ever since. Where do you think you are?'

That set the wheels going round again, but to no effect. At last he said, 'There's been no temperature change, so I couldn't have been taken very much north or south.'

'This hooker has a very efficient air-conditioning plant,' I said. 'You wouldn't know the difference. Do you like Chinese food?'

The switch confused him. 'What the hell! I can take it or leave it.'

'Have you had any lately?'

He was bemused. 'Why, yes—only yesterday I . . .'

I cut in. 'The ship has a Chinese cook. Do you know whose ship it is?' He shook his head in silence, and I said, 'It belongs to a man called Wheeler, a British MP. I take it you haven't seen him.'

'No, I haven't,' said Slade. 'I'd have recognized him. I met him a couple of times in . . . in the old days. What the devil is all this about?'

'Do you still think you are going to Moscow?'

'I see no reason to doubt it,' he said stiffly.

'Wheeler was born an Albanian,' I said. 'And his Chinese cook does more than rustle up sweet and sour pork. They're not your brand of communist, Slade. Right now you're in Malta and the next scheduled stop is Durazzo in Albania; from there I guess you'll be shipped by cargo plane straight to Peking. You'd better acquire a real taste for Chinese cooking —always assuming they give you any food at all.'

He stared at me. 'You're crazy.'

'What's so crazy about the Chinese wanting to get hold of you? What you have locked up inside that skull of yours would interest them very much—the secrets of two top intelligence services. And they'd get it out of you, Slade—even if they had to do it by acupuncture. The Chinese *invented* the term "brain-washing".'

'But *Wheeler*?'

'What's so odd about Wheeler? You got away with it for over a quarter of a century—why shouldn't someone else be as smart as you? Or smarter? Wheeler hasn't been caught— yet.'

He fell silent and I let him think it out. Yet I hadn't much time to waste so I prodded him again. 'It seems to me that your choice is simple. You come with me willingly or I kill you right now. I think I'd be doing you a favour if I killed you because I'd hate to see you after you'd been in the hands of the Chinese for a month. I think you'd better come with me and retire to a nice, safe, top-security wing in one of Her Majesty's nicks. At least you won't be having your brains pulled out through your ears.'

He shook his head stubbornly. 'I don't know if I believe you.'

'For God's sake! If Wheeler wanted you to go to Moscow then why didn't he transfer you to one of those ubiquitous Russian trawlers? In the Atlantic they're as thick as fleas on a mangy dog. Why bring you to the Mediterranean?'

Slade looked cunning. 'I've only your word for that, too.'

I sighed, and lifted the gun. 'You don't have much of a choice, do you?' I was getting mad at him. 'If ever I saw a man looking a gift horse in the mouth it's you. I haven't followed you from Ireland to . . .'

He cut in. 'Ireland?'

'That's where we were held together.'

'Lynch is Irish,' he said thoughtfully.

'Seamas Lynch? He works for Wheeler—he's an IRA thug with a dislike of the English.'

'He looks after me here,' said Slade. 'He's my guard.' He looked up and I saw that the strain of uncertainty was beginning to tell. 'Where are we now—exactly?'

'Anchored in Marsamxett Harbour.'

He made up his mind. 'All right, but if I get on deck and I don't recognize it then you might be in big trouble. You'll be wanting silence and I might take my chances on the gun in the darkness. Remember that.'

'How long is it since you've been in Malta?'

'Five years.'

I smiled humourlessly, 'Then I hope to God you have a good memory.'

Slade threw back the bedclothes and then paused, looking at me questioningly. There had been a creak which was not one of the usual shipboard noises. I listened and it came again.

Slade whipped the covers back over his chest. 'Someone's coming,' he whispered.

I held up the gun before his eyes. 'Remember this!' I backed off and opened the door of the lavatory and even as I did so I heard a key snap metallically at the cabin door. I closed the lavatory door gently and used my pen-light in a quick flash to see what I'd got into. As usual in lavatories there was no back door, just the usual paraphernalia of toilet, wash basin medicine cabinet and shower. The shower was screened off by a semi-transparent plastic curtain.

I switched off the light, held my breath, and listened. Lynch's voice was unmistakable. 'I heard voices—who the devil were you talking to?'

This was the crunch. If Slade was going to give me away he'd do it now, so I listened with care to what was arguably the most important conversation I was ever likely to hear.

'I must have been talking in my sleep,' said Slade, and my heartbeat slowed down to a mere gallop. 'I've been having bad dreams and I've got the makings of a headache.'

'Ach, it's no wonder, and you being cooped up in here all this while,' said Lynch. 'But rest easy, you'll soon be home.'

'Why have we been stopped all this time?'

'Something's gone wrong with the propellers,' said Lynch. 'But I didn't get the exact hang of it.'

'Where are we?'

'Now you know better than to ask that, Mr Slade. That's top secret.'

'Well, when will we be moving again—and when do I get my feet on dry land?'

'As to the first,' said Lynch, 'maybe it'll be tomorrow. As to the last, I couldn't rightly tell you. I'm not one of the bosses, you know; they don't tell me everything.' He paused. 'But you're looking so white and peaky, Mr Slade. Could I get you the aspirin?'

The hairs on the nape of my neck stood up and did a fandango as Slade answered. 'No, don't worry; I'll be all right.' It was borne heavily upon me that although I could hear Slade's voice I couldn't see what he was doing with his hands.

He might be saying one thing and pointing out to Lynch that he had an unwanted visitor.

Lynch said solicitously, 'Ach, it's no trouble at all. We promise to get you home in good condition; that's part of the deal. I'll get the aspirin for you.'

I ducked into the shower stall and drew the plastic curtain just as Lynch opened the lavatory door. He switched on the light and I saw his outline quite clearly through the curtain as he stepped forward to open the medicine cabinet. I had the gun trained on him all the time and I thought that I could dispose of him and Slade, too, if it came to the push. Getting out would be another matter.

I heard the rattle of pills in a bottle and then the rush of water as a tap was turned on. It was a relief to know that Lynch actually was getting aspirin and that Slade had not sold me out. Lynch filled the glass and turned to leave—he was so close that I could have touched him by only half-extending my arm and only the curtain was between us. Fortunately he was back-lit and I wasn't or he would have seen me had he glanced my way.

He went out, switching off the light and closing the door. 'Here you are,' he said. 'This should clear up your headache.'

'Thanks,' said Slade, and I heard the clink of the glass.

'Man, but you're sweating,' said Lynch. 'Are you sure it's not the fever you've got?'

'I'll be all right,' said Slade. 'You can leave the light on. I think I'll read for a while.'

'Surely,' said Lynch. 'Have a quiet night, mind.' I heard the cabin door open and close, and then the snap of the lock as the key was turned.

I was doing a fair amount of sweating myself as I waited for the trembling of my hands to stop. My stomach felt all churned up as the adrenalin sped on its appointed rounds gingering up my muscle tone and twanging my nerves like harp strings. At last I stepped out of the shower and gently opened the lavatory door.

Whether his sweating was due to a fright or fever Slade had used his wits when he had asked Lynch to leave on the main cabin light. It meant that I could see at a glance if the place was safe. Slade certainly didn't want to be shot by accident.

He lay in bed with a book held between slack fingers and his face was the yellow colour of old newsprint. 'Why didn't he see you?' he whispered.

I flapped a hand at him to keep him quiet and went to the door, still keeping the gun pointing in his general direction. I heard nothing so presently I turned and strode over to Slade. 'Where does Lynch live? Do you know?'

He shook his head and tugged at my sleeve. 'How the hell did he miss you?'

He found it difficult to believe that in a narrow space the size of two telephone booths one man could miss seeing another. I found it hard to believe myself. 'I was taking a shower,' I said. 'How was Lynch dressed?'

'Dressing-gown.'

That meant he hadn't come far and he probably had been allocated one of the cabins next door to be conveniently close to his charge. 'Have you any clothes?' Slade nodded. 'All right; get dressed—quietly.'

I watched Slade carefully while he dressed, principally to make sure he didn't slip a blunt instrument into his pocket. When he had finished I said, 'Now get back into bed.' He was about to expostulate but I shut him up fast with a jab of the gun. 'I want to give Lynch time to get back to sleep.'

Slade got back into bed and I retreated into the lavatory, leaving the door ajar. Slade had pulled the sheet up high and was lying on his side apparently reading his book. Everything would appear normal if Lynch took it into his head to come back. I gave him half an hour by my watch and during that time heard nothing out of the ordinary.

I stepped into the cabin and signalled Slade to rise. While he was disentangling himself from the bedclothes—it's really surprising how difficult it is to get out of bed when fully

212

dressed because the sheet wraps itself round one's shoes—I jimmied the lock on the door. I had to turn my back on Slade at this point but it couldn't be helped.

I turned and found him walking towards me slowly. When he approached he put his mouth to my ear and whispered, 'When I get on deck I'd better see Valletta.'

I nodded my head impatiently, switched off the light, and opened the door on to the darkness of the passage. The staircase was immediately to the left and I prodded Slade up it with the gun in his back, holding his right arm. I stopped him before we got to the top and cautiously surveyed the deck lounge. All was quiet so I urged him on his way and he went out on to the after deck.

I shone the light to give Slade some idea of the obstacle race he must run to get the twenty feet to the stern rail, and off we went again. Half-way across the afterdeck he stopped and looked around. 'You are right,' he whispered. 'It *is* Valletta.'

'Quit chattering.' I was edgy as I always am on the last lap. Once ashore I could turn Slade in to the Maltese Constabulary and the job was done, apart from wrapping up Wheeler and his mob, but we still had to get ashore.

We got as far as the stern rail and no further. I groped for the grapnel alongside the ensign-staff and couldn't find it. Then shockingly a blaze of light split the darkness as the beam of a powerful lamp shone vertically down on us from the boat deck above, and a voice said, 'That's far enough.'

I dug my elbow into Slade's ribs. 'Jump!' I yelled, but neither of us was quick enough. There was a rapid tattoo of feet on the deck as a small army of men rushed us and we were both grabbed and held. There wasn't a damned thing I could do—two of the three men who tackled me were trying to tear my arms off so they could use them as clubs to beat me over the head, and the other was using my stomach as a bass drum and his fists weren't padded as drumsticks are.

As I sagged and gasped for breath I was vaguely aware of Slade being dragged forward, hauled by two seamen with his feet trailing along the deck. Someone shouted and I was also hustled forward and thrust headlong through the doorway of the deck lounge. A burly black-bearded man whom I recognized as the skipper issued orders in a language whose flavour I couldn't catch. I was unceremoniously dropped to the deck and my assailants began to draw the curtains to the windows.

Before the last of them was drawn I saw a searchlight from the bridge forward begin to search the water around *Artina* and I hoped Alison had got clear. Someone handed my pistol to the skipper; he looked at it with interest, made sure it was cocked, and pointed it at me. 'Who are you?' His English was accented, but with what I didn't know.

I pushed myself up with wobbly arms. 'Does it matter?' I asked wearily.

The skipper swung his eyes to Slade who sagged against a chair, and then beyond him to the staircase which led below. 'Ah, Lynch!' he said, rumbling like a volcano about to explode. 'What kind of a guard are you?'

I turned my head. Lynch was looking at Slade with shocked amazement. 'How did he get here? I was with him not half an hour ago, and I made sure the door was locked.'

'The door was locked,' mimicked the skipper. '*Te keni kujdes*; how could the door be locked?' He pointed to me. 'And this man—he brought Slade out of the cabin.'

Lynch looked at me. 'By God, it's Rearden. But he *couldn't* have been in the cabin,' he said stubbornly. 'I'd have seen him.'

'I was in the shower, standing right next to you, you silly bastard.' I turned to the skipper. 'He nearly got himself killed. Not much of a guard, is he?'

Lynch made for me with blood in his eye, but the skipper got to me first, warding off Lynch with an arm like an iron bar. He dragged my head up by my hair and stuck the gun in my face. 'So you are Rearden,' he said, caressing my cheek with the barrel. 'We're very interested in you, Rearden.'

A cool voice said, 'He's not Rearden, of course.'

214

The skipper swung away and I saw the Chinese, Chang Pi-wu, who looked at me expressionlessly. Next to him stood a tall man with ash-blond hair, who, at that moment, was fitting a cigarette into a long holder. He dipped his hand into the pocket of his elegant dressing-gown, produced a lighter and flicked it into flame.

'Stannard is the name, I believe,' said Wheeler. 'Owen Stannard.' He lit his cigarette. 'So thoughtful of you to join us, Mr Stannard. It saves me the trouble of looking for you.'

CHAPTER TEN

I

'HOW DID YOU get hold of him?' Wheeler asked the skipper.

'Mehmet found a hook on the stern rail and a rope leading to the water. He removed it and told me. I set up a watch.'

Wheeler nodded. 'You didn't know whether someone was going to come on board or leave,' he commented.

The skipper waved his hand at me and Slade. 'We caught these two leaving. This idiot . . .' He stabbed his finger at Lynch. '. . . let them go.'

Wheeler regarded Lynch frostily. 'I'll talk to you later. Now get below.'

Lynch looked as though he was about to expostulate but he caught the cold glare from Wheeler's eye and promptly turned on his heel and went away, giving me a look of dislike as he went. I was beginning to improve physically; my shoulders no longer felt totally dislocated and although my belly was one massive ache I could now breathe more or less normally.

Wheeler said, 'Well, Mr Stannard; how did you expect to take Slade ashore? By boat? Where is it?'

'I swam out,' I said.

'And you were going to swim back,' he said incredulously. 'With Slade a cripple? I don't believe you.' He swung around to the skipper. 'Make a search for the boat.'

The skipper didn't move. 'It's being done.'

Wheeler nodded approvingly and crossed to Slade who had now sagged into a chair. 'My dear chap,' he said anxiously. 'What possessed you to leave with this man? Do you know who he is? If you had left the ship he would have put you in the hands of the police. And you know what that would mean— forty years in a British gaol. What sort of tale could he have told you?'

Slade wearily lifted up his head. 'I know you,' he said. 'We've met before.'

'Yes—in happier circumstances,' said Wheeler. 'Once at an EFTA conference and again, if my memory is correct, at a dinner given by some industrial organization or other—I forget which.'

'Your name is Wheeler; you're a member of Parliament. Why should you want to help *me*?'

'A good question,' I said. 'Answer him, Wheeler. Tell Slade why you are willing to commit treason.' I rubbed my sore stomach tentatively. 'As far as I know treason still carries the death penalty—it isn't covered by the Act of Parliament which abolished hanging for murder.' I grinned at him. 'But who should know that better than you?'

Wheeler didn't rile easily. He smiled, and said coolly, 'I am helping you because I don't recognize British law; because, like you, I'm fighting for a better world.' He put his hand on Slade's shoulder. 'Because, also like you, I'm a good communist.'

'Then why didn't I know about you?' asked Slade. 'I should have known.'

'Why should you have known? You didn't *need* to know, and therefore you weren't told. It was safer that way.' Wheeler smiled. 'You might have been important, Slade, but you were never as important as I am.'

I corrected him. 'As important as you *were*. You're finished Wheeler.'

Apart from gently shaking his head he ignored me. With his eyes fixed on Slade, he said, 'What nonsense has Stannard been filling you up with? You're a fool if you believe the enemy.'

Slade said, 'What are we doing here in Malta?'

Wheeler straightened and laughed. 'So that's the maggot he's put in your mind. I'm taking you home, of course. I spend my annual holiday in the Mediterranean; it would have looked damned suspicious if I'd gone to the Baltic this year. Even for you I wouldn't risk that.'

I said to Slade, 'Ask him if he's read any good thoughts lately—from the Little Red Book.'

'You're an Albanian,' said Slade flatly. 'I don't trust you.'

'So that's it,' said Wheeler softly. 'Does it make any difference?'

Slade nodded towards the silent Chinese. 'He does.'

I chipped in again. 'He makes a hell of a difference. Wheeler says he's taking you home. Home is where the heart is, and his heart is in Peking.'

That got to Wheeler. He said venomously, 'I think I'll have to shut you up—permanently.' He relaxed again and struck his hands lightly together. 'Not that it makes much difference whether you know or not, Slade. It made things easier as long as you believed you were going to Moscow—a willing prisoner is easier to handle. But we've still got you and you'll still get to your destination intact.'

From the look in Slade's eyes I doubted it. It wouldn't be beyond his capabilities to commit suicide somewhere along the way, and death would be far preferable to the information-extracting process awaiting him in China. Besides, under the circumstances it was his duty to commit suicide. Any man in his position knew that when it came to this sort of crunch he was expendable.

But Wheeler was ahead of us on that one. 'Your confinement will be more rigorous, of course. We can't have you hanging yourself by your braces.'

'Do I get to go along?' I asked.

Wheeler looked at me reflectively. 'You?' He shook his head. 'I don't think my friends would be interested in you. You've been out of the game too long to know much about recent developments in British Intelligence. A South African sleeper is of no consequence.' He half turned his head and said over his shoulder. 'What do you think?'

The Chinese spoke for the first time. 'He is of no use, but he is dangerous because of what he knows,' he said dispassionately. 'Kill him.'

I said something indescribably rude in Mandarin, and he opened his mouth in surprise. Orientals aren't all that inscrutable.

'Yes, Stannard; we must kill you. But how to do it?' Wheeler asked himself pensively. 'I have it. We discover a stowaway on board—an armed stowaway. There is a scuffle on his discovery and a shot is fired—the stowaway is killed with his own gun. We notify the police here and he turns out to be none other than Rearden, the British gaol-breaker.' He smiled. 'That would do a lot for my image; think of the headlines in the British press. What do you think of it?'

'Not much,' I said. 'If you turn me in to the police they'll want to know about Slade, too. He's a hell of a sight more important than I am. They'll want to search this ship, and they'll take it apart. You wouldn't want them to do that with Slade still aboard.'

Wheeler nodded. 'True. I'm afraid I must forgo that charming theatricality; my image must do without it. Besides, before you die there are some questions to be answered, such as what accomplices you have. That reminds me.' He turned to the skipper. 'What result of the search for his boat?'

'I'll find out,' said the skipper, and left the lounge.

I sighed. 'I came aboard alone.'

Wheeler nodded. 'You were alone at the beginning—I know that. But you might have picked up someone along the way. You realize that I must be certain.' He indicated the Chinese. 'My friend has ways of making sure, but you won't want to hear about that.'

I looked about the lounge casually. The departure of the skipper had reduced the odds against me, but not by much. There were two seamen behind me, one covering me with my own gun, and Wheeler and the Chinese were in front. The Chinese held his hand in his pocket and I was certain he, also, had a gun. I looked at Slade and wondered if he'd join me if it came to putting up a fight.

I said, 'I'd like to know how you got on to Mackintosh and

me so fast. You seem to know all about me—including my South African history.'

Wheeler chuckled. 'You British are a nation of amateurs—and that goes for your intelligence services. I was told about you, of course.'

I was genuinely bewildered. 'Who could have told you? There was only Mackintosh and me.'

'Precisely. And you didn't tell me.'

My jaw dropped and I stared at Wheeler incredulously. 'Mackintosh?'

'Who else could—as you point out. He was a little drunk and very indiscreet. I had no difficulty in flattering the fool. Towards the end he realized he was saying too much and shut up, but I got enough out of him.' He laughed. 'We were having a discussion on prison reform at the time.'

I was bewildered. Wheeler's description didn't fit the Mackintosh I knew, who was not a fool and certainly not susceptible to flattery. What in hell had Mackintosh been doing to blow things like that?

'He's dead, of course,' said Wheeler casually. 'I saw to that immediately as soon as I was certain we had you safe in Ireland. But we didn't have you safe, did we? Those IRA clowns are also amateurs. Never mind; here you are and all is well.'

I felt chilled to my bones. Whether Mackintosh was dead or not—and that was a moot point because I had told Alison to spread the word of his impending demise—I felt betrayed and utterly alone. Like a man who treads on a stair that isn't there. I felt jolted. I had to believe Wheeler because nothing else made sense, and yet Mackintosh's betrayal didn't make sense, either. Unless . . .

The skipper returned, breaking my chain of thought. 'No boat found,' he said.

Wheeler was fitting another cigarette into his holder. 'You may have been telling the truth, after all,' he said. He turned his head to the skipper. 'I want safe places for these two separately. What do you suggest?'

220

'Slade can go back to the cabin,' said the skipper.

'After what has just happened?' Wheeler lifted his eyebrows.

The Chinese said, 'He must be manacled to the bed, and a man must stay *in* the cabin all the time. He must not be permitted to make noise.'

Wheeler thought about it. 'All right; what about Stannard?'

'The forepeak; there's a steel bulkhead with a watertight door. He won't get out of there.'

Wheeler nodded curtly, then said to me, 'I'm afraid your interrogation will have to be postponed until we're away from land. The sound of a man screaming travels a long way.' He waved his hand and I found my arm held. 'By the way, were you responsible for what happened to our screws?'

'What's happened to your screws?' I managed to grin. 'Are they loose?'

'Very stiff-upper-lipped,' commented Wheeler. 'A quip in the face of death—very British. Take him away.'

I was hustled out of the lounge, a man on each side of me. I passed Slade whose face was yellowy-grey and who looked absolutely defeated and then I was thrust out on to the stern deck. There were now lights aboard *Artina* and, as we went forward along the side-deck, I saw that the man on my right still carried my gun. I didn't like the sound of that forepeak; from what I had seen of it on the plans of *Artina*'s sister-ship it was only four feet high—a hermetically-sealed steel box. The odds were I'd die of heat-stroke or suffocation.

But relish the prospect or not, the man next to me had a gun. The fact that he wasn't pointing it directly at me made not a ha'p'orth of difference—not while he gripped my arm and the man on the other side held me in a hammer-lock.

They pushed me along the deck until we were amidships and then there was a noise like a dud firecracker and the man with a gun gave a yelp and dropped it on to the deck. He stopped and looked at the blood oozing from the hole in the back of his hand, and let go of me. I'd heard that dud firecracker go off before.

I heard it go off again and saw a brief flash of light from the top of the deckhouse. The seaman who had me in the hammer-lock stumbled slightly and his grip loosened. He went down in apparent slow motion and I saw there was a dark red spot in the middle of his forehead.

'Jump, you damned fool,' yelled Alison, and I went over the side in an inelegant dive, arms and legs going every which way. I landed in the water with a hell of a splash and heard, two seconds later, another neater and more ladylike splash as Alison joined me.

I wasted no time in getting under the surface and swam in a circle searching for her. My hand touched her leg and she twisted in the water and grabbed my wrist. I pulled, leading her, and we swam deep and under *Artina*. It would be natural for anyone to look for us from the side of the ship from which we had jumped and I wanted to get away from there.

Matters were complicated by the fact that I was running out of air. Things had happened so fast that I hadn't had time to prepare myself by taking a good lungful of air, and that wasn't so good. I didn't want to come up within shooting distance of the ship. I compromised by coming up for air under *Artina*'s stern, hanging on to her rudder with just my nose and mouth above water. Alison joined me.

I took a few deep breaths and then allowed an ear out of the water. Things were going pop on deck; men ran along the deck in a seemingly confused way and the deep rumble of the skipper's voice held a note of menace. I prodded Alison under the chin so that her head came out of the water and whispered into her ear. 'Swim to Ta'Xbiex—under water as far as possible. I'll meet you at the place we left.'

She wasted no time in answering but sank under water and vanished. I took a last breath and followed her. Normally I like swimming but this was getting to be a bit too much; I like to swim in water I know to be clean. I took it easy, letting the air dribble from my mouth as the strain grew intolerable. When it finally became impossible to stay under any longer I surfaced face upwards, letting only my nose and mouth break the surface.

I cleared my lungs in four breaths and then risked a glance back at *Artina*. A searchlight was probing the water again but not in my direction. As I was about to go under again I heard a roar and ducked under just in time as a fast launch came hurtling in my direction. I struck out strongly to gain depth and the launch passed directly overhead, the disturbance of the wake buffeting me in the water.

Three times I had to surface before I came to the shore, or rather to the long line of yachts moored stern on to the wharf of the Lazzaretto Creek Marina. I came up under the bows of a floating gin palace, puffing and panting in an attempt to get my breath back, but I soon stopped that when I heard the pad of naked feet on the deck above.

Whoever it was seemed irritable. 'More uproar—everyone rushin' about in the middle of the night. What the hell do they think they're doin'?'

A woman said, 'I thought I heard fireworks earlier.'

'Fireworks be damned—they're tomorrow night. And who the hell lets off fireworks at this time in the mornin'?'

The launch came by again, going at a hell of a clip, and the boat I was holding on to rocked heavily in the swell of its passage. This provoked an outburst of rage from above. 'What the hell do you think you're doin'?' the man screamed, and I pictured him as a peppery, curry-voiced retired colonel.

His wife said, 'You're making more noise than anyone else, George. Come back to bed!'

There was the slap of bare feet on the deck as they padded away. 'All right; but a fat lot of sleep I'll get,' he grumbled. 'I'll see the manager tomorrow. We can't have this happenin' at night.'

I grinned and swam a couple of boats down the line before climbing ashore. Then I dog-trotted towards the place I'd assigned to meet Alison, hoping that she'd made it. I was worried about Alison for a number of reasons. Back in Ireland she had been distrustful of me and had wondered out loud if

I hadn't sold out to the Scarperers. Now I was distrustful of her.

If what Wheeler had said was true—that Mackintosh had blown the gaff—then I was really in trouble because Mackintosh wouldn't do a thing like that unheedingly. But why should I believe Wheeler? What incentive did he have to tell me the truth? In that case there was only one other person who could have sold out—Alison!

What brought that line of thought up short with a jerk was the recent episode on *Artina*. If Alison had sold out then why did she rescue me? Why did she pop off with that natty pistol of hers to wound one man, kill another, and get Stannard off the hot spot? That made even less sense. But I determined to keep a careful eye on Mrs Alison Smith in the future—provided she hadn't been run down by that launch.

2

I waited for fifteen minutes before she arrived. She was exhausted—so weary she couldn't pull herself from the water. I hauled her out and waited for a while until she recovered sufficiently to speak. Her first words were, 'That damned boat —nearly ran me down twice.'

'Did they see you?'

She shook her head slowly. 'I don't think so—they were just lucky.'

'They nearly got me,' I said. 'What happened to our boat?'

'I saw a man find the grapnel,' she said. 'And I knew you'd be in trouble. I went to the bows and climbed the anchor cable, and just let the boat drift.'

'Lucky for me you did. You're pretty handy with that popgun.'

'Six yards—no more. Anyone could do that.'

'Anyone wasn't there,' I said. 'You were.'

She looked about her. 'We'd better move. We could be picked up if we stay here.'

224

I shook my head. 'We're pretty safe. This harbour has so many inlets and creeks that Wheeler and his boys would have to search ten miles of coastline. But you're right—we'd better move on. It's a long walk back to the hotel and I want to get there before it's light. Do you feel fit?'

Alison got to her feet. 'I'm ready.'

It would take us, I estimated, a good hour to walk back to the hotel. We walked silently; I don't know what Alison was thinking but I was busy wondering what the hell to do next. At last I said, 'Well, I've fallen down on this one—my instructions were to bring Slade back or to kill him. I've done neither.'

'I can't see that you could have done differently,' said Alison.

'Yes, I could—I could have killed Slade on that yacht but I tried to bring him out.'

'It isn't easy to kill a sleeping man,' she said, and shivered. 'It isn't easy to kill anyone.'

I gave her a sideways glance and wondered about her. All that training must have produced something. 'How many men have you killed?'

'One,' she said, and her voice caught. 'To . . . night.' She started to shake violently.

I put my arm around her. 'Take it easy. It's a bad reaction, but it wears off in time. I know.' I damned Mackintosh for what he had done to his daughter. Yet at least he had made her into a professional and she would respond to the right stimulus just like one of Pavlov's dogs. To take her mind off what she had just done I said, 'We must leave the hotel.'

'Of course,' she said. 'But what then?'

'I'm damned if I know,' I admitted. 'It all depends on how much damage we've done to Wheeler's yacht. If she moves we're finished.'

'And if she doesn't?'

'We have another chance.'

'You can't go on board again—that won't work twice.'

'I know,' I said. 'I must think of something else.' We fell into a dispirited silence as we trudged along. We were both wet and it was cold in the early hours of the morning. We were also tired, and none of this helped us to think straight.

The sun was rising as we came into Floriana and there were a few people stirring in the streets. During our long walk our clothes had pretty well dried out and we didn't attract undue attention. Presently we passed workmen with ladders who were stringing up rows of gay bunting across the street. 'Those boys have started early,' I said. 'What's the celebration?'

'There's a *festa* today,' said Alison. 'They're always having them here.'

I remembered the man who had complained about noise in the harbour. 'They'll be having fireworks tonight, then.'

'Inevitably. The two go together in Malta.'

Something prickled at the back of my mind—the first stirrings of an idea. I left it alone to grow in its own good time. 'How much money have we got?'

'About three thousand pounds—including the five hundred I gave you.'

At least we were well equipped with the sinews of war. The idea burgeoned a little more, but I'd have to study the plans of *Artina*'s sister-ship a little more closely before I could bring it into the open.

A sleepy porter gave us our keys at the hotel and we went up to our rooms. At my door, I said, 'Come in here for a minute.' When we were inside I poured a big lump of scotch into a tooth-glass and gave it to Alison. 'Put that inside you and you'll feel better. Get yourself a hot shower and a change of clothing, but make it fast. We're evacuating—I want us to be out of here within a half-hour.'

She gave a wan smile. 'Where are we going?'

'We're going to ground—just where I don't know. But Wheeler will have his men checking the hotels; he might have started already. Just bring essentials—the money, passport and aircraft documents.'

226

When she had gone I followed my own advice. I knocked back a fast scotch and took a three-minute hot shower which chased away some of the aches and put some warmth in my bones again. My stomach was black with bruises. I dressed quickly and began to assemble the things I needed, not that there was much.

Then I sat down and began to study the ship plan. Fortunately it was scaled and I was able to measure distances fairly accurately. Not only was the idea burgeoning but blossoms were appearing. It all depended on whether Wheeler was immobilized in Marsamxett Harbour for another night.

Alison came back carrying one of those big bags which magically hold about six times more than they appear to. We left the hotel by a rear entrance and five minutes later we were at Kingsgate boarding a bus for Senglea.

Alison seemed brighter and said, 'Where are we going—and why?'

I paid the fare. 'I'll tell you when we get there.' The bus was crowded and I didn't want to talk about how I was going to kill Slade and Wheeler in public. The driver of the bus laboured under the misapprehension that his name was Jack Brabham, or perhaps he thought that the little shrine to the Virgin, so gaily decked in flowers, was a reasonable substitute for brakes. We got to Senglea in a remarkably short time.

Senglea is a peninsula jutting out into the Grand Harbour between Dockyard Creek and French Creek. Since the rundown of the Royal Navy and the demilitarization of the Naval Dockyard in Malta it seemed to be a reasonable place to find what I wanted—a boatshed, preferably with its own slipway.

It was still too early to do anything about that but the cafés were already open so we had breakfast, and very welcome it was. Over the bacon and eggs I said, 'Were you seen last night —seen to be recognized again?'

Alison shook her head. 'I don't think so.'

'Wheeler appeared to be uncertain about whether I had assistance,' I said. 'Of course, he knows now—but he doesn't know who. I think you're elected to do the shopping; it might not be safe for me on the streets.'

'What do you want?' she asked concisely.

'I want a boatshed. I only want it for twelve hours but we can't say so—we'll probably have to take it on three months' lease. I'm a boat designer and I'm working on a new type of . . . er . . . hydrofoil. I don't want anyone—my rivals, for instance—looking over my shoulder while I'm doing it, so I want discretion and security. That's the story.'

'Then what?'

'Then you push off and buy us a boat. Something about twenty feet overall and hellish fast, with big engines.'

'Outboard or inboard?'

'Doesn't matter. Outboards will be cheaper, but they must be powerful. You bring the boat round to the shed.' I looked through the window of the café. 'Over there is a scrap metal yard; I should be able to get most of what I want over there, including the hire of a welding outfit.'

Alison's brow wrinkled. 'So you have a fast boat and a welding outfit.' She waited patiently.

'Then you hire a truck. Can you drive a truck?' She gave me a look of silent contempt, and I grinned. She had probably passed her driving test with flying colours—in a Chieftain tank. I said, 'You take the truck and you buy enough fireworks to fill the boat.'

Now I had got her attention. 'Fireworks!'

'Big ones—especially the ones that go bang and throw out a shower of pretty lights. None of your paltry penny bangers; I want the big professional stuff. If they're so keen on fireworks here there should be quite a stock somewhere in this island. Think you can do that?'

'I can do it,' she said. 'Now tell me why the hell I should.'

I pulled out the ship plan and laid it on the table. 'I've been on board *Artina* and everything I saw fitted in with this plan, so I think we can trust it.' I tapped with my finger. 'The engine room, containing two 350 hp Rolls-Royce diesels which gulp a

228

hell of a lot of fuel. Under the engine room a supply of fresh water and the ready use fuel tank which holds 1,200 gallons.'

My finger moved on the plan. 'Forward of the engine room is Wheeler's cabin, and further forward are the crew's quarters. Under that, extending for twenty feet, is a double bottom containing the main fuel supply—5,350 gallons of fuel oil. We know she's just taken on fuel so the tanks are full.'

I did a bit of measuring with my finger-nail. 'To penetrate that tank we have to ram a hole at least three feet below the water line—preferably deeper. Her plating is mild steel, five-sixteenths of an inch thick—to punch a hole through that will need a hell of a lot of power.'

I looked up. 'I'm going to build a ram on the boat you're going to get me. At one time ramming was an orthodox naval tactic—all naval vessels had rams. But this is going to be a little different; it's going to be a combination ram and fireship. The boat will be full of big fireworks. When we ram the tank we let out the oil. It floats. The fireworks go off pop and set the oil on fire.'

'So you're going to smoke out Wheeler?'

I looked at her in silence for a moment, then I said, 'Don't be silly; I'm going to burn the bastard out.'

3

It all took time, and we had little enough of that. I was right in thinking that I could get a suitable boatshed in Senglea, but moving in quickly was something else again. A few enquiries made in the district soon turned up just what I wanted but the dickering promised to be protracted and it was ten-thirty that morning before the deal went through and only then because of the production of a hundred pounds in crisp, British fivers.

As time was getting short I sent Alison off to buy the boat, which I hoped wouldn't prove to be as difficult and time-consuming as renting the shed. In the meantime I went to the scrap metal yard and rummaged about until I found what I

229

wanted. I selected a few lengths of angle-iron, a lot of nuts and bolts and a steel bar, eight feet long and an inch and a half in diameter. I was also able to hire a welding outfit there, together with two full bottles of oxygen and acetylene and a pair of goggles.

As I paid out for this lot I reflected that the expense account for this lark was going to raise some Treasury official's hair. I could imagine him querying the purchase of perhaps a quarter of a ton of fireworks and acidly scratching out a memo asking Mrs Smith for further verification. But perhaps Mrs Smith also had training in cooking the swindle sheet.

I got all my equipment to the shed and waited around for Alison. I stared across the Grand Harbour to Valletta and wished I could see through it and into Marsamxett Harbour where *Artina* was still anchored—I hoped. At one-thirty I was still waiting and coming to a slow boil. Time was wasting and I had a hell of a lot to do.

It was nearly two o'clock before she arrived and the steam was blowing out of my ears. I caught the painter she tossed, and said curtly, 'What kept you?'

'I had to go to Sliema. Is she what you wanted?'

I studied the boat. She was a sleek, Italian-built job with two 100 hp Kiekhaefer Mercury outboard motors. Her lines looked good and those big engines would push her along at a fair lick. Alison said, 'I got more than thirty knots out of her on the way here.'

'You brought her from Sliema? You must have passed *Artina*.'

'She's still there.' I sagged a little in relief. 'They're doing a lot of work on her stern. When I passed they were hoisting out one of the propellers.'

'Were they, by God?' I laughed. 'Then it will be an all day job.' I jerked my thumb at the shed. 'There's a cradle in there. Help me get this thing up the slip and out of sight.'

We ran the cradle down the slip, floated the boat into it, and then winched the lot into the shed. Alison looked at her watch.

'I've arranged for the fireworks, too. They'll be ready to be picked up at three.'

'Then you'd better push off.'

She hesitated. 'Can you manage alone?'

'I should be able to. There's a block and tackle up there—I can use that to take the engines out.'

'There's a flask of coffee and a packet of sandwiches in the boat. And a bottle of whisky. I'll be back as soon as I can.'

She turned to go, and I said, 'Alison, there's just one more thing; see if you can get a big axe. A felling axe used for cutting down trees.'

She looked puzzled and then doubtful. 'I'm not sure they use those on Malta—there are not too many trees.'

'Do your best.' She left and I rescued the victuals before the bottle got broken, and then I uncoupled the steering cables on the boat and hoisted out the engines. I also used the block and tackle to turn the boat out of the cradle so that it lay upside-down on the trestles. I ate the sandwiches and drank the coffee while studying the problem; the whisky I left strictly alone because there was a job to be done, although I'd probably be glad of a stiff jolt before I set out.

I proceeded to get my hands dirty. The hull was of glass fibre and I began to ruin it by drilling holes in carefully selected places. The idea was to position the ram so that it was at least three feet below the water line when the boat was planing at speed, and it had to be fixed to the hull firmly enough so that it wouldn't come adrift on impact. If that happened then the momentum given by those big engines would be lost and the ram wouldn't penetrate *Artina*'s steel shell.

I cut up lengths of angle-iron and bolted them to the hull and through to steel cross-members which ran athwartship. Then I started to weld it up. It wasn't pretty welding and would have won no prizes at a craft school but, by God, it was strong—I made sure of that. When I had got that far there were two steel triangles built into the hull, the apexes of which were a little over three feet below the bottom. I took the long steel bar and welded it to the apexes of my steel triangles so that it was parallel to the bottom of the hull and projecting two feet in front.

Alison was back long before I had got that far and gave me a hand. It was hot and sweaty work and it took time. It was seven in the evening when I put the finishing touch to it. 'Did you get the axe?'

She produced just what I needed—a long-handled felling axe. I didn't need the handle and wasted no time in fiddling but cut it off with the welding torch. Then I took the blade and welded it vertically to the end of the steel bar—that was the cutting edge of my ram.

I stood back and looked at what I had done. Oddly enough it did look like a weird kind of hydrofoil, but I didn't like to think of what all that heavy ironmongery hung under the boat would do to her planing characteristics. I began to worry about the speed I was going to lose and if I could get her to plane at all.

'I could use a drink,' I said.

Alison poured some whisky into the cup from the vacuum flask and gave it to me. She looked at the boat, and said, 'It's going to be dangerous. I was wondering . . .'

'Wondering what?'

She turned to face me. 'I was wondering if this can't be done more simply—by the police.'

'That's a great idea,' I said sardonically. 'Can you imagine the local coppers believing us? Christ, Wheeler comes here every year and he's a respected figure, a British MP and an eminent capitalist. He's probably given prizes to the yacht club and I wouldn't be surprised if he's the sole support of a local orphanage. By the time we managed to convince anyone both he and Slade would have flown the coop.'

'There's still a body on *Artina*,' said Alison. 'That would take a lot of explaining away.'

'Same objection,' I said. 'Forget it. Let's have a look at the fireworks.'

232

There were a lot of them and they were big; rockets that would go up under their own power and maroons designed to be fired from mortars. 'This lot should add to the festivities,' I said in satisfaction. 'We must get the boat on to the cradle.'

I had to cut bits away from the cradle to accommodate our strange craft and it was forever ruined for handling normal boats. More expense for the Treasury. I installed the engines and hooked up the steering cables and tested them. When I jumped to the ground the boat, now right way up, looked a bit more practicable.

'How much did you pay for her?' I asked curiously.

'Fifteen hundred pounds,' said Alison.

I grinned. 'Guided missiles always are expensive. Let's put the cargo aboard.'

We filled up every spare inch of the hull with the big fireworks. Alison, as foreseeing as ever, had brought along a jerrican full of petrol and, after topping up the tanks, there was still half a gallon left, more than enough to start a fire to get things going. I now had a new worry; I had drilled a dozen holes in the hull to take bolts and had caulked them with putty, and I was wondering if I had sealed her tight. That couldn't be tested until we put her in the water and that wouldn't be until it was good and dark.

'When do they start shooting off the fireworks for the *festa*?' I asked.

'Two hours after sunset.'

'I'd like to ram *Artina* when the official fireworks are going full blast. It'll help to confuse the issue.' I sat down wearily and pulled out my ship plan; it was becoming worn and tatty and dirty at the creases, but it was still legible. 'The trouble is that I might hit one of the main frames,' I said. 'In that case I doubt if I'll get enough penetration.'

The frames were about two feet apart; statistically I had a good chance of missing—the odds were on my side.

Alison said, 'If we're going to do more underwater swimming we might as well do it comfortably.' She got up and dragged some scuba gear from the corner. 'I took the precaution of hiring this.'

'That slipped my mind.' I wondered what else I'd forgotten. I looked at the gear—there were two sets. 'I'm going to do the swimming,' I said. 'Not you.'

'But I'm coming with you,' she expostulated.

'For what? I don't need you.'

She flinched as though I had slapped her face. I said, 'You're right—it's a dangerous operation, and there's no point in both of us going. Besides, I need you for something else.' I thumped the side of the boat. 'Whether this works or not there's going to be ructions when these fireworks explode. If I don't get back someone must be around to have another crack at Wheeler—and you're elected.'

I reached out for the bottle and poured some more whisky. 'You can try going to the police; they might be interested enough by then to take you seriously.'

She saw the point, but she didn't like it. She set her face in a stubborn mould and prepared to argue. I forestalled her. 'All right; this is what you do. You wait here until nightfall and help me to get the boat into the water. Then you hop over to Ta'Xbiex and hire another boat—if you can get anyone to trust you.' I smiled. 'Looking as you do now I wouldn't trust you with a kid's bath toy.'

She rubbed her smudged face and distastefully inspected her fingertips.

'Thanks,' she said. 'I'll clean up.'

'If you can't hire a boat, steal one. There are plenty of loose boats at the Marina. Meet me at the seaward point of Manoel Island and then follow me in, but not too closely. When the balloon goes up watch out for Slade and Wheeler—they should be doing their best to jump overboard if all goes well. See they don't get ashore.'

'I lost the gun last night,' she said.

'Well, bat them over the head with an oar,' I said. 'I'll be around somewhere so keep your oar away from me.' I looked

234

at my watch. 'It'll be dark enough for launching in about an hour.'

That hour seemed to stretch out interminably rather like I'm told it does in an LSD trip; I wouldn't know about that —I haven't tried it. We didn't talk much and when we did it was of inconsequentialities. The sun set and the light slowly ebbed from the sky until at last it was dark enough to take the boat down the slip without anyone seeing it. Once it was in the water it wouldn't appear too abnormal.

I patted the wickedly gleaming steel axe-head which formed the tip of the ram and went to open the big double doors of the shed, and we steered the cradle down the slip and into the water. I released the boat and we took the cradle away and I turned to see how my handiwork had turned out.

It wasn't too bad; she was down by the head but not by too much considering the weight of iron under her bows, and she appeared quite normal apart from the bits of angle-iron which showed above water on each side of the hull. In another ten minutes it would be too dark to see even that, but even if I was picked up by a light in the harbour I doubt if anyone would notice anything particularly odd about her.

'That's it,' I said wearily. I was bone-tired; no sleep, a beating-up and a hard day's work did nothing to improve me.

'I'll go now,' said Alison quietly. 'Good luck, Owen.' She didn't kiss me, or even touch me. She just walked away, picking up her coat as she went.

I climbed into the boat and rearranged a few of the fireworks to make myself more comfortable. I put the scuba gear handy and checked my primitive system of fuses. Then there was nothing to do but wait another hour before I was due to move off.

Again it was a long wait.

CHAPTER ELEVEN

I

I CHECKED MY WATCH for the twentieth time in fifteen minutes and decided that time had come. I put on the scuba gear, tightened the weighted belt around my waist, and hung the mask around my neck. Then I started the engines and the boat quivered in the water. I cast off the painter and pushed the boat away with one hand and then tentatively opened the throttles a notch, not knowing what to expect.

At a slow speed she didn't handle too badly although there seemed to be something a little soggy about her response to the wheel. I switched on the lights because I didn't want the harbour patrol to pick me up for running illegally, and went down French Creek into the Grand Harbour. Here, in time past, the British Battle Fleet had lain, line upon line of dreadnoughts and battle cruisers. Now, there was another, but odder, naval craft putting to sea, but this one was in an earlier tradition—more like one of Drake's fireships.

Across the harbour Valletta was all lit up and there were strings of coloured lights spangling Floriana. Tinny music floated across the quiet water punctuated by the thumping of a bass drum. The merry-making was well under way.

I rounded the head of Senglea and steered to the harbour mouth. Nothing was coming my way so I decided to open up and see what the boat would do. The note of the engines deepened as I opened the throttles and I felt the surge of acceleration as 200 hp kicked her through the water. In terms of horse-power per ton of displacement this little boat was perhaps forty times as powerful as *Artina*; that's where the speed came from.

The steering was worse than bad—it was dreadful. The wheel kicked in my hands violently and my course was erratic, to say the least, and I went down the Grand Harbour doing a pretty good imitation of a water boatman, those jerky insects that run across the surface of ponds.

The damned boat wouldn't get on the step and plane and I don't suppose her speed was more than twelve knots, and that wasn't going to be enough. All the power going into the screws was doing nothing more than raising waves and I wasn't supposed to be in the wave-raising business. In desperation I slammed the throttles hard open and she suddenly rose in the water and took off, picking up at least an extra ten knots in as many seconds. But the steering was worse and there was a definite lag between hauling the wheel around and the corresponding reaction.

I throttled down again and she sagged into the water, and her speed dropped as though she'd run into a wall. This was going to be a dicey business. At a pinch I could get the speed, provided the engines didn't blow up, but I didn't know if I could steer her straight enough to hit my target. In spite of the flow of cooling night air I found I was sweating profusely.

If the only way to get her to plane was to run the engines at full bore I'd better not try that again. There would be no more trial speed runs because I was scared of the engines packing up, and next time this boat would be at speed again would be the last time. I'd have to handle the steering as best I could.

I dropped speed even further and plugged on towards St Elmo's Point. Fort St Elmo reared up starkly against the night sky as I passed between the point and the breakwater. Now I was in the open sea and the boat wallowed sickeningly. That heavy steel bar slung three feet under the water was acting as a pendulum. This lubberly craft was enough to give any self-respecting boat designer the screaming meemies.

I rounded the point and turned into Marsamxett Harbour, glad to get into sheltered waters again, and headed towards Manoel Island. Valletta was now to my left and I wondered from where they shot their fireworks. I checked the time and found I had little to spare.

As I approached Manoel Island I closed the throttles until

237

the engines were barely ticking over, just enough to give me steerage way. Not far away a light flickered and I saw that Alison was in position; she had struck a match and held it so that it illuminated her face. I steered in that direction and made contact.

She was in what seemed to be a small runabout driven by a little outboard motor. 'That's nice,' I said. 'Where did you get it?'

'I took your advice; I stole it,' she said, and laughed quietly.

I grinned in the darkness. 'It's our duty to save government money,' I said virtuously.

'How did you get on?' she asked.

'She's a bitch,' I said. 'As cranky as the devil.'

'She was all right when I brought her from Sliema.'

'That was a different boat. She's damned near uncontrollable at speed. How much time have we got?'

'About ten minutes.'

I looked about. 'I'd better get in position. We don't want to stay here or we'll be run down by the Sliema ferry—she's coming now. Is *Artina* in the same place?'

'Yes.'

'Then I'll be on my way. I'll go right down Lazzaretto Creek and turn around so as to get a good run up. You keep clear on the other side of *Artina*.' I paused. 'The steering is so bloody bad I might even miss her on the first pass. In that case I'll turn around and have a go on the other side. Don't be in my way or you'll get run over.'

'Good luck again,' said Alison.

I said, 'If you see Wheeler give him a good clout with my compliments. He was looking forward to seeing his Chinese friend operate on me. If things work out I'll see you in Ta'Xbiex—at the same place as last night.'

Gently I eased the throttles forward and moved off. I passed *Artina* quite closely; there were three men on deck—Wheeler, the Skipper and the Chinese, Chang Pi-wu. I could see them quite clearly because they were illuminated, but I was low on

238

the water in the dark and there was no chance of them recognizing me. I was just another ship passing in the night.

Mentally I made a cross on the place on the hull I intended to hit, and then I carried on down Lazzaretto Creek. At the bottom, near the Manoel Island bridge I turned with idling engines. I switched on the air from the scuba bottle and checked the demand-valve, and then bit on the mouthpiece and put on the mask. If things went well I wouldn't have time to do any of that later.

Behind me traffic passed on the road and presently a procession came by with a band of pounding drums and off-key brass. I ignored it and looked across to Valletta and the forthcoming firework display. There was what I thought to be a heavier thump on a drum but it was a mortar banging off. A maroon burst over Valletta in a yellow sunburst and in the echoing reflection from the water of the harbour I saw *Artina* clearly for a brief moment. The fireworks had begun and it was time for me to add my share to the festivities.

I advanced the throttles and moved off slowly as a rocket soared up and exploded in a shower of red and green fiery rain. I steered with one hand and with the other liberally doused my cargo with petrol from an open can, hoping to God that the sparks from the fireworks were totally extinguished by the time they reached water level. It only needed one of those in the boat and I'd go up in a cloud of glory.

Then I pushed open the throttles wider and by the time I was making any kind of speed the sky was alive with lights as the Maltese spent their fireworks with reckless abandon. *Artina* was clearly silhouetted as, with equal abandon, I jammed the throttles wide open.

The engines roared and the boat reared up in the water almost uncontrollably as she began to plane. The wheel kicked in my hands as I strove to keep her on course and I zig-zagged dangerously close to the line of yachts moored at the marina. I swung the wheel hard over but the bitch was late in responding and there was an outraged cry from the bow of one of the

239

yachts. It sounded like the curry-voiced colonel who must have got the fright of his life as I scraped his paint at twenty knots.

Then I was past him and heading out into the harbour, bucking and twisting and steering a course which would have brought tears to the eyes of any self-respecting helmsman. The fireworks banged and flashed overhead striking dazzling reflections from the water and my heart jumped into my mouth as a small runabout came out of nowhere and cut across my bows. I cursed him and swung the wheel and missed him by a whisker. That made two damned fools at large in Marsamxett Harbour.

As I swung the wheel hard over the other way I looked for *Artina* and saw that I was going to miss her by a sizeable margin. I cursed again at the thought of having to make another mad sortie. It occurred to me that with the steering being as crazy as it was then I'd better aim at anything but *Artina* and then I might have a chance of hitting her.

I estimated I was going to shoot under her stern but just then the hard-pressed port engine blew up and, with a nasty flailing rattle of a broken connecting rod, it expired. The boat checked a little in the water and her bow came over to aim directly at *Artina*. I hung on as she loomed over me and then, with a satisfying smash, my underwater ram struck her amidships.

I was thrown forward and bruised my ribs on the wheel but it saved me from going into the water. I still had one last thing to do. As I groped for my cigarette lighter I heard a shout on deck and I looked up into the eye-straining alternation of light and darkness and saw a movement as someone peered over the side to see what the hell had happened now. I couldn't see much of him but I must have been clearly visible as another batch of rockets went up.

I flicked the lighter and it sparked but there was no flame. In the rocket's red glare I saw that the boat's bow was smashed and broken with the impact against *Artina*'s side. The ram must have been deeply embedded because she showed no sign of wanting to drift away.

Desperately I flicked the lighter again but again there was no flame. There was a bang from above and a bullet smashed into the instrument panel next to my elbow, ruining the rev counter. I leaned forward and put the lighter right next to a bunch of petrol-soaked fireworks. The boat was making water and I had to start a fire before she went under.

I flicked again and the whole damned lot went up in a brilliant sheet of flame. It was only because I was fully equipped in scuba gear that I wasn't instantly incinerated. It went up, as suddenly ignited petrol does, in a sort of soft explosion—a great *whooof* of flame that blew me overboard. And as I went something hit me in the shoulder very hard.

Whether or not I was actually on fire for a moment I don't know. When I hit the water I was dazed, but the sudden shock brought a reflex into action and I struck for the depths. It was then I found that my right arm was totally useless. Not that it mattered very much; in scuba diving the flippered feet do most of the work. But it worried me because I didn't know what could be wrong with it.

I swam under water for a short while, then stopped because I didn't know where I was going. I was absolutely disoriented and, for all I knew, I could have been swimming out to sea. So I surfaced cautiously and looked around to get my bearings and to see what was happening to *Artina*.

I had not swum as far as I thought—she was about a hundred yards away, too close for comfort, especially in view of the little piece of hellfire that I had established amidships. My fireship was going great guns. With the ram stabbed into *Artina*'s side like a narwhal's tusk she was securely fixed, and the fireworks were exploding like an artillery barrage, showering multi-coloured sparks and great gouts of flame which licked up her side. Already a canvas deck awning was on fire and men were running about the deck every which way.

A big maroon went off like a howitzer shell, sending out a burst of green flame and sparks which reached out to patter on the surface of the water about me, hissing viciously as they were extinguished. I was close enough to be seen if anyone had the time to look, so I sank beneath the surface again after a last glance around, and struck out for the shore.

I had not done a dozen strokes before I knew something was wrong. I felt curiously weak and light-headed and my right shoulder had developed a dull throb which was rapidly sharpening up into a stabbing pain. I eased off and felt my shoulder with my left hand and the pain jabbed me with such intensity that I nearly yelled aloud which is a good way of getting oneself drowned.

So I surfaced again and drifted, becoming more light-headed and feeling the strength ebbing from my legs more swiftly every minute. The fire by *Artina* was still going strong but it all seemed blurred as though seen through a rain-washed window. It was then I knew that I was probably going to die, that I no longer had the strength to swim to the shore which was so close, and that I was drifting out to sea where I would drown.

I think I passed out for a moment because the next thing I knew there was a light flashing in my eyes from very close and an urgent whisper, 'Owen; grab this!'

Something fell across my face and floated in the water next to my head and I put out my left hand and found a rope. 'Can you hold on?' I knew it was Alison.

An engine throbbed and the rope tightened and I was being drawn through the water. Desperately I concentrated all my attention on to holding on to that rope. Whatever strength I had left must be marshalled and pushed into the fingers of my left hand so that they would not relinquish their grip. The water lapped about my head, creating a miniature bow wave as I was towed behind Alison's boat and, even in that extremity, I paid tribute to the efficiency of Alison Smith and Mackintosh's training. She knew she could not haul an almost unconscious man into the boat without either capsizing or, worse, attracting attention.

It was a ridiculously short distance to the shore and Alison brought up at a slipway. She rammed the boat up it, careless of the consequences, and jumped overboard into two feet of water and hauled me out bodily. 'What's wrong, Owen?'

I flopped down and sat into the shallow water. 'I think I was shot,' I said carefully, and my voice seemed to come from miles away. 'In the shoulder—the right shoulder.'

The pain washed over me as her fingers probed, and then I heard the rip of cloth and she bandaged the wound roughly but effectively. I wouldn't have been surprised if she had operated there and then, using a penknife and a hairpin to extract the bullet. I was becoming used to her surprising range of talents.

I said tiredly, 'What's happening to *Artina*?'

She moved away and I saw *Artina* in the harbour beyond. All the sea was on fire about her and above the yellow flames rose the rolling cloud of greasy black smoke that could only come from oil. The ram had done its work. Even as I watched there was a red flash just under the wheelhouse and then the wheelhouse vanished as an oil tank exploded in her vitals and blasted through the deck. A deep boom came across the water, echoed and re-echoed from the cliff-like fortifications of Valletta.

'That's it, then,' I said abstractedly.

Alison leaned over me. 'Can you walk?'

'I don't know. I can try.'

She put her hand under my left arm. 'You've been leaking blood like a stuck pig. You need a hospital.'

I nodded. 'All right.' It didn't really matter now. The job had been done. Even if Slade or Wheeler had survived they were done for. I would be asked why I had destroyed *Artina* and I would tell the truth, and I would be listened to very carefully. People don't wander around blowing up million-aires' yachts for nothing and what I had to say would be heard. Whether it was believed or not would be another matter, but enough mud would stick to Wheeler to make sure that hard, professional eyes would be on him for ever more. As for Slade, I had escaped from prison with him and if I was on Malta and said that Slade was around then he would be picked up in jig time. It's a small island and strangers can't hide easily.

As for myself I didn't know what would happen. Alison might give evidence *in camera* as to my part in the affair, but if Mackintosh was dead I didn't know how much weight that would carry. There was a strong possibility that I would spend the rest of my life in the maximum security wing of Durham Gaol. Right at that moment I was past caring.

Alison helped me to my feet and I staggered like a drunken sailor up the slipway, hanging on to her arm with a flabby grip. We had just reached the top when I paused and stared at the man who was waiting. He looked remarkably like that tough, young copper, Sergeant Jervis, who had taken such a strong dislike to me because I had stolen some diamonds and had not the grace to tell him where they were.

I turned my head and looked in the other direction. Brunskill was there with Forbes just behind him. Already they were striding out and coming towards us. I said to Alison, 'The end of the line, I think,' and turned to face Brunskill.

He stood in front of me and surveyed me with expressionless eyes, noting every detail of my disarray and the bandage on my shoulder. He flicked his eyes at Alison, and then nodded towards the harbour where *Artina* was going down in flames. 'Did you do that?'

'Me?' I shook my head. 'It must have been caused by a spark from the fireworks.'

He smiled grimly. 'I must caution you that anything you say may be taken down in writing and used in evidence.' He looked at Alison. 'That applies to you, too.'

'I don't think Malta is within your jurisdiction,' she said coolly.

'Not to worry about that,' said Brunskill. 'I have a platoon of the local constabulary on call.' He turned to me. 'If you had as many lives as a cat you'd spend them all inside. I'm going to wrap you up so tight this time that they'll have to build a prison just for you.'

I could see him mentally formulating the list of charges. Arson, murder, grievous bodily harm, carrying weapons—and worse—using them, driving a horse and cart through the Explosives Act. Maybe, with a bit of twisting, he could toss in piracy and setting fire to the Queen's shipyards. Those last two are still capital offences.

He said, 'What in hell did you think you were doing?' There was wonder in his voice.

I swayed on my feet. 'I'll tell you after I've seen a doctor.'

He caught me as I fell.

2

I woke up in the nick. It was the prison hospital, to be sure, but still inside thick walls, and they build walls thicker in Malta than anywhere else. But I had a private room and came to the conclusion that the local coppers didn't want the simple, uncomplicated Maltese criminals to be corrupted by contact with such a hard case as myself. This proved to be a wrong assumption.

An uncommunicative doctor performed a simple operation on my shoulder under local anaesthetic and then I lay waiting for the arrival of Brunskill and his inevitable questions. I spent the time thinking out ingenious lies to tell him; there are certain aspects of HM Government it is better for the ordinary copper not to know.

But it was a stranger and not Brunskill who was ushered into the room. He was a tall, middle-aged man with a smooth, unlined face and an air of quiet authority who introduced himself as Armitage. His credentials were impressive; I read a letter of introduction from the Prime Minister and pushed back the rest of the bumf unread.

He pulled up a chair to the bedside and sat down. 'Well, Mr Stannard; how are you feeling?'

I said, 'If you know my name is Stannard then you know most of the story. Did Alec Mackintosh send you?'

'I'm afraid not,' he said regretfully. 'Mackintosh is dead.'

I felt a cold lump settle in my stomach. 'So he never came out of hospital.'

'He died without recovering consciousness,' said Armitage.

I thought of Alison and wondered how she'd take it. The love-hate relationship she had with her father made it difficult to estimate her reaction. I said, 'Has Mrs Smith been told?'

Armitage nodded. 'She took it quite well.'

How would you know? I thought.

'This is all going to be difficult,' said Armitage. 'Your activities—particularly in the Irish Republic—could put the Government into an awkward position.' He paused. 'Should they be fully disclosed.'

I could imagine that they could. Relations were already strained over what was happening in Ulster and the Press would have a field day with garbled stories of a British agent on the rampage in the sovereign State of Ireland.

I said ironically, 'Not to mention my own awkward position.'

'Just so,' said Armitage.

We stared at each other. 'All right,' I said at last. 'Who blew the gaff? This operation had the tightest security of any I've been on. How did it fall apart?'

Armitage sighed. 'It fell apart *because* of the tight security. It fell apart because Mackintosh was constitutionally unable to trust anyone.' He held me with his eye. 'He didn't even trust you.'

I nodded, and Armitage snorted. 'He didn't even trust the Prime Minister. All through he played a lone hand and deceived everyone regarding his motives.'

I said quietly, 'I have a big stake in this. I think you'd better tell me the story.'

It all started with the spate of prison escapes which worried the people at the top. Mountbatten investigated the prison service and security was tightened, but the vague rumours of the Scarperers' organization kept the worries on the boil and Mackintosh was put in charge of doing something about it.

'I didn't like that,' said Armitage disapprovingly. 'And I said so at the time. It ought to have been left to the Special Branch.'

'Mackintosh told me they'd tried and failed,' I said.

Armitage nodded impatiently. 'I know—but they could have tried again. Mackintosh was too much the lone wolf—too secretive.'

I could see what stuck in Armitage's craw. He was a top level civil servant—a Whitehall mandarin—and he liked things to go through channels in an orderly way. In particular, he didn't like the idea of the Prime Minister having a private hatchet man. It offended his sense of what was fitting.

He leaned forward. 'Unknown to anybody Mackintosh already had his eye on Wheeler but he kept his suspicions to himself. He didn't even tell the PM. We'll never know what went through his mind, but perhaps he thought he wouldn't be believed. Wheeler was coming up fast in popularity and influence; in fact, the Prime Minister was on the point of making him a Junior Minister in the Government.'

'Yes,' I said. 'I can see Alec's problem. How did he get on to Wheeler?'

Armitage shook his head. 'I don't know. I believe the Prime Minister reposed full confidence in Mackintosh regarding certain measures of top level security.' He sounded even more disapproving.

So Mackintosh was running security checks on the élite. That was one answer to the question: *Quis custodiet ipsos custodes?* I could imagine the Prime Minister might expect Mackintosh to turn up some member of the radical Left or Right as a potential risk, but who would suspect a bourgeois capitalist who firmly trod the middle road of being a Maoist? The idea was laughable.

'So Mackintosh had unprovable suspicions,' I said. 'He didn't want them getting back to Wheeler so he kept his mouth shut until he could catch Wheeler in the act.'

'That must have been the size of it,' conceded Armitage.

'He brought you in and put you next to Slade by means of the diamond robbery.' A slight smile mitigated his severe expression. 'Ingenious. But he didn't tell you about Wheeler.'

'I wouldn't expect him to,' I said flatly. 'At that stage I didn't need to know.' I rubbed my chin. 'But I'd expect him to tell Mrs Smith.'

'He didn't—but I'll come to that later.' Armitage leaned forward. 'When you and Slade escaped, Mackintosh went to see Wheeler. We have established that he saw Wheeler at his club. They had a conversation in the course of which Mackintosh disclosed who you were. That's how . . . er . . . the gaff was blown.'

I blinked, then closed my eyes and lay back on the pillow. 'He did it deliberately?' I asked softly.

'Oh, yes. He wanted to stampede Wheeler into ill-advised action. He wanted to catch him *in flagrante delicto*. Apparently you were expendable.'

I opened my eyes and looked at Armitage. 'I always was. It's an occupational hazard.' All the same I thought that Alec Mackintosh was a ruthless son of a bitch.

'Wheeler was stampeded, all right, but I'm not sure that Wheeler's action was ill-advised,' said Armitage reflectively. 'Mackintosh was run down by a car the same day. We've impounded all Wheeler's cars for forensic examination and I'm pretty sure we'll turn up some evidence even at this late date. I think the job was done by his Irish chauffeur.'

'Or his Chinese cook.'

Armitage shrugged. 'So Mackintosh was unconscious in hospital. He was run down on his way to his office where Mrs Smith was awaiting him. Whether he was going to tell her what he'd done we'll never know. At all events, at this time no one in the Government knew about Wheeler. Do you see what I mean about the security of the operation being too tight?'

I said, 'A top-rank Whitehall man, such as yourself, doesn't turn up in Malta out of the blue so opportunely. Something must have come up.'

'It did. Mackintosh died. He'd taken out insurance. He wrote out a full account of his actions and posted them to his lawyer just before he saw Wheeler. The snag about that was that the sealed envelope was inscribed, "Only to be opened in the event of my death."'

Armitage stared at me. 'And Mackintosh was in the hands of the doctors. He wasn't dead, but you'd hardly call him alive although in the legal sense he was. He was a vegetable maintained by modern medical techniques and the doctors' duty by the Hippocratic Oath, and that was something he hadn't calculated for. That damned envelope was in the lawyer's hands for two weeks before Mackintosh died and by then it was nearly too late. It would have been too late were it not for your actions.'

'That's all very well,' I said. 'But how did that lead you to me? Mackintosh didn't know where I was.'

'We went straight for Wheeler,' said Armitage. 'We were just wondering how to tackle him when you took the problem out of our hands.' He smiled slightly. 'Your methods are direct, to say the least. It was thought that you might be around, so we brought along people who could recognize you.'

'Brunskill and company,' I said. 'So you've got Wheeler.'

He shook his head. 'No; Wheeler is dead, and so is Slade. You saw to that very effectively, if I may say so. The Special Branch is working on the ramifications of Wheeler's organizations—those that are legal and those that are not. I think it will be a lengthy task, but that is none of your concern.' He leaned back in his chair. 'However, you do present a problem to the Government, which is why I am here.'

I couldn't suppress the smile. 'I bet I am.'

'It's no laughing matter, Mr Stannard,' said Armitage severely. 'Already the Press has become alerted to the fact that there is something in the wind.' He stood up and wandered over to the window. 'Fortunately, the worst of your . . . er . . . crimes were committed outside the United Kingdom and to those we can turn a blind eye. But there is the matter of a diamond robbery which may well prove awkward to handle.'

I said, 'Were the diamond merchants paid out by their insurance company?'

Armitage turned and nodded. 'I should think so.'

'Well, why not leave it at that.'

He was affronted. 'Her Majesty's Government cannot connive in the cheating of an insurance company.'

'Why not?' I asked reasonably. 'Her Majesty's Government is conniving in the murder of Wheeler and Slade. What the hell's so sacred about a few thousand quid?'

That didn't sit well with him. Property rights come before human rights in British law. He harrumphed embarrassedly, and said, 'What is your suggestion?'

'Wheeler is dead and Slade is dead. Why shouldn't Rearden be dead, too? He can be killed while evading arrest—it shouldn't be too difficult to stage manage. But you'll have to gag Brunskill, Forbes and Jervis, and you can do that under the Official Secrets Act. Or you can throw the fear of God into them; I don't think any of that gang would relish being transferred to the Orkneys for the rest of his days.'

'And Mr Stannard comes to life again?' he queried.

'Precisely.'

'I suppose it could be arranged. And how do we explain the spectacular death of Wheeler?'

'It must have been those rockets they were shooting over the harbour,' I said. 'One of them must have gone out of whack and hit the ship. It was being repaired at the time—I'll bet there was some fuel open on deck. I think the Maltese Government ought to be ticked off for not keeping proper control.'

'Very ingenious,' said Armitage, and took out a notebook. 'I'll suggest that the Navy offer a ship and a diver to help lift the wreck. We'll choose the diver, of course.' He made a note with a silver pen.

'You'd better,' I said, thinking of that ram which was probably still embedded in *Artina*'s side. 'A sad end to a popular MP. Most regrettable.'

Armitage's lips twitched and he put away the notebook. 'The organization for which you worked before Mackintosh pulled you out of South Africa apparently thinks highly of you. I am asked to inform you that someone called Lucy will be getting in touch.'

I nodded. How Mackintosh would have sneered at that.

'And the Prime Minister has asked me to pass on his sincere thanks for the part you have played in this affair and for the way you have brought it to a conclusion. He regrets that thanks are all he has to offer under the circumstances.'

'Oh, well; you can't eat medals,' I said philosophically.

3

I sat in the lounge of the Hotel Phoenicia waiting for Alison. She had been whisked to England by the powers-that-be in order to attend Alec's funeral. I would have liked to have paid my respects, too, but my face had been splashed in the pages of the British newspapers with the name of Rearden underneath and it was considered unwise for me to put in an appearance until Rearden had been forgotten in the short-lived public memory. Meanwhile I was growing a beard.

I was deriving much amusement from an intensive reading of an air mail edition of *The Times*. There was an obituary of Wheeler which should put him well on the road to canonization; his public-spiritedness was praised, his financial acumen lauded and his well-known charitableness eulogized. The first leader said that in view of Wheeler's work for the prisons his death was a blow to enlightened penology unequalled since the Mountbatten Report. I choked over that one.

The Prime Minister, in a speech to the Commons, said that British politics would be so much the worse for the loss of such a valued colleague. The Commons rose and stood in silence for two minutes. That man ought to have had his mouth washed out with soap.

Only the Financial Editor of *The Times* caught a whiff of

something rotten. Commenting on the fall of share prices in the companies of Wheeler's empire he worried at the question of why it was thought necessary for the auditors to move in before Wheeler's body was cold. Apart from that quibble Wheeler had a rousing send-off on his journey to hell.

Rearden came off worse. Condemned as a vicious desperado, his death in a gun battle was hailed as a salutary lesson to others of his kidney. Brunskill was commended for his perseverance on the trail of the villainous Rearden and for his fortitude in the face of almost certain death. 'It was nothing,' said Brunskill modestly. 'I was only doing my duty as a police officer.'

It was hoped that Slade would soon be caught. There were full security wraps on Slade's death and I had no doubt that in another ten or twenty years any number of criminologically inclined writers would make a fair living churning out books about the Slade Mystery.

I looked up to see Alison coming into the lounge. She looked pale and tired but she smiled when she saw me. I rose to my feet as she approached and she stopped for a moment to survey me, taking in the cast on my arm and the unshaven stubble on my cheeks. 'You look awful,' she said.

'I'm not feeling too bad; I can still bend my left elbow. What will you have?'

'A Campari.' She sat down and I whistled up a waiter. 'I see you've been reading all about it.'

I grinned. 'Don't believe everything you read in the papers.'

She leaned back in the chair. 'Well, Owen; it's over. It's all over.'

'Yes,' I said. 'I'm sorry about Alec.'

'Are you?' she asked in a flat voice. 'He nearly got you killed.'

I shrugged. 'He miscalculated the speed and direction of Wheeler's reaction. But for that it was a good ploy.'

'Even though he was selling you out?' Her tone was incredulous.

'God damn it!' I said. 'We weren't playing pat-a-cake. The stakes were too great. Wheeler *had* to be nailed down and if the way to do it was to sacrifice a man in the field then there was no choice. Wheeler was striking at the heart of the State. The Prime Minister was considering him for a ministerial position, and God knows where he could have gone on from there.'

'If all statesmen are like Alec then God help Britain,' said Alison in a low voice.

'Don't be bitter,' I said. 'He's dead. He killed himself, not me. Never forget that.'

The waiter came with the drinks and we were silent until he had gone, then Alison said, 'What are you going to do now?'

I said, 'I had a visit from Lucy. Of course I can't do much until the shoulder heals—say a month to six weeks.'

'Are you going back to South Africa?'

I shook my head. 'I think I'm being considered for the active list.' I sipped my drink. 'What about you?'

'I haven't had time to think yet. There was a lot to do in London apart from the funeral. Alec's personal affairs had to be wound up; I spent a lot of time with his solicitor.'

I leaned forward. 'Alison, will you marry me?'

Her hand jerked so that she spilled a few drops of red Campari on to the table. She looked at me a little oddly, as though I were a stranger, then said, 'Oh, no, Owen.'

I said, 'I love you very much.'

'And I think I love you.' Her lower lip trembled.

'Then what's the matter? We're very well suited.'

'I'll tell you,' she said. 'You're another Alec. In twenty years —if you survive—you'll be sitting in a little, obscure office pulling strings and making men jump around, just like Alec. You won't be doing it because you like it but because you think it's your duty. And you'll hate the job and you'll hate yourself—just as Alec did. But you'll go on doing it.'

I said, 'Someone has to do it.'

253

'But not the man I marry,' said Alison. 'I told you once that I was like a Venus Fly Trap. I want to be a cabbage of a housewife, living, perhaps on the green outskirts of an English country town, all tweedy and *Country Life*.'

'There's no reason why you shouldn't have that, too,' I said.

'And stay behind and be alone when you went on a job?' She shook her head. 'It wouldn't work, Owen.'

I felt a sudden resentment, and said abruptly, 'Then why did you come back here—to Malta?'

A look of consternation crossed her face. 'Oh, Owen; I'm sorry. You thought . . .'

'You didn't say goodbye, and Armitage told me you'd be coming back after the funeral. What was I supposed to think?'

'I was flown to England in an RAF transport,' she said quietly. 'I've come back to pick up my plane . . . and to say goodbye.'

'To say goodbye—just like that?'

'No,' she flared. 'Not just like that.' Her eyes filled with tears. 'Owen, it's all going wrong.'

I took her hand in mine. 'Have you ever been to Morocco?'

She looked at me warily, taken wrong-footed by the sudden change of subject. 'Yes; I know it quite well.'

'Could that aircraft of yours fly to Tangier from here?'

'It *could*,' she said uncertainly. 'But . . .'

'I need a holiday,' I said. 'And I have a year and a half of back pay which I need help in spending. I'm sure you'd make an efficient guide to Morocco. I need one—I've never been there.'

'You're trying the blarney again,' she said, and there was laughter in her voice. 'Maeve O'Sullivan warned me about that.'

Maeve had also told me that I wasn't the man for Alison Smith. She could be right, but I had to try.

'No strings and no promises,' said Alison.

I smiled. Six weeks together was all the promise I needed. A lot could happen in six weeks.